BODIES IN THE BOOKSHOP

Investigate the killer plots of twenty mysteries – nearly all specially commissioned and all with a literary flavour – published in honour of Heffers and independent bookshops everywhere. Chase down the criminals in new stories featuring Carole & Jude, Gary Goodhew, the Good Thief, and the redoubtable Baroness 'Jack' Troutbeck, by their respective creators: Simon Brett, Alison Bruce, Chris Ewan, and Ruth Dudley Edwards.

BODIES IN THE BOOKSHOP

BODIES IN THE BOOKSHOP

by

L C Tyler & Ayo Onatade

Magna Large Print Books
Long Preston, North Yorkshire,
BD23 4ND, England.

British Library Cataloguing in Publication Data.

Tyler, L C & Onatade, Ayo
Bodies in the bookshop.

A catalogue record of this book is
available from the British Library

ISBN 978-0-7505-4167-1

First published in Great Britain by Ostara Publishing 2014

Published in Large Print 2015 by arrangement with
Ostara Publishing

Magna Large Print is an imprint of Library Magna Books Ltd.

Printed and bound in Great Britain by
T.J. (International) Ltd., Cornwall, PL28 8RW

Contents

Foreword

Trawling second-hand bookshops is a favourite occupation of mine. An excursion, many years ago, turned up a copy of John Blackburn's excellent 1963 thriller, *Blue Octavo* – a fascinating impression of the 1960s' London book world! The suicide of a rare book dealer is a surprise to bookseller John Cain – not only had he inherited the dead man's collection but several days earlier he'd witnessed his benefactor's excessive bid for an innocuous volume on mountaineering. If books could kill – and working in my over-laden study, with mysteries stacked from floor to ceiling, there's always that possibility – even more so, if you've a mind to murder in locating every copy of a particularly rare volume!

The premise for this collection, was to serve as a tribute to independent bookshops everywhere, especially Heffers and its annual *Bodies in the Bookshop* event. The brief to the contributors was for a story based on any or all of four themes: bookshops, Cambridge, books and libraries. We succeeded with the first three, but, in the absence of any library-based offering, two stories on other themes sneaked in, though not undetected! Authors are constantly either researching, writing or promoting their work, so we were delighted by their positive response. Their works, collectively, feature every crime in the book – from the laugh-out-loud humorous to the tragic; from stories steeped in local colour to tales from farther afield – with familiar or new detectives, and plots that linger in the mind.

The tranquil aisles of fictional bookshops provide perfect cover to a host of writers staging all kinds of death and deconstruction, as evidenced in *The Best Revenge* by Kate Charles, in the setting of a Cambridge bookshop's crime writers' evening. A little learning too can be murderous, as testified in *The Storytellers* by Suzette A Hill, where a youngster's imagination runs riot. There's no shelving the evidence after three shops frequented by town, gown and tourist, are targeted in *The Enemy Within* by Ruth Dudley Edwards.

Farther afield, in a Cotswolds village bookshop, shady practices appear to be prevalent in *Brought to Book* by Judith Cutler. A nocturnal walk with the dog results in a shock to the system for two octogenarians spotting a body on the bookshop floor, in *The Body in the Bookshop* by Simon Brett. Driving a book-filled VW caravanette across Northumberland proves to be no picnic for an ex-cop-now-storyteller in *Killing Your Darlings* by Ann Cleeves, An author comes under scrutiny by her own characters in Ruth Downie's *The Strange Affair at Sheepwash.* A customer-poor second-hand bookshop, stocked with musty old tomes, is refreshed by someone with an entrepreneurial streak, in Martin Edwards' *Lucky Liam.*

The city of Cambridge provides a rich setting for detective stories with the colleges of Trinity, St

John's and King's sharing the distinction of being the most popular. There's something decidedly dodgy with a copper on the trail of an absentee don in *Murder in Trumpington* by L C Tyler. A sinister side of the city is revealed at Grafton Investments, housed in a Georgian property off Midsummer Common, in *The Photocopier Murders* by Susanna Gregory and Simon Beaufort; a hit-and-run incident on Maids Causeway occupies DC Gary Goodhew in *Death of the Author* by Alison Bruce; whilst the harsh reality of life on the city's streets is vividly portrayed in *The Stain* by newcomer Jenna Hawkins.

As well as a booty of biblio-mysteries and first degree Cambridge murders, several stories offering a delicious frisson of uncertainty have been included too. The quiet surroundings of Kensal Vale cemetery provides perfect sanctuary for both the living and the dead in *Waiting for Mr Right* by Andrew Taylor. A golden couple's path to wedded bliss is put on hold in *The Guest List* by Stella Duffy and a weightier problem confronts a philanderer in *Remember My Name* by Christopher Fowler. Death takes passage when three men, all at sea, muse on the perfect murder, in *The Problem of Stateroom 10* by Peter Lovesey, whilst a claustrophobic travel writer is hampered by his fear of flying in *Flotsam and Jetsam* by Michael Gregorio.

All in all twenty splendid pieces of storytelling, rich in their diversity, colour this collection from authors at the top of their game. I've often thought, though, that any writers scratching their heads for a new storyline might do well to consider the opportunities offered when a bookshop undergoes building work – as Heffers has done several times. Reader, I buried them!

Richard Reynolds, 2014.

Acknowledgements

My heartfelt thanks to:

Ayo Onatade and L C Tyler for agreeing to be editors, and for their extreme generosity with their time and their expertise in putting this collection together.

Simon Brett, Alison Bruce, Kate Charles, Ann Cleeves, Judith Cutler, Ruth Downie, Stella Duffy, Chris Ewan, Martin Edwards, Ruth Dudley Edwards, Christopher Fowler, Michael Gregorio, Susanna Gregory & Simon Beaufort, Elly Griffiths, Jenna Hawkins, Suzette A Hill, Peter Lovesey, Michelle Spring, Andrew Taylor and L C Tyler for being so generous in providing their stories and for their patience.

Those who've kindly offered advice and support along the way: Susie Dunlop, Broo Doherty, Mike Ripley, Jon Gifford, Nancy-Stephanie Stone, Philip Robey, Christopher & Paulette Catherwood and Pippa Macallister.

To my wife, Sally, for her constant encouragement and support, correction of my grammar and so much more.

To Andrew Cocks of Ostara Publishing for his generous advice, kindness and for agreeing to publish this collection

To my colleagues at Heffers for their friendship

and support.

Richard Reynolds, Cambridge

Introduction

When Richard Reynolds asked me if I would help co-edit this anthology with Len Tyler I did not hesitate to say yes. I mean who would want to turn down such an amazing opportunity? I certainly did not. All the stories in this collection have been written by crime writers whom I admire, and I am really pleased to have had some part in putting this collection together. Thank you all for your stories I am sure that they will be enjoyed by all that read them.

In this collection two things come to mind – books and Cambridge. In my opinion short stories are a blessing. I am a big supporter of them, as I believe that they are a wonderful invention and they are in my belief one of the best ways to read a story. They can be used for example to introduce a character who later goes on to star in their own series and they can also be easily read in one sitting on a train journey. It is something that I frequently do.

The collection is extremely eclectic and I am sure that like me you will enjoy all the stories. It is brilliant for example to have the very first *Good Thief* short story by Chris Ewan. Michelle Spring tantalises us with a story about a dedicated reading group that manages to outfox a supermarket whilst Elly Griffiths entertains us with a story about someone who hates books.

So, settle down, inhale, and prepare to indulge yourself with some really good stories. It bears repeating that the crime fiction community is the best and I am proud to be part of it.

Ayo Onatade
September 2014

The Body in the Bookshop
by Simon Brett

'There was definitely a body lying on the bookshop floor,' said Renée.

'There definitely was,' Valerie agreed.

The two sisters were among the more unusual members of Jude's clientele. As a healer, she had come across a wide variety of humankind but Renée and Valerie were the only ones who had ever insisted on attending sessions together – and indeed both being healed at the same time.

And yet when she had met them, the idea made perfect sense. They had lived in the West Sussex seaside village of Fethering much longer than Jude herself had – they'd been born there in fact – and they did everything together. From their similarities in appearance and their intuitive understanding of each other one might have thought they were twins, but Renée was the older by two years. Their manner might also have made them be taken as a pair of spinsters, but in fact both had been happily married, though neither had had children. When their husbands had died within a year of each other, the two women, then in their sixties, had moved back to Fethering to a house very similar to the one in which they had been brought up, and some twenty years later they were still there. They made a familiar sight walking along Fethering's parade of shops and beach, two tiny figures with matching tiny chihuahuas. The octogenarians were known locally by the compound word 'RenéeandValerie'.

Jude had first met them when they approached her one morning on Fethering parade, asking if she was 'the healer who had moved into Woodside Cottage?' As soon as she had assured them that she was, they had launched into a litany of the pains caused to them by arthritis, speaking as ever in an alternate sequence of overlapping sentences. This had led to Jude taking the pair of them straight back home with her. There she had exposed the treatment couch in her cluttered sitting room and done what she could for each sister in turn. Arthritis, she recognised, was not a condition that could be cured, but she knew some forms of massage therapy that could alleviate the women's discomfort.

'We definitely did see the body,' Renée reiterated.

'Well, you seem pretty clear about that,' said Jude.

That morning they hadn't come round for a healing session. Jude had had a call quite early from Renée, saying that she and Valerie had something 'very important' they wanted to discuss with her. It was the kind of thing they wondered whether they ought to 'go to the police about'. But they thought maybe 'asking Jude first' might be a good idea. After all, you and your next-door neighbour Carole Seddon 'have got involved in murder investigations from time to time, haven't you?'

Jude had played down this suggestion, but still agreed that RenéeandValerie should come round to Woodside Cottage as soon as possible. And so it was that she found herself being told about the body the two old ladies had seen in the bookshop.

'You see,' said Valerie, picking up the baton, 'last night we were taking Churchill and Montgomery out for their late evening walk...' Jude knew that Churchill and Montgomery were the names of the two chihuahuas.

'We always do,' Renée continued, 'about half past nine ... you know for them...' she blushed '...to do their business.'

'Yes,' said Jude, reassuring them that she was not shocked by this revelation.

'And,' Valerie went on, 'we always walk along the parade, because there's good street lighting from our house to there ... you know, for safety reasons.'

'Not that we're pussy-footed,' insisted Renée.

'Oh no, by no means pussy-footed.'

'Anyway...' said Renée, 'you know, along the parade are all the shops...'

'Yes, I do walk there quite often,' said Jude. Every day, in fact.

'And usually...' it was Valerie's turn, 'all the lights are switched off...'

'Well, except in the estate agent's windows, they stay on all night...'

'Which always seems a bit odd to me, doesn't it, Renée?'

'Well, so you always say, Valerie, and I do so agree with you.'

'Because do you think the estate agents really get a lot of potential customers checking out the details of a country cottage in Fethering at three a.m. in the morning?'

Valerie giggled, and Renée joined in. Clearly this was a private joke between them. Renée stopped giggling first and went on, 'Well, anyway, last night we were going past the bookshop ... you know where the bookshop is, don't you?'

Jude assured them that she did. 'Called "Book and Candle".'

'Yes. It's run by that woman with red hair,' said Valerie.

'Lorna Philpott,' Jude supplied.

'Mind you, I don't think it's natural red,' said Renée.

'No, nobody's born with hair that colour,' her sister agreed.

'And if they had been, it wouldn't still be that colour at Lorna's age.'

'No. She's married, though,' said Valerie, as if this were a slightly unusual state for a woman with dyed red hair.

'Yes, the husband doesn't seem to be around much, though.'

'I don't think I've ever seen him.'

'No, nor have I,' said Renée.

There was a natural pause at the end of this little rattle of duologue. Then Valerie looked searchingly at Jude. 'You know her name, do you actually know Lorna Philpott?'

'Yes, I've been in the shop a good few times. She has an excellent "Mind, Body and Spirit" section.' Jude didn't mention that Lorna was a client, for whom the menopause had brought great misery as a final confirmation of her childlessness. Although her husband Mike had apparently never voiced any word of complaint or reproach, she felt that she had let him down. Healing had helped Lorna Philpott through a difficult time.

'Well, normally,' said Renée, picking up momentum after the brief lull, 'Book and Candle has all its lights off when we take Churchill and Montgomery for their little night-time walk to...'

'Do their business,' Jude filled in helpfully, sparing Renée's blushes.

'Yes, exactly.'

'But last night,' Valerie picked up, 'the lights were on...'

'The blinds were down...'

'Oh yes, they always are when the shop's closed.'

'And we were *intrigued...*'

'So we thought maybe the woman who runs it...'

'Lorna Philpott.'

'Exactly, Valerie. We thought maybe she might be working late...'

'You know, stock-taking or whatever...'

'Anyway, there was a little space between the edge of the blind and the window frame...'

'So Renée, who's always been very nosey–'

'It takes one to know one, Valerie.'

'Touché! Renée crept up to the window and peered through the crack...'

'And there I saw a dead body lying on the floor of the bookshop.'

'So I had a look too. And there it was – no question about it – a body lying on the floor. It was a woman, lying on her front...'

'With a jewelled dagger sticking out of her back.'

'There was blood all over her...'
'Blood all over her...'

'Well, really, Jude,' said Carole. 'I'm surprised that you take anything those two say seriously. They're completely gaga.'

'I disagree. All their marbles are firmly in place.'

They were sitting in the antiseptically clean kitchen of High Tor, the home of Jude's next-door neighbour Carole Seddon. By the Aga her Labrador Gulliver snuffled contentedly in dreams of killing hostile seaweed on Fethering Beach.

'Well, they always seem to be gaga to me,' announced Carole in a manner that defied argument. After a long career in the Home Office, she was a pragmatist, disapproving of flights of fancy – in anyone, and particularly in herself. 'And really! A woman's body lying on its front with a jewelled dagger sticking out of her back? It sounds like a scene from the local amdram's latest Agatha Christie.'

'Well, I believe them,' said Jude doggedly.

'But if RenéeandValerie really were witnesses to this "scene of the crime", why don't they go and tell the police about it?'

'I think they're worried they might be laughed out of court.'

'With justification, Jude. And they claim to have seen this gruesome tableau last night?'

'Yes.'

'Well, I'd have thought the first thing they should have done was to go to Book and Candle again this morning and see if there were any signs of their body.'

‘Oh, they did that before they rang me.’

‘And?’

‘And there was no sign of anything untoward. The bookshop’s blinds were up and everything looked exactly as normal.’

‘Well?’ Carole Seddon shrugged, as if her point had been made.

‘So they said they’d be embarrassed to go to the police.’

‘I don’t blame them. A very sensible decision, I would say. The police can be very patronising to people who see themselves as amateur sleuths.’ Carole spoke with feeling. She’d had a few uncomfortable encounters with the authorities during her investigative career.

‘But they’re still utterly convinced of what they saw,’ Jude persisted.

‘Jude, there are people in this great country of ours who are utterly convinced that they’ve seen spaceships landing and little green men climbing out.’

‘Well...’ Carole’s neighbour jutted out a stubborn lower lip. ‘I still feel inclined to investigate what RenéeandValerie saw.’

‘Please feel entirely at liberty to do so,’ said Carole with infinite condescension. ‘So long as you don’t expect me to participate at any level.’

‘Well, yes, I could go it alone...’ said Jude dubiously.

‘That’s the only way you can “go it”, I’m afraid. I’m certainly not getting involved.’

‘That’s a pity.’

‘Why a pity?’

‘Because RenéeandValerie were very keen that

you should be involved.'

'Oh?'

'Yes, they said...' Jude lied, 'that, though they'd appreciate the kind of intuitive input I might bring to the case...'

'Yes?'

'What they really wanted to tap into was your analytical and deductive skills.'

'Did they?' said Carole, interest beginning to kindle in her pale blue eyes behind their rimless glasses.

Jude was a great believer in synchronicity, so she was unsurprised later that morning to receive a call from Lorna Philpott, asking to arrange an appointment as soon as possible. The diary for the rest of the day was empty, so it was agreed that the bookshop owner would come to Woodside Cottage at three.

When Lorna was laid out on the treatment table, Jude ran her hands up and down the woman's body, not touching but just probing for the tensions and knots. The sitting room's curtains were drawn and the lights kept low. The fire was alight and aromatic candles burned on the mantelpiece.

'Hm, it's the shoulders and the small of the back,' Jude observed. 'Like it was the last time.'

'Yes. Can you make it better like you did the last time?' There was a lightness in Lorna Philpott's tone, which couldn't fully disguise the desperation in her plea.

'Hope so,' said Jude lightly. 'I'll start with just a basic massage to loosen you up, then see where we go from there. If you wouldn't mind just stripping down to your underwear...?'

Jude kept a very strict dividing line between her professional work as a healer and her hobby of investigation. She wouldn't have dreamt of asking one of her clients directly about a case. And rather like a Catholic priest in the confessional, she would never have revealed anything said during a healing session to anyone else – even Carole.

On the other hand, she had frequently gleaned useful information from casual conversation with people on her treatment table.

As her firm hands kneaded into the tightness of Lorna Philpott's shoulders, she said, 'And I presume you haven't come back for the same reason as last time?'

'No, no. I won't say it's gone away. There is an enduring sadness about having no children. Haven't you ever felt it, Jude?'

'I can honestly say I haven't, no.' Though Jude had had two husbands and many lovers, she had never met anyone with whom she had felt the need to make the commitment of a family. 'But I do understand the feeling. Just turn on your side, facing the fire, would you...?'

As her fingers probed into the tension along Lorna's collar bone, Jude asked, 'And how's everything going at Book and Candle?'

A long sigh preceded the answer. 'Oh, I suppose no worse than any other bookshop is doing at the moment. In other words, pretty badly. People come in and browse, find the books they want, then go home and buy them cheaper from Amazon. And of course the explosion of Kindles and other e-readers hasn't exactly boosted the sales of old-fashioned books.'

'No, but you're surviving?'

'Just about, I suppose. I do my best, set up events, readings, quizzes, Crime Evening, even book launches... I did one back in September for Tilly Thwaite – she's local and she had a book out then, and she's very efficient when it comes to publicity. So I do try, but it's an uphill struggle.'

'When we had our last sessions...' Jude knew she had to put the next bit delicately, '...you implied that, if you went through a bad patch with the shop, Mike'd always bail you out in the short term.'

'Yes, but I never wanted to go running to him.' Lorna responded with some asperity. 'However much he might have liked that.'

'Oh?' Jude made the monosyllable sound light and incurious.

'I'm afraid Mike has always wanted to dismiss Book and Candle as a wealthy woman's indulgence. He doesn't realise how seriously I take it as a business. Book and Candle is my baby. He doesn't realise that. Nothing would have given him greater satisfaction than having to bail me out.'

The only response was a non-committal 'Ah', but Lorna's words did stir a memory from their previous sessions. Jude remembered getting the impression then that all was not entirely comfortable in the Philpott marriage. That Mike was a rather unimaginative and demanding husband, and that for him Lorna's inability to bear children was not her only shortcoming.

'Oh well,' Jude continued in a comforting tone. 'I'm sure you'll weather out the recession, just like a lot of other businesses.'

'It's not just the recession,' said Lorna grimly. 'It's a fundamental shift in the way people access their reading material.'

'You don't just sell books, though, do you? You've still got the candle side of the business.'

'Yes, but that's only really there to justify the store's name. I never sold that many candles. And now, given all the new knick-knacky kind of shops that are springing up all over the place...' The sentence didn't seem worth finishing.

'Hm.' There was a silence while Jude's hands continued to do their magic. Then she said, 'So I suppose that's part of the tension...?'

'Hm?'

'The reason you've come to see me. Worries about the financial stability of Book and Candle.'

'That may be part of it, yes. Certainly I've got to find some way of making more out of the business.'

'A way that presumably doesn't involve you eating humble pie and asking Mike to help you out financially?'

Lorna Philpott jutted out a rueful lower lip. 'Fat lot of good that'd do now.'

'Oh?'

'The fact is, Jude, that Mike's lost his job.'

'Oh, I'm sorry. I thought he worked for a bank.'

'If you think that's still a guarantee of job security, you're behind the times.'

'Yes, I probably am. He wasn't involved in one

of the big banking scandals, was he?'

'Oh God, no. Mike's been on the marketing side for some years now. With the same bank since he left school. And done pretty well out of it, good income, quite a bit of foreign travel, no surprises. But now there's been some kind of "rationalisation" – that's what they call it these days – and apparently the "rational" thing was to chuck Mike out on his ear.'

'But surely with his experience, he could get something else, couldn't he?'

'You'd think so, wouldn't you? The trouble is, a lot of other people have also been "rationalised" recently. And many of them are rather younger than Mike. And considerably less expensive. Not many openings for the over-fifties.'

'But he must get some kind of compensation, mustn't he?'

'You'd have thought so, wouldn't you? But no, he doesn't get a lot. Little more than a year's salary. And then there's rather an ugly gap without any income until his pension kicks in. So Mike's going through all those processes you keep reading about in the papers, registering with head hunters, scouring the "Appointments" pages, trying to re-contact old friends in the banking business, applying for everything in sight. And very rarely even having an acknowledgment of his application. He's getting very depressed. Someone like him thought he'd got a job for life. And Mike's not good at change. Even if he got something new, I think he'd have a terrible adjustment to working in an unfamiliar environment.'

'I can see why you're stressed, Lorna.'

'Thank you.'

'And, er...' cue for a little more delicacy '...things are all right between you and Mike?'

'Oh yes. As ever.' But the airiness of Lorna Philpott's words was belied by the instinctive tensing of her shoulder muscles under Jude's fingers. Further questioning about the marriage would be required at some point, but now wasn't the moment.

Lorna went on, 'Mind you, it's a bit cramped with the two of us currently living in the flat over the shop.'

'I thought you'd got that big house over on the Shorelands Estate.'

'Rented,' said Lorna. 'And before long probably have to be sold.'

'I am sorry. I'm sure something'll come up.' It was automatic reassurance; Jude had read too much recession gloom in the papers to be optimistic about Mike Philpott's job prospects.

'Huh,' said Lorna. The sound summed up her hopelessness, and the mounting stress which had led her to seek the comfort of healing hands.

Since her client was being so forthcoming about her circumstances, Jude thought it might be the moment to try a more direct line of questioning. 'I heard about something strange happening at your shop last night ... at Book and Candle...'

Well, don't ask me about it,' came the tart reply. 'I wasn't there last night.'

'Oh?'

'I needed to ... get away from things for a while, so I went to my sister's in Hove and stayed there the night. Mike was on his own at Book and Candle.'

Carole and Jude had agreed to meet for an early evening drink at the Crown and Anchor, Fethering's only pub. Carole was determined to make it just an early evening drink. She knew how easily a couple of glasses of Chilean Chardonnay with Jude could lead to staying in the pub for supper. And Carole Seddon's temperament resisted such self-indulgence. In her fridge at High Tor there was a bowl of left-over chicken and rice which would heat up perfectly for an austere, solitary supper over the six remaining clues in a particularly recalcitrant *Times* crossword.

At the Crown and Anchor they were greeted by the landlord Ted Crisp, his hair and beard more haystack-like than ever. Once he had served their drinks, characteristically he treated them to the last joke he'd heard at the bar at lunchtime. 'Two fortune tellers meet on the seafront at Brighton. One says, "Lovely weather."

'"Yes," says her friend. "Reminds me of the summer of 2024."'

Once the two women had finished groaning, they moved across to sit in one of the pub's alcoves. Jude did not reckon the revelation that Mike Philpott had been alone in Book and Candle the previous evening constituted a breach of client confidentiality, so she told Carole.

'Hm. So he was alone in the bookshop – or the flat – with a woman,' came the response.

'What woman?'

'Well, the one who got stabbed – obviously.'

'Carole, I thought you didn't believe that RenéeandValerie had actually seen a body.'

'Well, the more I thought about it, the more I thought: why would they bother to make up a story like that?'

'Exactly. And what else did you think?'

'The usual things you'd think when a man is in the marital home alone with a woman not his wife.'

'But "the usual things" don't usually involve murder, do they?'

'No.' Carole was thoughtful for a moment. 'A sex game gone wrong, perhaps?'

'Really! You've been reading too much of the *Daily Mail.*'

Jude's neighbour was affronted. 'I do not read the *Daily Mail.* As you know, I'm a *Times* reader.'

Yes, but a lot of your attitudes are out of the *Daily Mail.* Jude had the thought, but didn't say it out loud. She didn't want their conversation to be sidetracked into irrelevant arguments.

'The other thing I've been thinking,' Carole went on, 'is: why was Lorna Philpott away that night?'

'She was at her sister's. She said she wanted a little time on her own.'

'Was her sister away then?'

'I don't think so. Why?'

'Well, when you want "time on your own", you don't go and see someone else, do you?'

'From Lorna's tone, I think for "time on her own" you could read "time away from Mike".'

'Oh? Problems with the marriage?'

'I don't know any details, but I got the impression Lorna was finding Mike's constant presence in the tiny flat over the shop a bit wearing. She's not used to having him around so much. He used to travel quite a bit for his work.'

Carole's antennae caught something there. '"Travel quite a bit"? Opportunities for a bit of extra-marital straying there perhaps...?'

'I've no idea.'

'And you didn't tell Lorna about what Renée-andValerie had seen?'

'It wouldn't have been appropriate. She was with me for a healing session.'

'Yes.' Carole couldn't keep the disappointment out of her voice. On many previous occasions she'd wished her neighbour might have been a bit more lax about the boundaries between her professional life and the business of investigation. She sighed. 'Well, it sounds like you've got all the information you're going to out of RenéeandValerie. So the only person who can actually tell us what happened last night at Book and Candle is Mike Philpott himself.'

'Yes. And it's a slightly difficult conversation to open with someone you've never met.'

'Oh, I thought you had met him...?'

Jude shook her head. 'Bit tricky to go up to him and say "Did you murder a woman in your wife's bookshop last night?"'

'I take your point. So there's nobody else we can ask, is there? Nobody who knows the couple well and might be able to cast a light on their relationship?'

'No there's no one who... Oh, just a minute!' A smile irradiated Jude's plump features. 'Yes, there is someone we could ask.'

'Who?'

'I'll tell you,' said Jude, reached for the menu in the middle of the table, 'when we've sorted out what we're going to have for supper.'

'I wasn't really intending to–'

'Go on.'

'Oh, all right,' said Carole. The chicken and rice could live to feed another day.

Tilly Thwaite had interviewed Jude when she'd been writing an article about alternative therapists in West Sussex, and the two women had stayed in touch. Tilly was a bundle of writing energy who would literally turn her hand to anything. After a couple of years as a cub reporter on the *Fethering Observer*, she had gone freelance, inventively rooting out stories and selling them to a variety of local newspapers and, increasingly, nationals.

When the market for freelance articles began to diminish as editors used their in-house staff more, Tilly had shifted to writing books. At first, like the one which had included Jude, they'd been manuals and listings, extended versions of the stuff she'd used to write articles about. Then she'd moved on to fiction, having minor success with a few chick-lit novels. When that genre blew itself out, Tilly Thwaite had metamorphised yet again, and started writing crime novels. For these she had used backgrounds that she had researched in her journalistic days.

She did not endue writing with any mystique; it was simply the means by which she could make a living. She had no sentimentality about her craft.

Nor did she show any sentimentality in her private life. Jude had heard many women saying they'd like to have a more masculine approach to relationships, but here was someone who actually put that theory into practice. Tilly Thwaite picked up men for sex and, as soon as she'd lost interest, dropped them. She never went on holiday with a man, travelling on her own to expensive hotels in exotic locations. If she met someone out there for a brief fling, fine. If not, she was perfectly content with her own company.

Tilly was also an indefatigable self-promoter, constantly plugging her wares on Facebook, Linkedin, Twitter and any other available platform. Jude, whose circle of friends was wide and varied, had huge admiration for Tilly's pragmatic approach to her work and life.

The attraction between the two women was mutual and Tilly, who lived in the nearby coastal village of Smalting, readily agreed to meet Jude for coffee in the Copper Kettle there the following morning.

'Can't be too long,' she said as they ordered their cappuccinos – and a croissant for Jude, whose breakfast seemed an age ago. 'I've got to keep up my word count on the new book.'

'How much do you demand of yourself per day?' asked Jude.

'Two thousand words.'

'Sounds a lot to me.'

Tilly, a small woman with skilfully blonded hair and perfect make-up, shrugged. 'It's less than I'd do when I was writing articles.' Characteristically, she moved straight to practicalities. 'Anyway, what is it, Jude? Why did you want to meet?'

'I believe you know Lorna and Mike Philpott...'

'Yes, sure. I've done a couple of promotional gigs down at Book and Candle. I'm doing one of Lorna's Crime Evenings in a couple of weeks.'

'What form does a Crime Evening take?'

'Oh, Lorna wheels out a couple of crime writers ... usually local, sometimes from a bit further afield. We do a bit of chat and some readings, then her regular clientele ask questions. It's all very low-key, but hopefully I shift a few books.'

'Funny, I haven't seen any adverts for the Crime Evening round Fethering.'

'No, that's not Lorna's way. She relies on word of mouth. Has this very loyal group of supporters – mostly female – who turn up to all her events. And I think she's very happy with that situation.'

'You say there's one of these Crime Evenings coming up?'

'Yes, a fortnight today. Lorna always does her Book and Candle events on Thursdays.'

'Hm.' Jude tapped her chin thoughtfully. 'You know Mike and Lorna quite well, don't you, Tilly?'

'Not very well. I know Lorna. Mike I've only met a couple of times.'

'And did you get the impression that everything was all right with the marriage?'

Tilly Thwaite grinned. 'Very direct, Jude. If anyone else asked me a question like that, I'd come up with some fudge by way of an answer. With you, though, I'm assuming you have some reason for asking it.'

'Thank you. Yes, I do.'

'O.K. Well...' She paused to marshall her thoughts, before continuing, 'The impression I got was that it had been a very workable marriage.'

'"Had been"?'

'Wait, Jude. Let me finish. All right, the lack of children was a sadness, certainly for Lorna. I really don't know Mike well enough to know how much it affected him. But the marriage worked well, in a kind of semi-detached way. Mike worked long hours, travelled a lot, they didn't really spend a great deal of time together. And Lorna had her separate life, most of which revolved about Book and Candle. That gave free rein to her imagination, and from everything I've ever seen of him, Mike doesn't possess an imagination. So, not a relationship of great burning passion, so far as I could see, but – to use the word I used before – "workable". Probably happier than the average marriage.' The note of cynicism in the last words made Jude wonder whether Tilly had had a husband at some stage in the past, before she developed her very satisfactory independent lifestyle.

'But then of course,' the writer went on, 'Mike lost his job.'

'I heard. And that upset the apple cart?'

'Totally, so far as I can tell. Having to let the big house, living on top of each other in that poky little flat over the shop, Mike paranoid about being unemployed ... hardly a recipe for marital bliss.'

'No.' Jude was silent, then went on, 'I wonder, Tilly, do you think it likely that Mike Philpott has ever had an affair?'

That suggestion elicited a bark of disbelieving laughter. 'You can't be serious, Jude! Mike? Have you met him?'

'No.'

'Well, if you had you'd know he'd never have an affair. He's so shy. Gauche, really. I often wonder how he ever summoned up the courage to ask Lorna out in the first place.'

'Yes, but–'

'Jude, if you're about to say: "It's the quiet ones you have to watch out for"...'

'No, I wasn't.' But in fact she had been on the verge of saying something not a million miles from that. 'I was just thinking, if Mike's as shy as you say, how on earth did he get into marketing? I would have thought that was the kind of work that required a degree of flamboyance.'

Tilly Thwaite shrugged. 'I've no idea. I think he's apparently very good on detail, entirely reliable, trained as an accountant. But in those traditional banking set-ups people often get promoted through the system, and he'd been there all his working life. What's that management thing about people being "promoted to their level of incompetence"?'

'"The Peter Principle".'

'Right. Well, I think Mike Philpott could have been an example of that in action. A safe pair of hands, a plodder. Certainly hard to see him in the role of marketing whiz kid. Maybe he was lucky to hang on to his job for as long as he did.' Tilly looked at her watch. 'Going to have to go shortly. Only done a hundred and seventy-four words so far this morning. I should be up to five hundred by eleven.' She gathered up her handbag. 'Now is there anything else you need to ask me?'

To Jude's disappointment, she realised there wasn't. And it seemed that her conversation with Tilly Thwaite had not advanced her investigation in any way.

Carole Seddon must have been watching for the taxi coming back from Smalting, because within a minute of Jude's return, she was round knocking at the door of Woodside Cottage. In a state of high excitement, she held out a copy of that day's *Fethering Observer*. 'ReneeandValerie weren't the only ones,' she said breathlessly. 'Look!'

Jude did as instructed and read:

'BODY OR NO BODY?

AN ANONYMOUS CALL TO FETHERING POLICE STATION ON TUESDAY REPORTED THE APPEARANCE OF A DEAD BODY IN "BOOK AND CANDLE", FETHERING'S ONLY INDEPENDENT BOOKSHOP. INVESTIGATION BY THE POLICE DISCOVERED NOTHING SUSPICIOUS ON THE PREMISES. "MAYBE SOMEONE HAD HAD A FEW TOO MANY AT THE CROWN AND ANCHOR," SUGGESTED THE SHOP'S PROPRIETOR, MIKE PHILPOT. "OR MAYBE SOMEONE WAS GETTING TOO EXCITED ABOUT 'BOOK AND CANDLE'S FORTHCOMING 'CRIME EVENING' ON THURSDAY 23 FEBRUARY AND LET THEIR IMAGINATION RUN AWAY WITH THEM."'

'Do you think it was ReneeandValerie themselves?' asked Carole.

'Who reported to the police? But, if so, why

would they be anonymous? Also, they said they were talking to me *rather* than going to the police.'

'They might have gone to the police after they'd talked to you.'

'Doesn't sound likely, Carole. But I'll ring them and check.'

Renée answered. Using a telephone was one of the rare occasions when the sisters could not share the conversation. But Renée, on her own, confirmed that no, they hadn't made any contact with the police. 'But now we know we didn't make up what we saw,' she said excitedly, 'because there's something about it in the *Fethering Observer.*'

Full of coffee from the Copper Kettle in Smalting, Jude decided it was near enough lunchtime to open a bottle of Chilean Chardonnay. Carole made her customary demur about 'drinking in the middle of the day', but still accepted a glass and quaffed away merrily while she was brought up to date with the little information gleaned from Tilly Thwaite. There was, Jude noticed while she was talking, a kind of impatience in her neighbour's manner, as if Carole had some revelation of her own she was waiting to unfold.

And so it proved. After commenting on the poor pickings from Tilly, she announced, 'I, however, have managed to move the investigation on a little.'

'Oh?'

'Yes,' Carole said airily. 'I contacted Mike Philpott.'

'Did you?'

'Mm. Which is why I shouldn't really be

drinking now.'

'Oh?'

'I've fixed to meet him for a drink early evening in the Crown and Anchor.'

'Good for you. What excuse did you invent for having the meeting.'

'I said I'd seen the thing about the Crime Evening in the *Fethering Observer* and I'd like to know more about it.'

'And he agreed to meet you, just like that?'

'Yes.' Jude wondered whether Mike Philpott, like his wife, would use any excuse to escape the confines of the flat above Book and Candle.

Carole looked slightly embarrassed as she said, 'It'll just be the two of us. Mike Philpott and me.'

'Fine.' Jude couldn't suppress a smile at the Carole's words. Had it been the other way round, she knew that her hypersensitive neighbour would have been deeply affronted not to be included in the interview. But Jude had the kind of nose that remained permanently in joint.

That afternoon Carole rang a friend from her time in the Home Office. Richard Franks was one of the few of her colleagues to whom she had warmed. Younger than her, he had seen the light round the time of Carole's early retirement, and left the Civil Service to set up his own business, which had thrived and seemed to be in a continual state of expansion.

Richard was delighted to hear from her, assuming at first that the call was professional. But when she told him the reason for her making contact, he listened intently to what she had to say.

Though pleased to be conducting this part of the investigation on her own, as six o'clock approached, Carole began to wish that she would have Jude with her for the forthcoming confrontation. Her neighbour, she knew, was more instinctively empathetic than she was. Carole's own spiky manner could put people off. Still, she had made her statement and she was going to stick by it.

A measure of her anxiety was that she had made little headway on the *Times* crossword by the time she set out for the Crown and Anchor. She arrived characteristically early, but as she sat in an alcove with her glass of Chilean Chardonnay, the clues remained stubbornly impenetrable.

As well as the *Times,* Carole had a copy of the *Fethering Observer,* open at the page with the report of the body – or lack of body – in Book and Candle. She had told Mike Philpott she'd have it on the table to help him identify her.

He was a thin, ascetic-looking man whose short haircut and severe glasses would have gone better with a suit than the green fleece and brown corduroy trousers he was wearing. He introduced himself with uncomfortable heartiness, said he was very sorry that he hadn't arrived in time to buy her a drink, and he was dying for a pint. But when he came back from the bar he was carrying a glass of mineral water.

'You said you were interested in the Crime Evening, Carole...'

It was a minor shock. She had almost forgotten

the pretext on which she had set up their meeting. But she recovered herself quickly enough and tapped the *Fethering Observer.* 'This is rather handy publicity for the event, isn't it?'

Mike Philpott beamed, as if he had been given a personal compliment. 'Doesn't hurt, does it?'

'Interesting, though. In the paper you are described as the "owner" of Book and Candle. I thought your wife ran it.'

'Lorna is more hands-on than I am, but it's always been a joint venture.'

'Ah.'

'I mean, it was my money that bought the place, but I've had to take a back seat over the years. Now, though, I'm going to be more closely involved.'

'Oh?'

'Yes, I've taken early retirement so that I can devote more time to Book and Candle.'

'I see.' So that was the story he wanted to make public. Fair enough.

Mike gestured towards the *Fethering Observer.* 'And it was that that got you interested in the Crime Evening, was it?'

'Yes.'

Again he beamed. 'Well, spread the word, won't you? More people we can get along, the better.'

'Right. I'd sort of got the impression that the Book and Candle events were, kind of, fairly exclusive, that more or less the same group of people went to all of them.'

'That's maybe how it was in the past,' said Mike Philpott, 'but things are going to change now I'm more personally involved. My background is in marketing, you see.'

'And you think you can build up the business?'

'Of course. The Body Shop just started from one shop.'

As he said that, Carole realised the full extent of Lorna and Mike Philpott's problems. She thought of the description Jude had relayed from Tilly Thwaite. 'A safe pair of hands, a plodder.' And now the plodder was hoping to rebuild his lost income from developing his wife's little bookshop. Mike was a fantasist, not probably a dangerous fantasist, but one for whom the only thing that lay ahead was disappointment. And a big threat to an already fragile marriage.

Once again Carole pointed to the report in the *Fethering Observer*. 'This was very clever of you,' she said, 'setting up the dead body in the shop.'

This prompted no denial, but another beam. What she was saying bolstered his self-image. 'Well,' he said in mock self-deprecation, 'you sometimes have to take the unconventional route to achieve success.'

'I'm sure you do. And I dare say you felt pretty secure that someone in Fethering would see the tableau you'd set up, and it'd be round the village in no time?'

He nodded, still in a state of self-congratulation. But then his face clouded. 'Mind you, nobody did seem to see it. I set the tableau up with a shop's dummy when it got dark, about nine o'clock, I suppose, and tidied everything away round three in the morning. I was awake all night, expecting the police to arrive, but they didn't come. Nobody saw it.'

Carole could have reassured him that his handiwork had at least been witnessed by Renéeand-Valerie, but it wasn't the moment. Instead, she said, 'You clearly haven't spent much time in Fethering. Very few people go out here after dark.'

'Well, I was rather annoyed,' said Mike peevishly. 'Eventually I had to make an anonymous call to the police myself.'

'Pretending to be someone who had seen the body in the bookshop?'

'Exactly.' He brightened. 'Still, the police did come round, and I explained to them that it hadn't been a real body and I'd just been preparing a display for the Crime Evening. And they were very friendly about it, and we had a good laugh at the way people in Fethering over-react to things.' His face clouded again. 'So as it turns out, I needn't have bothered setting up the tableau, since nobody saw it and I had to call the police myself.'

'And did you have to phone the *Fethering Observer* too, to get this story in?'

'Yes. Anonymously, of course. But they seemed to be pleased to have the story.' The *Fethering Observer* is pleased to have any story, thought Carole.

Mike Philpott's pride was returning as he said, 'Well, you have to do unconventional things in the world of marketing. None of the world's great entrepreneurs ever played by the rules.'

Under different circumstances Carole might have laughed. The man was so pitiable – someone who'd trodden down the paths of convention his whole life, comparing himself with 'the world's great entrepreneurs'.

'Well, congratulations, anyway,' she said. 'I hope the Crime Evening's a big success.'

'Oh yes.' Mike Philpott grinned. 'I've got a whole lot of other publicity stunts up my sleeve.' Inwardly Carole shuddered.

But she showed no outward sign of her reaction as she gently steered the conversation in another direction. 'You say your background was as an accountant, Mike...?'

'That's right.'

'Funny, I was talking to a friend of mine this afternoon who's in that line of business...'

'He'll fit the bill,' said Richard Franks' voice from the other end of the line.

It was two weeks later. Carole had been in High Tor rattling through a rather easy *Times* crossword when the phone rang.

'Really, Richard? Oh, I am pleased.'

'Each time I open a new office, no problems with getting the juniors – I'm inundated with applications. But getting someone to head up the operation is more difficult. You know, someone older, with a bit of *gravitas,* but not too much ambition. Not the kind of guy who's always going to be looking to move to a better-paid job in another company. Someone who's ... I don't know...'

'A plodder?' suggested Carole.

'Not to put too fine a point on it, yes. And Mike Philpott fits the brief exactly. So I was ringing to say thank you very much for suggesting he should send me his c.v. He's accepted the job. It's less money than he was getting at the bank, but he doesn't seem too worried about that. And the branch he's heading up is only in Worthing, so he won't have to move house or anything.'

No, he'll be able to move back into his existing house on the Shorelands Estate, thought Carole.

'And everything all right with your financial well-being?'

'You should know the answer to that, if anyone does.' Richard was her accountant and advised Carole on the management of her small but healthy portfolio of shares.

He chuckled. 'Anyway, so far as Mike Philpott's concerned, a good result all round.'

'I fully agree, Richard,' said Carole. Particularly for the man's wife.

A week later there was a call to Woodside Cottage from Lorna Philpott. She was so busy she couldn't make the next healing session she'd booked. And no, she didn't really feel she needed to reschedule it.

As Jude put the phone down, there was a satisfied smile on her generous lips.

Carole went to pick her neighbour up at quarter to seven. They were both going to Lorna's Crime Evening at Book and Candle. Jude wanted to see Tilly Thwaite, apart from anything else. She had an open bottle of Chilean Chardonnay and suggested a drink before they left, 'in case there isn't any booze at the bookshop' (there was, as it turned out, plenty).

Jude raised her glass to Carole and they clinked. 'A very satisfactory outcome.'

'Oh, I agree, Jude. Have you heard any more

from RenéeandValerie?'

'We'll see them tonight.'

'Oh?'

'Yes, nothing's going to keep those two away from the Crime Evening. They're convinced they're going to find dead bodies on every shelf.'

'Hm...' Carole was wryly thoughtful. 'Pity, though...'

'What?'

'Well, that there never was a dead body. No crime was committed. No one got murdered.'

'No,' Jude agreed. 'On the other hand, a death was averted.'

'Whose death?'

'The death of a marriage,' said Jude, and she took a long swallow of Chilean Chardonnay.

Death of the Author
by Alison Bruce

Charlie Trace leant against the frame of his open front door and let the dregs of the guests squeeze out past him. He was aware that they turned back to wave, but his attention was only on the phone call now. 'I don't write anything that I'm not happy to own, and I don't say it either,' he growled.

Bill Hammond grunted in reply. He'd been Charlie's agent for almost twenty years and that meant they knew one another well – well enough for Charlie to know what Bill really meant. Then, for good measure, Bill said it anyway, 'Charlie, you're full of shit.'

Charlie let the words settle. He ran his tongue over his teeth and considered Bill's perspective. 'I'm standing in the doorway of my new house, you really should see the view Bill.' Charlie's house faced onto Midsummer Common, which made it prime Cambridge property, and which, come to think of it, pretty much amounted to prime property nationwide. He glanced over his shoulder, the last two guests were undergraduates. Young enough to hang on to his every word, but comfortably old enough to count as legal. 'Prime property Bill. That's what I've earned for both of us.'

'And is that,' snapped Bill, 'the signal for me to

kowtow to the best-selling Charlie Trace and just be thankful?'

'You work it out.'

'I have. I am severing our agreement. That interview went too far...'

'It will blow over, it was a great piece.'

'No, it was crass. You went too far and if you're going down I'm not going with you.'

Charlie still had the phone to his ear when Bill cut him off. 'Bastard,' he breathed.

He left the front door open and headed for the kitchen. Alesha and her friend leant close over their flutes of bubbly, they looked less keen and more cunning now. The night had rapidly turned sour. He took their glasses, poured them into the sink and asked them both to leave.

Each patient's television viewing was displayed on a small, flat screen mounted like an anglepoise lamp so that it could twist and tilt its way across the bed. Miriam Lloyd's had been pushed to one side but the screen was still in Goodhew's line of sight and only a couple of feet from his chair near her bed. It silently displayed the BBC News channel, the same stories rotated every few minutes, flickering in the unmoving room and creating the impression that time had been trapped in a fifteen minute loop.

Goodhew had been in the loop for six hours; since she'd left surgery and been stabilised enough for this bed. Before that she'd belonged to the paramedics as they'd fought to save her from dying on the tarmac of Maids Causeway. The driver who'd hit her had been a breath under the drink-drive limit but a breath under the speed limit too; driver and pedestrian both possibly saved by those two breaths.

She'd *run from nowhere,* but then, the driver would say that. The call had come in at 11.42 but no other motorist on that perpetually busy stretch of road, or any occupant from any of those windows facing onto the street, had seen a thing. Just one student had come forward because she'd heard the bang of car on person. *Like a small explosion.*

The road had been cordoned off, but the saturation of blue pulsing and bright white pools of light, would have been visible from the other side of Midsummer Common, drawing the curious until one of them noticed an open doorway and caught sight of the other body.

Goodhew had arrived at five minutes before midnight. Now, a total of eleven hours later, his tired gaze settled back on the national news and he watched a repeat of the first news' footage. A reporter stood in the dark, near a line of police tape, with floodlights and a police tent two hundred yards behind that. A red banner of text rotated at the bottom of the screen. CHARLIE TRACE *MURDER. Celebrated but controversial author killed in Cambridge knife attack.*

Goodhew checked his phone; #CharlieTrace-Murder was trending on Twitter too, along with *#DeathOfTheAuthor,* probably, he guessed, the gleeful creation of a first year English literature student. A new hash-tag had sprung up since he'd last checked; *#TraceMurderSuspect* followed by variations and re-tweets of a woman being questioned by police.

Being questioned wasn't how he would describe it. He looked up from his phone, to Miriam Lloyd. She had been unconscious at the scene of the accident and remained so. He knew, from her notes, that she was 52 years old and an administrator for one of the many English Language schools in Cambridge centre. She drove an older model VW Golf and lived with her nineteen-year-old daughter in a rented house five miles out, in Barton. On the face of it she seemed to have had little in common with Trace, but the blood coated knife in her jacket pocket said otherwise.

Just then her lips parted as she tried to form words.

'Mrs Lloyd? Miriam?'

She took a few seconds to respond, then her eyelids flickered. 'Tony,' she whispered.

Kincaide had led them into the corridor and closed the door behind him. He continued to grip the handle as though he thought it might be pulled open from the other side. Unlikely, Goodhew thought, since Miriam Lloyd was still barely conscious, heavily medicated and attached to a drip.

But, as PC Sue Gully had commented, it was all about effect with Kincaide. There were days when the way Kincaide answered the phone, held a pen and probably even breathed that irritated her too. It was a shame she wasn't here right now; she always enjoyed the moments when Goodhew found it impossible to contain his distaste for Kincaide.

'I'm not prepared to back you up on this,' Goodhew told him.

'Gary, her eyes were open, it counts as an arrest.'

Goodhew shook his head, 'She's not in a fit state.'

'She spoke when I asked her if she understood and confirmed her name.'

'You can't ask her any questions when she's drugged up like that.'

'We would if she was an assault victim about to die. We'd get whatever we could from her and use it in court. I don't see the difference.' Kincaide set his jaw and stared past Goodhew, along the corridor towards A and E and the exit. 'I'll be speaking to Marks in a few minutes, requesting that we charge her.'

DI Marks wouldn't go for it, at least not without more to back it up. Goodhew shook his head but didn't reply, he knew his breath would be wasted and, instead, found himself studying the limp lapel of Kincaide's knock-off suit and its pretentions of being the real thing.

'Stay with her,' Kincaide instructed. A smile flickered in one corner of his mouth, 'I know I can trust you to keep notes of anything useful.'

Goodhew nodded, 'I'll grab a coffee and go back in.' He turned from Kincaide, he didn't need a drink, just needed to be out of Kincaide's orbit until he was sure that Kincaide really had left the building.

Miriam Lloyd thought she would have known nothing about the time she lay unconscious, but, as she adjusted to the stripes of sunlight that cut between the blinds, she knew that smells of the ward, the footfalls on the hard tiled floor and even her own immobility all made sense.

She wasn't alone either. She didn't see anyone at first but instinctively knew that she only had to turn her head towards the shady corner of the room and she would find someone there.

Not her daughter though. She would have spoken as soon as Miriam stirred, or pulled closer to reach for her hand. She turned her head a little, enough to glance at her fingers and make sure that no one was holding them. Then she looked at the man in the visitor's chair.

He looked almost too young to be there for any genuine reason, young enough to be looking to someone older for answers. She guessed therefore that he'd been told to sit there, to wait for her to wake then fill in whatever pedantic form he might be about to produce.

'Mrs Lloyd?' His voice was firm and clear; her opinion of him wavered and changed almost instantly. 'I'm DC Gary Goodhew. How are you feeling?'

'Almost awake.' He held her in sharp focus and she could tell then that he'd come for information. She exhaled slowly, hoping to buy enough time to gather her thoughts. Her mind flashed to anecdotes of people in peril, their minds racing and constructing escape routes with only milliseconds to spare, but it flashed a single image back to her; Charlie Trace. Dead. Curled on the floor as though he'd clutched his stomach, fallen to his knees then tipped to one side. He hadn't reached out or attempted to crawl away, he'd just stayed still with his hands wasting their last seconds trying to hold back the blood that slipped effortlessly between his weakening fingers.

The blood had pooled. Miriam blinked as she remembered the smell of his urine as it slid along the channels between the glossy floor tiles.

Charlie Trace had deserved to die.

'Mrs Lloyd?'

She opened her eyes and studied him some more. He leant forwards, resting his elbows on his knees. 'I need to ask you some questions about last night.' His physique was strong and he seemed serious beyond his years. She revised her estimate of his age up to late-twenties. 'Do you know why you are in hospital?'

'Something hit me. Feels like it could have been a bus.'

'It was a car. The driver claims you ran into the road. What do you remember before the accident?'

'Feeling crushed and elated all at once. I wasn't the only one who hated him, and I felt as though the world had improved simply because he no longer breathed.'

'Who?'

'You know who.'

'For my notes.'

'Charlie Trace.' She expected Goodhew to react at hearing Trace's name spoken so openly, but his expression gave away nothing. 'He made a name for himself by humiliating others; I wanted to do something about it.'

'Tell me what happened.'

'I visited his house.' She started her next sentence then paused, her head was rapidly clearing now. It was telling her that she needed to be careful. *Say nothing.*

'Mrs Lloyd?'

She pressed her lips together. *Say nothing.* Say nothing until she had worked out what had happened. And what they knew.

He tried coaxing her with questions, but she succeeded in locking him out until his phone bleeped with an incoming text. He glanced at the screen and, finally, stood to leave.

She relaxed, but a little too soon because he turned back at the door. 'So, who's Tony?' he asked.

'My daughter.' And, for a moment, her mask slipped. 'Has something happened?'

'It was the name you spoke as you were coming round.'

He hadn't even realised it had been a female name, let alone her daughter's. She managed a small smile; she was out of her depth already. 'Toni, short for Antonia of course. She was Rudy's sister, but she didn't kill Trace.'

Before tonight Goodhew had known the name Charlie Trace, he'd never read anything he'd written and never planned to. In the last ten years Charlie Trace's writing career had taken a backseat to his partying and rent-a-gob appearances on TV and radio, debating everything from the future of publishing to the future of the country's youth. He still produced novels, still sold them to a loyal body of fans who seemed to stay with him no matter what scandal followed, despite the claims of plagiarism from a young writer, despite the suicide of that same writer.

'Rudy Costello?' he asked her.

'That was his pen name, Rudy Lloyd to us.' She sighed as her head sank back on the pillow. 'He is why Charlie Trace deserved to die.'

'And is that why you went to his home? To kill him?'

She nodded slowly, 'I suppose it is.'

'And did you?'

She looked straight at him but didn't reply, no discernible emotion appeared on her face. Not fear, or satisfaction or guilt, just curiosity at what Goodhew might say next; she was clearly hoping that he had the answer to something.

'It was his housewarming, but you weren't a guest. So was it a coincidence that you chose tonight or did someone tell you?' She held his gaze too solidly and he knew he was warm. 'Did Toni tell you?'

A small smile touched her lips, curling with an equally subtle tinge of irony. 'I heard, that's all.'

He needed to find the right topic, and if her daughter was off limits perhaps her son wouldn't be. He settled back in his chair. 'So, tell me about Rudy.'

The sharp tangent seemed to throw her, but her expression softened immediately. 'Rudy?' She tilted her face towards the ceiling and closed her eyes, mouthing his name. She smiled as she remembered. 'He was so talented. Funny too. And he adored his sister.' Her eyes reopened but her gaze slipped past Goodhew. 'His father used to say that Rudy thought in rainbows, that nothing was dull or impossible to him. And I believed Andy, until close to the day Rudy died.'

'When Charlie Trace accused him of stealing his work?'

She looked back at him and to Goodhew's surprise, she shook her head. 'Not really, well I don't think so. It wouldn't have been so hard for Rudy to prove that the work was his; his writing was as good as his fingerprint. No, it was the betrayal, Rudy loved Trace, he considered him to be his ally and mentor but then Trace turned and humiliated him in public. People who had been his friends refused to speak to him. His agent and publisher dropped him and his career was over barely before it had begun. All Rudy wanted to know was why Trace had done it.'

'Professional jealously perhaps?'

'Maybe. But my ex-husband knew Charlie Trace back when he was plain Gareth Cooper, said he'd do anything for attention.'

'So he thinks Trace wanted publicity?'

Her eyes darkened. 'I don't know what he thinks. He cleared off after Rudy's death. For Toni and me it was like we'd been bereaved twice.'

'Does she know you're here?'

Miriam ignored the question and, instead, struggled up onto one elbow. 'How could that bastard Trace think he had the right to hold up his head? To push himself right under our noses? The last thing we want is to risk seeing him, or having the press in our faces again, or to be left jumping at shadows in our own home town.'

PC Sue Gully found Goodhew in Addenbrooke's Hospital's main concourse. He sat alone with his coffee to one side and a sheet of paper directly in front of him. She glanced at it as she took the seat opposite.

He'd only written two words, *'WHY NOW?'*

'Prolific eh?' He glanced up, 'What do you have?'

'We've been in contact with the last couple of guests, Alesha Hart and her friend Emily Malik. They left after Trace had a telephone argument and became verbally abusive.'

'To them?'

'Yes and no. He was furious with the caller and continued to vent afterwards, shouting obscenities down the phone even after the man had hung up.'

'So they saw a less charming side to him and cleared off?'

'Uh-huh.'

'But they knew it was a man?'

Gully grinned, 'Yep, Bill Hammond, Literary Agent.' She passed a phone number on a Post-it note across to Goodhew.

'Does Marks have this?'

'He's chasing down Miriam Lloyd's daughter Toni, so I left him a message. And unfortunately I can't seem to find Kincaide, so that's all yours.'

She watched Goodhew as he moved to a quieter area. He spoke for several minutes, turning his back on the concourse and facing a noticeboard each time he needed to concentrate. He seemed more thoughtful when he returned.

'Well?' she asked.

'Bill Hammond dumped him, he said. Wanted

to put as much distance as possible between himself and Trace before the shit hit the fan.'

'What shit?'

'What fan more like.' Goodhew drew his sheet of paper closer to him. 'Trace made a documentary and it was due for broadcast next week. He refers to the aftermath of Rudy Costello's death as a *"career highlight"* and, according to Hammond, when the interviewer gave him the opportunity to show compassion, Trace claimed that the suicide was no more than Costello's admission of guilt. He was unrepentant and Hammond wanted out before his client became a total pariah.'

Gully nodded towards Goodhew's two word question, 'That answers that then. Now what?'

Goodhew smiled, 'Hammond told someone about the interview. We cross our fingers and hope he also tells them that we're about to charge Miriam Lloyd.'

'And are we?'

'Only if she's guilty.'

Miriam had said little since Goodhew's brief reappearance, this time a policewoman in uniform came with him and it was she who now sat near the window. She was polite when she spoke but mostly silent.

It was almost an hour since they'd spoken, when Miriam had asked again whether her daughter was on her way. PC Gully had promised to find out, had left the room for less than a minute, then returned with the message, *she'll be here soon.*

So this was a waiting game; Miriam could feel it. Her thoughts began to drift, picturing scenarios that filled her with fear, then calming herself a little when she imagined the words she might use if the time came to confess.

Just then she saw PC Gully's attention turn to the door, so she followed her gaze. Goodhew was back. 'You have a visitor,' he said, 'You have two minutes together. You are both under caution and I will be in the room the whole time. Do you understand?'

Miriam nodded as PC Gully slipped quietly outside.

Goodhew held the door a little wider and Miriam managed to push herself into a half-sitting position, expecting for her daughter, Toni, to appear.

'How are you Miriam?'

She froze with her cannula-free hand halfway through straightening the thin hospital blanket. 'Andy?'

He'd lost weight since she'd last seem him, but aside from that he hadn't changed much. He wore a blue shirt with narrow white stripes and it looked like one she'd bought him ten years ago.

Her ex-husband stopped near the foot of her bed, 'I'm so glad I reached him first.' She glanced at Goodhew, then back at Andy who seemed to read her thoughts. 'I've told him what I did,' he said. 'I had no intention of letting anyone else take the blame for this. Bill told me about the interview and I told Toni. I wanted you both to be prepared for the pain, I should have known you might snap...'

'I didn't snap, I calmly decided to kill him.'

'Miriam.' He repeated her name once more and

both times sounded as though it was meant as a full and complete sentence, filled with sentiment. He moved to the side of the bed and she watched him take her hand. 'I'm sorry I ever introduced Rudy to Charlie Trace. I couldn't guess what would happen, but I knew Trace, I should have seen it was a bad idea.' His hand squeezed hers a little harder. 'I'm sorry I left you and Toni, and I'm sorry I haven't been much of a father ever since. But I'm not sorry I killed him. I'm just so glad I got to him before you.'

And so glad it wasn't Toni, she added silently. Miriam pressed her free hand over his. 'Thank you,' she whispered.

The Best Revenge
by Kate Charles

First of all, let me say that I have never aspired to be either a crime writer or an actual detective. Aspiring to be a priest was challenging enough for me, and I've only just achieved that.

And it's been an uphill struggle all the way. Not because I don't have the ability – false modesty aside – but because people don't take me seriously. They never have. People have an annoying tendency to judge other people on what they look like, and I don't look like anyone's idea of a priest. Or even a person with a brain, actually. I'm short, way heavier than I should be, and I have what some might delicately refer to as an over-developed chest. Huge boobs, to put it bluntly. And I'm blonde. Not just kind of blonde, but 'blessed' (or so my mother has always claimed) with Shirley Temple ringlets. There's nothing I can do with them but let them curl.

So I got into all of this because of Nicky. Because Nicky is just about the only person who *does* take me seriously. Even if he doesn't love me. At least not in the way I love *him*.

I fell in love with Nicky the moment I saw him, our first day at theological college. I mean, who wouldn't? He's gorgeous, and clever, and funny. He's also gay, which is a major drawback when it comes to our relationship.

But that doesn't stop us from being friends, and that's what we are. Best friends. We do all sorts of things together, and enjoy each other's company. And if, one day, a miracle were to occur and he were to wake up straight, and in love with me – well, then, life would be perfect. My other friends tell me it isn't going to happen, but ... you never know, do you? Believing in miracles is part of my job.

So. About a year ago, last summer, during our final term at theological college in Cambridge, Nicky came to me with a flyer he'd picked up in town. 'Look at this, Tamsin,' he said. 'A one-day workshop on crime writing. In conjunction with Heffers' annual "Bodies in the Bookshop" event. Let's sign up for it.'

I stared at him. 'Why on earth would we want to do that?'

'Because,' he said, 'it's being taught by Jake Striker and Dougal McPherson. *Jake Striker*, Tam. I mean – a whole day with Jake Striker!'

Jake Striker, world-famous, mega-best-selling author of crime thrillers. I'd never read one of his books, or even been tempted to, but of course I knew the name. As far as I was aware, Nicky hadn't read any of his books either. 'But why?' I repeated.

'He's so ... hot,' Nicky explained patiently, rolling his eyes, showing me the flyer.

Looking at the photo he was pointing to, I caught on. Not my idea of an attractive man at all, with that designer stubble and the leather jacket. Mean and moody. But I knew that Nicky had a weakness for the type. 'Isn't he married?' I pointed out. 'To that bimbo from the telly?'

Nicky waved it away. 'I don't want to *marry* him, Tam. I just want to stare at him for a few hours.'

I shook my head, and a look of low cunning crossed his beautiful face. 'Well, if you don't want to go, I could always ask Callie instead.'

Callie Anson, one of our circle of friends. I didn't think she would be in the least interested, but at that point I gave up. 'All right,' I said. 'I'll do it.'

It might be amusing, I told myself. I'd be able to spend a whole day with Nicky. And there was the added attraction of Dougal McPherson, the author of a popular series of twee Scottish detective stories which have long been a guilty pleasure of mine, to be read furtively in bed at night. I confessed to myself that I wouldn't mind meeting Dougal McPherson – though I wasn't about to admit it to Nicky.

As things worked out, though, my curiosity about Dougal McPherson was not destined to be satisfied. When we arrived on the day at the room where the workshop was to be held, it was hard to miss Jake Striker, holding forth in the centre of the room, filling the space with his over-sized personality, drawing people to him like moths to a flame. But the man next to him wasn't the avuncular, elderly Scotsman I'd seen in so many book jacket photos. He was a fairly weedy-looking youngish chap in jeans, trainers, and a tee-shirt which proclaimed 'Writing Well is the Best

Revenge', be-spectacled and wearing a somewhat apologetic – almost self-effacing – expression.

All was made clear eventually. 'Dougal McPherson wasn't able to be with us today,' Jake Striker announced when the clock reached the appointed starting time. 'Something to do with the Edinburgh Book Festival.' There were a few murmurs of disappointment, but Striker continued. 'Instead my "partner in crime"' (he laughed, of course) 'is my colleague Tim Billings.'

The weedy chap bowed his head in acknowledgement. I looked at Nicky, who shrugged and raised his eyebrows. No enlightenment there, then.

Like I said before, I'm not interested in writing a crime novel. What I *am* interested in, though, is people, and what makes them tick. Apparently some writers are interested in that, as well, so the workshop itself had more to offer than I'd expected.

I found it fascinating that everyone, including Nicky of course, was totally focused on Jake Striker, and the pearls of wisdom he dispensed. He did most of the talking, while his acolytes scribbled down his words like they were the Ten Commandments being handed to Moses. 'Thou shalt not use too many adjectives' – that sort of thing. Holy Scripture, revealed Truth.

Tim Billings barely got a look-in. As far as I was concerned, though, when he did say something, it was worth listening to.

That, along with my natural curiosity (which some call nosiness!) and a certain stubborn streak of independence from the herd mentality, led me to choose Tim Billings as my lunch companion, when a couple of trays of sandwiches and bowls of crisps were brought in at midday. Nicky followed everyone else to the table where Jake Striker established himself. I was the only one to sit at the second table, across from the other crime writer.

I smiled at him, but before I had a chance to introduce myself, there was a great commotion at the other table. 'Who,' Jake Striker shouted, holding his sandwich aloft with a dramatic gesture, 'is trying to kill me?'

For a second or two, you could have heard a pin drop. All eyes were on the famous writer.

'I told them no prawns. NO prawns!' He threw the sandwich down on his plate. 'And what do they send? Bloody prawn mayonnaise!'

One of the women at the table said something to him, too quietly for me to hear.

He didn't lower his voice. 'It isn't just that I don't like prawns. I'm deadly allergic to them. One prawn would be the end of me!'

'Thank goodness you noticed before you took a bite!' another woman contributed, looking at him with an awe-struck expression. 'I think there are plenty of other sorts of sandwiches here, Mr Striker. Here's a nice ham and cheese.'

Tim Billings raised an amused eyebrow at me across the table; I stifled a giggle.

Belatedly I introduced myself. 'I'm Tamsin Howells,' I said.

He nodded. 'Tim Billings. You've never heard of me, have you?' he said conversationally, reaching with deliberation for a prawn sandwich.

I didn't want to hurt his feelings, but had to be honest. 'No,' I admitted.

'I'm not surprised.' He gave me a sweet, rather wistful smile. 'My first novel, *Death of a Civilised Man,* was published the same day as Jake Striker's *Bloody Murder.* By the same publisher, actually. And guess which one got the better reviews?'

'Yours?' I hazarded a guess, figuring I had a 50/50 chance of getting it right.

Tim nodded, looking pleased. '"A lyrical work which transcends the crime genre." That's what the TLS said. They didn't actually review *Bloody Murder* at all.'

I didn't know what to say. *What happened?* was the question I wanted to ask, but it seemed a bit rude.

'But *Bloody Murder* was on the best seller list for ... well, practically forever. By the time it dropped out of the top ten, *Death of a Civilised Man* was already remaindered.' His mouth twisted in a smile which was no longer wistful.

Then he told me, between bites of his prawn sandwich and in a few concise words, how the publishing business works. For whatever reason – his rugged good looks, his celebrity wife, his commercially popular style – the publishers had decided to put their money on Jake Striker. Literally. After giving him a huge advance, they'd splashed out on publicity, investing in billboards, display ads in newspapers both highbrow and lowbrow, and advantageous placement in bookshops. They'd sent him on an international tour, got him on every television talk show in America.

They had made him into a global best-selling superstar. Every book he wrote – and he seemed to churn them out with great rapidity – went straight to the top of the list. Jake Striker had a mansion in St John's Wood, a country house in Cheshire, a farmhouse in Provence, a *pied-à-terre* in Manhattan, and a villa in L.A. 'He even has his own jet,' Tim confided quietly. 'And I ... I live in a bed-sit. In Lewisham.'

I know that life isn't fair, but this struck me as egregiously unjust. 'Isn't there anything you can do?' I demanded. 'Show the publishers your reviews. Tell them how much better your books are than his!' I was sure that they were, even though I'd never read one.

Tim took his time answering, finishing his sandwich first. Half of a prawn had dropped out and lay on his plate. He picked it up, contemplated it, then placed it carefully on his serviette. 'They don't care,' he said at last, and now his expression was bleak. 'They honestly don't care. Quality means nothing to them. The numbers are all that matter, and the numbers are a self-fulfilling prophecy. The publishers decide who is going to be the best seller, and then they make it happen.'

'But why can't there be *two* best sellers? Or three or four?'

He shook his head. 'There's only room for one, you see. Winner takes all. So the only way you'll ever see my name on the best seller list is ... if something bad happens to Jake Striker.' He gave an ironic laugh.

I felt sorry for him, but I didn't think it was very funny. 'Don't you believe what it says on your tee shirt?' I asked him, pointing.

Tim looked down at his chest. 'Writing well is the best revenge.' He grinned. 'Oh, yeah. Right.'

Something bad *did* happen to Jake Striker, of course. I'm sure you've heard all about it – seen it on the news, read about it on the internet. It shut Twitter down for the better part of three hours, there was such an overload of traffic on the site. Shock, horror. Conspiracy theories, weeping and wailing. How could someone so young, so talented, so good looking, so rich, be cut down like that, in his prime?

It happened at 'Bodies in the Bookshop', in Heffers. I wasn't there – I was working on my heuristics essay that evening – but Nicky was a witness, and I heard about it afterwards. One minute Jake Striker was signing books for his hordes of fans, and the next minute he was on the floor, in anaphylactic shock. An ambulance was summoned; he was rushed to hospital, but was dead on arrival.

A tragic accident, the inquest said. Somehow he'd ingested a bit of prawn, and the severe allergic reaction had been fatal.

For a while afterwards, his book sales went through the roof. Everyone who hadn't read Jake Striker before was reading him now. The same thing happened to Michael Jackson, you remember – he hit the top of the charts after he died, prompting the comment that death was a good career move for him.

There was one Jake Striker book still in the pipeline, it transpired. *Slash and Die* was published in time for Christmas gift-giving and sold in the millions – you probably got a copy or two from your nearest and dearest.

But things move on, and after a few months the millions of copies of *Slash and Die* started finding their way into charity shops.

A few weeks ago I saw a sign on the side of a double-decker bus for a new book called *Blood Fugue* – an intriguing title, with a hint of cleverness. The next time I went past a bookshop, copies of *Blood Fugue* were stacked in the window. And I saw that the author was Tim Billings.

On impulse, I went in and bought a copy. I read it over the next few nights. It was terrific.

Several days ago, surfing the internet, I came across the latest best seller list. The book at the top of the list was *Blood Fugue*.

Sometimes I wake in the middle of the night, and just for a moment I wonder.

Accident?

Or not?

I wonder…

Should I say something to anyone?

Maybe...

But like I said before, no one takes me seriously. I'm just a blonde vicar with big boobs. What do I know about ... murder?

And it *was* a very good book.

Maybe writing well really *is* the best revenge.

Killing Your Darlings
by Ann Cleeves

The idea came to me overnight. Not in a dream because I didn't sleep much those days. It appeared more as a vision, an epiphany. I'd been struggling to find an occupation, something to suit my restlessness and my need for an audience. A narrative to explain myself. Suddenly I had the image in my head of a battered van driving down the military road in Northumberland. In the back of the van I saw a stock of stories, new books in brightly-coloured boxes. I would become a mobile bookseller. Fiction has been my stock in trade and my downfall. Why not play to my strengths and make story-telling my living at least for a while. After years in the city I craved space and a sharp, easterly wind. An excuse to be on the road, moving every day. I'd always had a romantic passion for the place of my birth and now I longed to be north in the borders again.

I bought an old VW caravanette. It had been owned by an elderly hippy, was painted canary yellow and had room inside for me to sleep and to store the books. I had two wild days in London, chatting to publisher friends, haggling over discounts, deciding which titles would work best with the ladies who lunch in the smart market towns and with the struggling sheep farmers in the hills. I had most fun choosing the children's stories and imagined the response I'd receive when I pulled picture books from the boxes like a magician fishing a rabbit from a hat. Performance was part of my old world too.

It was early spring when I drove north and began touring with my travelling circus of stories. I pitched up in village halls, scout huts and rural schools, giving my spiel to anyone who turned up. Telling my tales, singing my songs, selling my books. Word spread. My website was printed on the side of the van and each night there'd be a new invitation from a playgroup, a WI or an enterprising librarian. If there were kids in the audience I'd read the picture books, playing the parts with different voices, making them howl with laughter. For the first time in years I was happy. Here I was: Roddy Fellowes, drop-out cop and pied piper to the culturally deprived.

I noticed her first in Amble. I'd set up in a café ... close to the harbour. It was mid-April, unseasonably warm, the trees heavy with blossom. By now I could lay out my stock in minutes – I was fitter than I'd been in my undercover days. I'd carried out the boxes and changed into my costume of black jeans, black T-shirt and the flamboyant silk jacket made for me by an ex-lover who was wardrobe mistress for a TV company. That evening there was an adult audience. The café served wine and freshly caught fish and I was the after dinner entertainment. When the diners were settled with their coffee I started my pitch. I'd chosen books with a watery theme and read three poems from the new Jen Hadfield collection, scraps from a weird contemporary novel about a mermaid and a couple of pages from Du Maurier's *Jamaica Inn* for the traditionalists.

She was sitting at the back and even when I was reading my attention was drawn to her. The café was lit by candles but still she shone out to me. I've always been attracted to dark, Celtic women and she had hair that was almost black and impossibly pale skin. In the dim light I couldn't make out the colour of her eyes but I knew they'd be flinty blue. When I finished reading I was surrounded by a crowd of buyers and by the time the room had cleared the woman had gone.

After that she was often in the audience. She never had children with her, but she even turned up to gigs in schools and playgroups. There was no rhythm to her appearance. Sometimes there was a gap of more than a week, but I came to expect my mysterious stalker and if I didn't see her when I bounced onto my stage I was ridiculously disappointed. These days I was sleeping better and she haunted my dreams. I didn't make a move on her though. I know the value of patience and there was something self-contained about her. I could tell that she'd have to approach me in her own time and her own way.

We first spoke after an outdoor gig in the Tyne Valley, close to Hadrian's Wall. It was dusk and bats were flying between the trees. I'd packed away the books and was sitting in the doorway of the caravanette, thinking of food and beer and sleep. I'd noticed her at the event of course, but I'd assumed she'd disappeared as usual. Then she walked out of the darkness and was standing in front of me.

'I think you can help me.' Her voice was as I'd imagined it. Deep and thoughtful with that lightness that the Northumberland accent always gives.

'Why me?' I didn't wait for an immediate answer. Instead I went inside the van and brought out an empty plastic box that usually held books, turned it upside down to make a seat for her. Then I went inside again and came back with two beers.

'I recognized you,' she said. 'That first night in Amble. You used to be a police officer.' She sat on the box. She wore a long skirt over boots and a short leather jacket. I opened the beer for her and she took a drink. 'I never expected to see you doing this.' She gestured towards the van. 'Why did you leave the police?'

I paused for a moment. I still wasn't used to the question. 'I was invalided out. No physical injury. Madness.' I looked up at her but there was too little light for me to see her reaction to that. I went on, keeping my voice easy. 'I ended up undercover, spent too long pretending to love women I didn't love, taking up causes I wouldn't have supported in a million years. Eventually it gets to you. And then a close friend committed suicide. That sent me over the edge.' I was tempted to ask how she'd known I was a cop, but still I didn't want to push her.

She nodded as if she understood. 'You arrested me once,' she said. 'A long time ago. You were kind.'

Suddenly I was back in the magistrates' court

in Newcastle. One of my first times giving evidence, which is probably why I remembered it so well. I'd dropped out of my good university and become a policeman. Another romantic whim. She'd been about seventeen years old and it was *her* first time in court too. She'd been skinnier and her hair had been a mess, choppy, not nearly so sleek. I'd caught her shoplifting in a designer outlet just outside the city. She'd had style even then. She hadn't stolen anything cheap or fake. It had all been classy and the real deal. She'd been given probation.

'You've done well for yourself,' I said. It wasn't a question. She might be casually dressed but every garment had quality.

She nodded again, not a person to waste words.

'What do you do for a living?'

'Me?' She gave a little laugh. 'I'm a kept woman.'

'How do you think I can help you?' I'd drained the bottle but didn't want to fetch another beer. I still thought she might escape.

'I want you to find someone for me.' I'm not sure what I'd expected but it wasn't that. It was properly dark now. A tawny owl was calling in the trees beyond the van.

'Who?'

'My mother.' She put the empty bottle on the ground beside her. 'I lost touch when I was a teenager. Usual story. I didn't get on with my stepfather. And he tried too hard to get on with me.'

'So you ran away?'

'And now I'd like to meet her again. I've changed a lot. Perhaps she has too.'

I still wasn't sure how to respond. 'There must

be people who can help you,' I said. 'Friends. Neighbours. Relatives.'

'We didn't have any relatives,' she said. 'The gruesome stepfather is dead. I did hear that on the grapevine, years ago. Mam might have remarried. She didn't like being on her own.' A beat. 'A bit like me.' There was a longer silence. 'You'd have access to official records. You'd know where to start.'

'I'm not a cop anymore.'

'I could pay.' Her voice was as close to desperate as she'd ever get. 'You can't earn much doing this.'

'I don't need much.' I could tell my reply was too sharp and I added: 'I'm a very simple sort of chap.'

There was another silence but I was already running through the steps I could take to find her mother. It shouldn't take long. A couple of hours with a computer and a few phone calls to old friends.

'My husband thinks I'm crazy,' she said. 'He thinks he should be enough for me.'

I didn't answer that. Instead I asked for her mother's maiden and married names and date of birth. Her last known address.'

'I'm sorry,' I said. 'I've forgotten *your* name.'

'Melanie Cooper. Mel. When you knew me I was James. Melanie May James.'

I stood up. 'Where will I find you?'

She hesitated. 'I'll find you. I'll come to another of your performances.'

'You'll be bored,' I said. 'You'll have heard it all before.'

'Not at all.' Even in the dark I could tell she was smiling. 'I love reading. That was why I came to Amble and how I recognized you. It was quite by chance. Things might have been very different if someone else had arrested me. Or if I weren't a reader. I believe in serendipity.'

'You didn't buy a book that night.' Suspicion has become second nature now and I question everyone's motives.

'I was shy. And it took me a while to decide that you might be the person to help me.'

I was going to ask about her favourite authors. There's something very intimate about sharing a love of books. But she stood up, gave me a little wave and ran off into the night. I stared after her for a while. At the height of my psychosis occasionally I'd see people and things that weren't real. Only the empty beer bottle beside the upturned box persuaded me that Melanie had been there at all.

It wasn't as easy to trace Mel's mother as I'd imagined. She seemed to have disappeared, much as her daughter had done the night before. There was a record of Susan James having been born, giving birth to a daughter as a single woman and then marrying Derek Oldfield. Oldfield had died seven years earlier after a stroke, but if Susan had taken up with another man she hadn't married him. I still had friends in the police service and they told me that the woman had never been in trouble with the law. Nor had Mel since that first charge of shoplifting years before. I couldn't find Susan on any of the electoral registers in Northumberland, but perhaps she was like me and had lost faith in the power of the vote. Mel didn't turn up at my following night's gig but perhaps that was just as well because I would only have disappointed her with my lack of news.

I found Susan Oldfield the next morning quite by chance when I was unpacking new stock. Another example of serendipity. When I saw her she was using the name Suzie May, but I was convinced she was the woman I'd been seeking. I liked the idea that she'd stolen her daughter's middle name. It showed she must still feel something for Mel. I saw Suzie on the jacket of a novel. Her face jumped out at me. The physical likeness to Mel was astonishing. The face had the same bone structure and the same white skin. There was a brief author history. It said that Suzie was a widow with one daughter. I suppose the back of a novel isn't the place to admit that you haven't seen your only child for twelve years or that your dead husband tried to abuse her.

Called *The Collier's Mistress,* the book wasn't to my taste. It was a romantic novel set against 50s Tyneside. I read the first chapter but there were too many adverbs. I hate adverbs: all tell and no show. It had obviously sold well though and a few pages of a second novel were printed at the back of my paperback as a taster. The subject matter seemed very similar. I googled Suzie May and saw that her website included a list of appearances – signings at bookshops, library events and book festivals. For the hell of it I sent her an e-mail: 'I'm a travelling bookseller. My audience would love to meet you. Any chance you could come to one of my events?' Then listing the next month's dates and venues. Not thinking that the message would get through to her personally. If I expected a response at all I thought I'd get an automated message asking me to contact her publicist.

When I checked my emails the next morning, though, there was a message from Suzie: 'I love the idea of a travelling bookseller and I always support independent shops. I'm free on the evening of the 20th and I'd be delighted to come along.'

The 20th was a week away and that gave me time to make plans, to buy in books for Suzie to sell at her gig and to work out how best to handle the situation. Mel turned up at my next afternoon event. This was in a library and, apart from one elderly man who sat in the front row and snored throughout, the audience was made up entirely of women. Afterwards Mel lingered at the book stall until the place was empty.

'Any joy?' For someone who gave so little of herself away, her desire for news was intense. It made me feel a bit dirty, as if I was seducing this woman with the promise of contact with her mother.

I pulled out my copy of *The Collier's Mistress* and turned to the back cover. I showed Mel the photo without speaking. There was a moment of silence. I wondered if I'd got the whole thing wrong. Perhaps the likeness between the women was coincidental.

'That's her,' Mel said at last. She paused again. 'It seems as if she's reinvented herself.'

'Like you.'

‘Perhaps.’ She was still staring at the photo. ‘How can I find her?’

‘You don’t have to.’ I explained that Suzie was coming to speak at one of my events. I didn’t tell Mel about the website, that direct contact was only a mouse click away. I wanted to be the person who brought them together. I hoped that Mel would be grateful and I wanted to be sure that she turned up to the event on the 20th. She’d become the only audience that mattered to me.

Newbiggin where the event was to take place is working Northumberland. There used to be pits close by but they’ve all been closed now. A few people go fishing for crabs. There’s still sea coal washed up on the beach. I was performing in the Marine Centre, right by the water with a view of The Couple, the sculpture of two lovers that stands in the middle of the bay. It seemed a perfect backdrop to the meeting of mother and daughter. I’d arranged for wine to be served. People started to arrive early and when Suzie May turned up many of the seats had already been taken. Suzie was still beautiful. She looked as I imagined Mel would be in twenty-five years’ time.

I’d wondered all day how I should play this; should I tell Suzie that her long-lost daughter might appear in the audience? In the end I said nothing. There were too many people around to overhear the conversation. And I was only the go-between. If I’m honest I didn’t much care what effect the reunion would have on the mother. It seemed she hadn’t tried very hard to track down Mel the teenager and all my focus was on the daughter.

Mel hadn't arrived when Suzie started speaking and I was starting to feel anxious, the sort of crippling anxiety that had marked the start of my illness. Perhaps all my efforts had been wasted and Mel was having second thoughts. But she slipped in to the back when the author was talking about the process of editing a novel. 'Sometimes it can be painful,' Suzie said. 'You put time and emotion into creating a character but if they don't work out you have to let them go.' A pause and a little laugh. 'You have to kill your darlings.' There was a scatter of applause and in my heightened state it annoyed me that she didn't credit another writer with the words.

At the end she sat beside me signing her books; I did a good trade. It was hard to imagine her as a dysfunctional mother with a runaway daughter – she chatted easily to the readers – but I couldn't think of any reason why Mel would have lied about that. Mel was last in line, clutching the book that I'd given her.

'Hello mam.' Her voice had slipped back to the broad accent of her youth.

I left them to it. Of course I was interested in how things played out between them but it wasn't my place to intrude. They went outside to talk. It was dark when I'd finished packing up my stock and I saw them walking on the beach in the moonlight, so close that they formed one silhouette. I assumed things had been sorted out between them. Perhaps they had a lot in common now as strong, successful women and they could let the past go.

I was still parked next to the centre. There was

a sign that said *No Overnight Parking* but I knew that the Newbiggin police would have more to worry about than a VW caravanette overstaying its welcome. I laid the tiny table in the van with Northumberland cheeses, oatcakes and two glasses and put a bottle of wine in the fridge. There was always a possibility that Mel would just slip away to her husband but I thought she would call in to see me, even if it was only to tell me how the meeting had gone.

There was the sound of an engine starting. I was listening out for the second car when there was a tap at the door. In the moment before opening it tried to persuade myself that Suzie not Mel might be outside. I've always thought it was bad luck to be optimistic.

'Come in,' I shouted in my performer's voice, not quite crossing my fingers behind my back.

Mel stood there. I could tell she was mine if I wanted her. That was why she hadn't driven straight home. I reached into the fridge for the bottle and poured wine, all the time prattling like Peter Wimsey at his goofiest. She saw I was nervous and put her hand over mine to calm me.

That was when I got serious. We sat across the table, our knees almost touching, and both sipped the wine. I began my pitch. I hadn't been entirely honest, I said. I *had* been ill. A good friend had committed suicide when his business collapsed and on top of the stress of the job I'd gone a bit mad for a while. But I hadn't been invalided out. I was still a cop.

'You're under cover?' She wasn't stupid. She knew where this was going.

'We've had access to your bank account. All those payments to Amazon and to the bookshop in Corbridge. We worked out that you were a reader.'

'You set up all this to track me down?' She nodded towards the boxes at the back of the van, the silk jacket hanging from a hook on the wall.

'Well not you, exactly. Your husband. And I didn't know you were looking for your mother. That was a bonus.' I allowed myself another sip. 'In another life the travelling bookshop would be my dream, but we thought you might be prepared to negotiate a deal. This was the best way we could think of to make contact without raising your husband's suspicion.'

It was very quiet. Outside in Newbiggin a dog barked. I thought I could hear waves breaking on the beach. For Mel it was a moment of decision. She started talking. I put up my hand to stop her and put a small digital recorder on the table between us. She nodded her agreement to the recording and began again.

She told me everything I needed. Much I knew already: her husband was an accountant who laundered money for organized crime. He'd been overlooked for years because he wasn't based in London. Robert Cooper also set up his own scams and one of his fraudulent deals had put my best friend out of business. My friend's suicide had given me a very personal reason for wanting him caught. Mel gave me dates, account numbers and contacts, the kind of details we'd never hoped for. It was as if, once she'd decided to talk, she couldn't stop. I had the image suddenly of a woman bringing a dowry to a marriage. This was her gift to me.

When it was over I went outside and phoned my handler. I was watching Mel's face in profile through the uncurtained window throughout the conversation. Then I went in and poured more wine.

'You shouldn't go home tonight,' I said. 'My colleagues will be on their way to your house already.'

She nodded as if she'd worked that out too. I couldn't believe how calm she was.

'Don't you care?' I asked. 'You've been with him for a long time.' Our research had painted Cooper as charming, and the marriage as happy, stable.

She hesitated and then smiled. 'As mam said, sometimes you have to kill your darlings.'

The words hit me. In that moment I knew that she'd set up her husband to be the apparent leader of the organization. She was the inventor of the schemes, the writer of the stories that had hooked in so many unsuspecting victims. And she'd conned me. She'd known all along who I was and what I was doing. I'd become one of her darlings too.

Brought to Book
by Judith Cutler

When I saw my first novel on the shelves at Heffers I knew at last that I was a real writer. Of course I had already held a copy before that – several copies, in fact, when the cardboard box arrived from my publisher and was peeled open, layer by precious layer of padding to reveal the pristine covers. That was one of the best experiences of my life, to tell the truth – akin, I should imagine, to holding a new-born baby – but it was pleasure in a vacuum. The books were cherished, but they were to be given away – to family and friends holding out rapacious but doubting hands. Sure old Tim had written a book at last, and sure some fool of an agent had been conned into representing him and had in turn persuaded some gullible publisher to take a punt, but that didn't mean anyone would buy it. Look at the old fool now. He wasn't even selling them, just handing them out as freebies.

But now my book was in not just any bookshop, but one known the world over. There was no argument: bookshops wouldn't stock a book unless they thought they could sell it to Joe Public, would they? (It was only later I learned about the grim realities of being remaindered.) Dare I do what other authors did, and sign every copy on the shelf? I actually reached for my pen

– but in the end I decided that since my writing L plates were bigger than my advance, I didn't have the temerity, and I crept quietly away.

Enough people bought the book, whether from Heffers or from elsewhere, to persuade my publisher to offer me another contract – for two books this time. But somewhere along the line someone – my agent? my editor? – dropped out that they never expected me to be a best seller: they saw me as a good, reliable mid-lister, who would produce a reasonable book year after year, to the delight of librarians and borrowers. I mustn't expect to see myself in the front windows of major national chains, not as long as publishers had to pay for that sort of publicity. I wouldn't be doing promotional tours, unless I paid for them myself, and I might as well forget about TV appearances and all the other perks of being a Famous Author.

I didn't feel it necessary to share all these truths with my doubting friends. If they ever bothered to wonder out loud why I wasn't off to the States to puff the latest book – it might have been the fifth or the sixth by then – I could sigh and allude sadly to my Ageing Parents who couldn't be left this year. Or any year, of course, if my royalties were expected to support me on transatlantic jollies. My parents, incidentally, come from exceptionally long-lived stock, and in their nineties are currently on a cruise to Antarctica. So it was not from them but from a kindly Premium Bond that I got enough money to give up my mind-numbing local government job – not, in fact, that there was any choice, since redundancy had already started to sweep the country like a Biblical plague. At least I was old enough to qualify for a little pension: if the books continued to sell I'd be solvent.

Realising that pottering round pretty places in the UK – officially in easy reach of the APs should they need me in an emergency – was tax-deductible so long as I claimed it was for research, I set out on regular trips. Often I'd tie them in with talks at public libraries, in the days when they still lent real, as opposed to virtual, books and moreover could still offer a modest fee to a guest speaker. There were still independent bookshops too, to offer a jobbing author a chance to meet his readers, and sign a couple of books for them. (The ambiguity is deliberate.)

The Book Wormery was one such. Personally I might have thought of a more enticing name than something I associate with vegetable peelings being transformed into compost by a mass of bright red wriggling creatures that always make me think of Hamlet's words about Polonius' last known location. Set picturesquely on a steep hill in a well-heeled village in the Cotswolds, it kept afloat by selling not just new books, but also a second-hand array that would have had Oxfam salivating. There was even an area set aside for modern first editions, most of which were in an elegant Georgian display cupboard, the surrounding lighting rightly subdued to the point of being nonexistent. As I waited for my audience to cram itself into the space Mr Grace had organised, I peered closely at the products of my illustrious predecessors. My cousin was particularly partial to the novels of the Midlands writer John Moore, and here was a signed first edition of *The Waters under the Earth.* There was no obvious and indecent indication of the price. Since Mr Grace was still busy – it was amazing how long it took him to seat and serve wine to nine people – I thought I'd take a look. The cabinet, however, was locked.

'My dear Mr Griffiths,' Mr Grace said, swiftly putting his hand between me and my prey, 'those are not *genre* books.' As if a crime writer, producer of lower order literature, read nothing else and should not soil such precious and unattainable volumes with his heretical gaze. 'And your audience is waiting,' he added propelling me by the elbow to take my place.

My talk was enlivened by the presence of a cat in a creaking wicker cat basket, intermittently reminding the man beside it that it had had enough of captivity, and a woman who required tissue after tissue for her streaming nose and eyes, caused, she insisted resentfully, by a cat dander allergy. So I gave the matter no more thought. At last, however, once Mr Grace's till had rung agreeably and I had signed no fewer than twelve copies of my latest book and four from my backlist, I thought it was time to mention the John Moore. However, it transpired that Mr Grace had set it aside for a regular customer, and that our table was waiting for us in the Blue Gates, an establishment, he assured me, which would see us well fed and watered. It did. What I hadn't realised was that he expected us to go Dutch; at least subsistence expenses were tax deductible, I told myself, and thanks to people like Mr Grace sales were still good enough for me to have to pay tax.

As you will be all too aware, there have been major developments in the world of books, with repercussions on the ordinary book store. All too many shops on what had become my small but regular annual circuit had become charity shops, with the proud former owners now volunteering amongst the ranks of tatty paperbacks better suited to landfill but at least bringing in the odd fifty pence for Cancer Research or whatever. But the Book Wormery still flourished, and had been joined on its fertile journey by the Book Wormery II, occupying a prime site in another village so much photographed the locals told me that even on Christmas Day several coaches would debouche their loads of camera and phone touting Japanese tourists. On its website, Book Wormery II proudly boasted that it was open every day except 25th December, but on even that special day it would welcome overseas visitors by appointment.

As I found out when I went there to puff my twelfth crime novel – a constant mid-lister, I was still waiting breathlessly to be an overnight success – I found that the Book Wormery II was considerably bigger than its older sibling. There was plenty of space, and this time not just wine but also canapés. In the absence of both feline and allergic presence, my talk went well and the tills again rang loud and clear – more accurately the card terminals purred with satisfaction long enough for me to inspect the rest of the shop until the punters could form a queue for me to sign their purchases. Though this shop wasn't sullied by mere second-hand volumes, there was an area set aside for collectors' books. Once again the first editions were behind glass. A pretty copy of George Moore's *Esther Waters,* which I dimly remembered from my schooldays, caught my eye. Since Mr Grace's services were still required at the first shop, this establishment was run by a quiet and earnest young manager by name of Jethro, his accent, however, far from the agricultural burr the Christian name suggested, to me at least. Jethro was in no haste to close the shop and there was no invitation to eat at the local pub – a mercy since it turned out to have a Michelin star and prices to match. But he seemed no keener than Mr Grace to let me range carte blanche amongst the treasured volumes. At last he consented to respond to my very specific request to handle the George Moore.

'You're sure that this is four hundred pounds?' I asked, managing neither to drop the volume nor to squeak.

'A collector's item,' he intoned, taking it from me before I could check its condition and replacing it with a reverence that even its excellent condition hardly deserved.

I was silenced. I knew too little about antiquarian books to argue. But then I remembered that the customer was always – perhaps, in these benighted times, especially – right, and so I pointed at one or two other books, asking for their prices too. Even a battered nineteen sixties Folio edition of *Wind in the Willows* topped the three hundred mark.

My mind raced: when I'd moved house and shipped crates of books to charity shops and church fetes, had I given away a potential fortune, thinking it no more than a mess of pottage?

At least my pride was mollified when I discovered that however many book dealers my Google-guided explorations found, none charged as outrageously as the dear old Wormeries. But now my interest was piqued. Did they ever sell any of their treasures? I presumed they must have done, or the two flourishing shops would have gone under years ago; there'd certainly be no talk of a third Book Wormery opening soon in Chipping Norton. If so, who were the customers willing to pay ten, even twenty times what the books were worth? Was it a simple case of clever marketing and the Emperor's new clothes?

On impulse I turned to the books by my fellow crime writers to see what they were fetching on line. Of course, the market leaders' books fetched good sums, but you could get a mint, signed first edition of a PD James for under a hundred. So why were the third Book Wormery asking over five hundred pounds for *Still Waters?* Judith Cutler's a good friend of mine, but I think even she would have been surprised to the point of shocked to learn that someone valued her work quite so highly. So would John Harvey, who'd written a book with an identical title.

By now I dimly realised that some sort of scam must be in operation.

One of the questions I always get asked at my talks is whether a police procedural or an amateur detective novel is more realistic. Usually I manage to suppress my retort, which would be the riposte of a much more famous crime writer: if you found a corpse in your kitchen you'd call not Miss Marple but nine-nine-nine. I'm not even an amateur sleuth – so what could I do? I'm only a mid-list crime writer. Maybe a top of the range writer like a Val McDermid or a Peter James would have known what to do in real life as well as in fiction, and would have plucked out the bloody entrails of our perpetrator. I might well myself, of course, but I'd do it off stage, as it were – and I'd have to work out first what crime was being committed.

For by now I was sure that money was being made not so much out of but via the books sitting in splendid isolation. In a classic Golden Age detective novel the villains might have been involved in espionage, which I bravely discounted in these post-Cold War days. I'd once read a wonderful short story – was it by Sara Paretsky? – in which the denouement featured a microdot doubling as a full-stop in a sought-after book. Might that be a possibility? But surely even a microdot would these days be old hat compared with the latest and most sophisticated electronics. Drugs? They seem to be freely imported into the UK in industrial quantities.

My only clue – my apologies for such a retro term – was that so far all the books I'd even touched, let alone handled, were associated with water. What if I asked to see other precious volumes unrelated to such a topic? I'd make a point of it when my next book was released and I was making my regular pilgrimage to one of the Wormeries. It was due out in a month or so: I sat back and awaited my invitation.

It did not come. Some publishers offered their authors the services of a publicist. Mine didn't – or at least they didn't offer me one anymore. So I contacted each Wormery in turn to offer my services, and was in turn rejected – poor sales, a desire for more thrusting, up-and-coming writers, generally poor budgets for that sort of thing. Much as I wanted to leap up and down and refute any or all of their reasons, I was impotent. And it was true: Tim Griffiths, dear cuddly old Tim Griffiths, rarely saw the light of day in bookshops and lurked more and more on library shelves. As long as libraries had book budgets, they would be my spiritual home, even if I did have to give my talks for expenses only these days. The librarians were as committed and charming as ever. One in particular, in a town some thirty miles from my own, was a lady whose company I came to relish more than anyone else's: Leonora.

Out of the commercial world I might be, but I still wrote a couple of books a year: my publisher and my agent got on well with each other and as I fulfilled each three book contract, my agent conjured another. I like long-running series, and was happy to keep two in play, one featuring a cunning curate, the other an honest estate agent. At least I could jog along with professional respectability and personal satisfaction. Research – increasingly on line these days – still occupied much of my non-writing time. I had friends both within the

Crime Writers' Association and outside it; I played golf; I took jive classes to remind me of my energetic youth. Life was good, especially now I had found that *Guardian*-reading and now retired companion with whom it might just be possible to share the rest of my life.

But those books and what they might contain niggled away. I had to find the answer.

What would my crafty curate do?

He would discuss the problem with his attractive magistrate line-dancing side-kick, of course, with whom he has a long term will-they-won't-they relationship. (He has issues with his past; her concerns are more with their future.) So in a moment of post-coital bliss, I risked all and asked the lady in my life the most pressing question on my mind.

Leo – I'd soon learned her full name had been bestowed on her by an opera-loving godmother – accepted another glass of champagne... No, she didn't. She preferred a cup of tea. Despite her name, Leo was the most gentle of creatures, with none of the macho elements with which I've endowed my female protagonists. The only thing she'd ever stab was her tapestry.

'Let me think,' she said, in a voice I'd not heard before – one that suggested some form of direct action in the line of a young Georgette Heyer heroine, not a lady touting a bus pass to match mine.

I've always written of the frisson of fear my curate feels when his magistrate puts herself forward to assist, but never truly understood it. Now I did. I knew that however much I was intrigued by the wretched books, compared with Leo's safety they mattered not one jot.

Leo was tapping away on her smart phone, endearingly putting on my reading glasses to see better and making little notes.

'And you've never actually handled any of the books?'

I shook my head. 'And any I wanted to buy have been reserved.'

'It's true you can order on line,' she said, showing me the screen. 'But what interests me is that the site invites you to enter a code – here, can you see?'

'Not without my glasses,' I admitted.

Absent-mindedly she passed me hers.

'I often shop on line,' she said, 'particularly if there's some sort of special offer. Sometimes you have to type in an offer code, or your customer number, to ensure it's you that's getting the discount, not someone else. But it's funny to see it here.' She pointed. 'I wonder what happens if you put one in...'

'No, I beg you – don't take any risks. What does it matter if someone's smuggling drugs or gold or ivory or jewellery or–'

'Surely you'd have felt the weight or noticed some distortion if they were smuggling those. I did read a book about someone stealing miniatures the other day–'

'I know. I gave it to you. The author's a friend of mine.'

'So you did. And of course it was fiction. That's the end of that theory. Come on, Tim, what's small and portable and extremely valuable?'

Cue for some conversation of interest only to the parties involved.

Which is how – eventually – Leo conjectured that there might be something like photos in the books.

'As in "feelthy pictures"? Surely it's easier to circulate them on-line,' I demurred.

'True... So maybe it's something written in the books themselves – do they still use invisible ink?' she asked. But she didn't wait for a reply. 'Heavens, is that the time? I ought to be heading home.'

'Not in this snow,' I said. 'Far too dangerous to drive. Why not stay over – again? And, come to think about it, why not put an end to all this driving and do the green thing – move in with me?'

Later that year, the weather, which had been the immediate if not the fundamental reason for Leo to take her first step on the road to becoming Mrs Griffiths, changed radically. We moved from a hose-pipe ban to floods within weeks, after rain in Biblical quantities. First one then another part of the country succumbed either to a steady and inexorable inundation or to the horror of flash floods. It wasn't until one particularly soggy weekend when we couldn't even pretend to garden and the paint in our redecorated bedroom was steadfastly refusing to dry that Leo raised the issue of the unnaturally valuable books.

I hadn't forgotten about them but I hoped she had.

'I think it's time we took a trip to one of the

Book Wormeries,' she said without preamble. 'At least, you may drive me, but I will take the trip. They'd batten down the hatches at once if they see you. But they won't know me from Eve–'

'Except that you will be better dressed, my love.'

'So I shall be able to ask to look at the rare books with impunity. And with luck,' she added frankly. 'You said water might be a theme – and there's enough of that today. I've checked on line and there's a history of English watercolours that's caught my eye. And a Victorian illustrated guide to waterfowl. I might offer cash. And I shall insist on a thorough inspection.'

'And what will you be inspecting for?' I tried to keep my tone light but I was sick with anxiety. Literally queasy.

'Remember the conversation that started all this?' she said, her gesture taking in the chaos of redecorating and a few of her still unpacked removal boxes. 'Something small. Very small.'

'Please don't take any risks. Heavens, in this weather even driving to the Book Wormeries – any of them – involves risks.'

'So did agreeing to marry you.'

That was actually a point I wasn't aware we'd reached but I let it pass.

So we found ourselves heading towards the nearest Book Wormery, which turned out to be the first, where I'd met Mr Grace. The rain would have made Noah start herding the animals aboard; the water in the ditches rose and oozed in the verges. Puddles at either side of the lanes joined in the middle.

'I've never driven through a flood before,' I said, inching the car forward.

'Live a little,' Leo said.

No, she didn't, any more than she swilled champagne after sex. Only one of my heroines would have said that. In actual fact, with a squeak she pointed at a wheelie-bin bobbing down the road towards us.

'Isn't there something I should do with the brakes?' I asked.

'Something about drying them out? I've no idea how.' Then she added, in a terrified voice, 'Dear me: we have company!'

We did. My rear view mirror was completely occupied by a fire appliance, giving me blues, but not twos. There was nowhere for him to overtake, after all, since if I pulled over I risked putting myself in the ditch hidden beneath the swirling waters. I pressed on, going far faster than I suspected was safe.

At last we reached the village, and I could let the monster pass me. I tried to dry the brakes, but whether I succeeded or not, I don't know. And never will now. Even as I pulled on the handbrake to park, the street became a torrent, as suddenly as if someone had turned on a tap. The car began to bob, like a plastic duck on a bath.

'Out!' yelled Leo, grabbing her handbag.

We got out. We were in each other's arms at the side of the street before we knew it, icy water up to our thighs. The car dipped and ducked away, like a courtier making apologetic little bows as he left our presence. Other items, large and small, joined it in an irregular flotilla. There was a dog basket, a foot stool, cushions, saucepans, photo albums: people's lives, writ large and small. Leo and I intercepted as many as we could, joining an impromptu human chain passing them back to relative safety. Soon the current threatened to slice our feet from beneath us; the rain came down with the force of a giant hosepipe. The human chain now became a human net, hauling its links and thus itself on to higher ground. Leo and I were dragged with them, willy-nilly. But then other items still drifted down. One in particular caught my eye. It was a book cupboard, sadly battered about the edges as if someone had tried desperately to drag it from danger. It wasn't just any book case, of course. It was the one Mr Grace had refused to let me inspect, all those years ago. In it, in their own tank of water, the collectors' books jostled for comparative safety.

If I could bring that ashore, the questions that had irritated me over the years would be answered.

Holding tightly to Leo, I leant into the torrent and guided the cupboard towards the rest of the rescuers, who uncurled themselves and once more strove heroically to effect a rescue. But my hands were icy, the wood wet and the current too strong.

Book case, books and answers slipped inexorably from my fingers.

Should I have tried a moment's heroism, diving after it and saving it? Leo's urgent cries, the shouts of the villagers and my own simple cowardice gave me one implacable answer. Let it go.

I did. I would never know what secrets those books had concealed.

As it happens, I did. I did what anyone could have done. Should have done. I told the police. It must have been a quiet day crime-wise, because they did look for the cupboard amongst all the other detritus from the deluge and indeed they found it. The contents were by then very little more than papier mache, but one nosy officer peeled apart a copy of *River of Destiny* leaf by soggy leaf he found a stamp. Fifty thousand pounds worth of collectible stamp. Valueless now, of course. As were all the other precious stamps in all the other ruined tomes he and his scientific colleagues managed to extract: over a million pounds worth of postage memorabilia in all. Heaven knows how many others had changed hands more efficiently via the Book Wormeries' transactions. My actions had tied up a case for them: but there was to be no punishment for the perpetrators. Mr Grace's efforts to save the book case had caused a fatal heart attack. Jethro, until recently still managing the second shop, had prematurely departed for the big library in the sky after a tangle with a combine harvester. Some might say that there was such a thing as divine retribution. As for the third Book Wormery, the new manager there somehow convinced the understaffed police that he, like others before him, knew nothing, and was just acting in accordance with company policy when he overpriced certain books.

As for me, my hesitancy, my tardiness in taking action denied me the reward once offered.

But at least I had an idea for a new novel, which both my agent and my publisher thought might be my longed for break-through book to promote me from the ranks of mid-listers and back into the book shops. If it does, with Leo at my side I will make a pilgrimage back to Heffers and make sure I sign every single copy on their shelves.

The Strange Affair at Sheepwash
by Ruth Downie

'Here she comes. Dead woman walking.'

The rattle of the taxi's engine faded away down the lane. The girl paused to push her hair out of her eyes and then tottered towards the house on unsuitably high heels. Garrett said, 'It might not be her.'

The girl's suitcase was patterned with pink flowers as if it had been wallpapered. It caught and jolted on the rough path as she struggled to tow it.

'That's her,' McMahon insisted. 'I can always tell.'

Garrett wondered whether to step forward and offer help with the suitcase, but then decided the high heels were too irritating. She said, 'Do you ever get tired of this?'

'Uh?' McMahon was still eyeing the girl.

'Must be just me, then.'

'Yeah.'

'I need a transfer.' Garrett watched the girl change hands on the case. 'Fraud would do. Regular hours. Nice warm office. Nobody dies.'

'They won't let you go,' McMahon told her. 'You're the token woman.'

Garrett snorted. 'That makes you the token old man.'

At last the girl caught sight of the two police

officers eyeing her from the doorway, and stopped. 'Is something wrong?'

'Now you've frightened her,' Garrett murmured.

'Me? Why me?'

Garrett stepped forward. 'Just a routine visit,' she said. 'Are you here for the writing course?'

The girl looked relieved. 'Am I too early?'

'No miss, you just go on in,' McMahon pushed the heavy door open. 'Tea and coffee in the kitchen. Mugs on the drainer.'

'There won't be any biscuits,' Garrett warned her. 'Not if he's got there first.'

The girl adjusted her grip on the suitcase, glanced at McMahon as if wondering whether he might help, then gave it one last heave over the threshold. 'Oh!'

'Nice, eh?' McMahon offered, looking over her shoulder. 'Traditional farmhouse kitchen. My missus fancies a place like this. Oak beams, big table, one of them burner things.'

'Aga?' Garrett suggested.

'Whatever. Don't see a lot of them in Peckham.'

The girl said, 'You're from Peckham?' in a *what are you doing here?* tone.

'He's just moved down,' Garrett stepped inside to find the light switch. 'I'm showing him around. Dank old afternoon, eh?'

'I thought Devon would be sunny.'

'Not in November,' Garrett told her, guessing the girl went abroad for holidays and mentally divided her homeland into *London* and a vague otherworld which was *Not London*.

'I've never been to the West Country,' said the

girl, confirming Garrett's suspicions. 'But I got offered a free place so I thought, why not? I'll give it a try.'

'Right,' said McMahon. 'Why not?'

Garrett, who had worked with McMahon often enough to know exactly why not, avoided his gaze.

'I never thought for a minute that they'd pick me. I've never written a poem before.' She glanced around the kitchen. 'Am I allowed to put the kettle on?'

Garrett's opinion of her rose, which was not good. There was no sense in getting attached to them. 'Thanks, but we need to be going,' she said, moving towards the door and holding it open until McMahon submitted and tramped out past her. 'Enjoy your stay.' She clamped the door firmly shut behind her. They were halfway down the path before she said, '*Peckham?*'

'It just came to me.'

Garrett sighed. 'It's always like this with BK. She forgets the details in between books. Where did your drink problem go after Book Three?'

'It's in the past,' McMahon assured her. 'Writing course, eh?'

'Think about it. BK hasn't had a proper job for years. Writing is the only thing she knows. She probably thinks she can make it sound interesting.' Garrett checked the radio clipped to her shoulder. 'You think I could use this to call a taxi? She's written us miles from anywhere.'

McMahon paused to gaze around him. Gently sloping pastures were dotted with white sheep. Beyond them, dense woodland faded into soft mist. 'Must be nice here in the summer.'

Garrett gave an involuntary shudder inside the stab-proof vest. She tried not to think about pitchforks and farm machinery. About being trampled by large hooves. About deep, stinking slurry pits, and shotguns, and bodies being eaten by pigs, and the fact that out here, nobody could hear your screams. 'I hope she isn't going to be tortured.'

She realised McMahon had stopped. He was staring at her. 'It's not *real,'* he pointed out. 'That girl's no more real than we are.'

'Even so. I don't like to think about it.'

'You're getting soft.'

'I hate it when they do that. It's so cheap. What's wrong with a quick and simple poisoning? A nice country house murder mystery with a knife in the back and no blood? Colonel Mustard in the library with the candlestick?'

'Colonel Mustard doesn't sell,' he reminded her. 'People want gritty crime now. Books with lots of black on the covers. Gruesome injuries in widescreen HD.'

Garrett sniffed. 'She's written you a terrible haircut. Are you going bald under that hat?'

'She's written you bad breath.'

Garrett raised both hands and cupped them over her nose and mouth, but before she could test the truth of his accusation she was distracted by the arrival of a green Fiesta. The crop-headed man who called, ''Scuse me?' out of the open window looked no more than twenty-five.

'Scuse me, Garrett felt, was a good start. Better than *Oi.*

'I'm looking for a girl, blonde hair, big flowery suitcase?'

Instead of replying, McMahon kept perfectly focused on the young man and took in a slow breath, expanding his chest under the stab-proof vest. It was supposed to impose his authority, but Garrett decided it just made him annoying. She would have to watch that. Everything seemed to be annoying today. She hoped BK wasn't going write her as an irritable old cow.

'Me and Nat had a row,' the lad explained, leaning one tattooed and muscular arm out of the window. 'She won't answer my calls. Her flatmate says she's come here on some course. So is she here, or not?'

When neither officer answered he added, 'Look, I'm not a stalker. I'm Jaz. I'm her boy-friend.'

This last word was said, Garrett felt, with unwarranted confidence.

'We'll be seeing you shortly, then,' McMahon told him. 'You'll be the first and most obvious suspect.'

'Suspect?' Jaz was out of the car. 'What's happened?'

'Nothing,' said Garrett. 'Take no notice of my colleague.'

'Is Nat all right? Where is she?'

'In the kitchen,' Garrett assured him. 'Making tea.'

'It's all right, son,' McMahon assured him, holding up a defensive hand. 'It probably won't be you. This isn't real life, this is crime fiction.'

Jaz's brow creased, as if frowning would help

him to make sense of things. 'Fiction? Are you making a series? Like – *Luther? Broadchurch? The Wire?*'

'Not very much like them,' admitted McMahon.

'Where's the cameras?' Jaz looked around, suspicious.

'We're not filming,' Garrett told him. Not for want of trying: BK's agent had been trying to sell the rights for years, in the hope of reviving her income and BK's flagging backlist.

Jar tried again. 'Is it like one of them Murder Mystery weekends?'

McMahon said, 'That's more like it.'

The furrow vanished. A childlike smile spread across the young man's face. 'I get it. You guys are playing the police.'

'That's right.'

'You're good. You had me going there for a minute.'

'We've had lots of practice,' Garrett assured him. She had appeared in six novels for BK so far. Not to mention working in various guises for other crime writers who wanted a bright female police officer they could adapt to their own purposes.

'Nat's in the kitchen?'

McMahon pointed back towards the heavy oak door under the porch. 'Just through there.'

Jaz bounded up the path, leaving the window of the Fiesta open. Garrett said, 'Have I really got bad breath?'

'Don't stand too near anybody.'

'Liar,' she guessed.

McMahon took his hat off and ran a hand over

the top of his head. 'I'm not bald either,' he said. 'But she's written me on a bloody diet. Here we are in the land of cream teas and pasties, and I can't touch 'em.'

Garrett shrugged. 'Where would you find a cream tea around here? This is the middle of Devon, not the seaside. I was in a foot-and-mouth novel around here once.' She stopped, not wanting to dwell on the fact that these days, she was offered more work than he was.

He said, 'Maybe we could phone for a curry.'

'I hope she's written us a Land Rover,' she observed, glancing at the sky. 'That lane'll flood if we get much rain.'

They stepped aside as a mud-spattered white Peugeot swerved into the yard. 'Speak of the devil,' said McMahon. 'And our author arrives.'

'Same car, more dents.'

'What did I tell you? Her books aren't selling. Last time she did a signing, four people turned up. One of them was the mum of the bookshop manager and the others had come for Ian Rankin and got the wrong week.'

The car door creaked open and one heavy purple lace-up boot emerged, followed by a large woman draped in an array of bright clothing that made it hard to tell where the person ended and the fabric began.

'That's it, boss, have a good stretch,' McMahon murmured. 'Wrecks your back, sitting at a computer all day.'

The woman held the door pillar with one hand and bent to reach into the car. She dragged out a battered canvas handbag and, more carefully, an orange Sainsbury's carrier. The carrier clinked as she carried it past them up the path and into the house. She showed no sign of being aware of their presence, which was just how Garrett liked it. When authors weren't concentrating on you, you could do whatever you wanted.

'Maybe I could get myself written into one of those foreign things,' she said. 'You know. The Scandinavian ones where everybody's glum and it rains a lot.'

McMahon said, 'I hear there's a French series on the box where the cops get to take drugs and have sex with beautiful women and shoot the suspects.'

'Do you speak French?'

'I could, given the right author.'

Garrett said nothing. They both knew that BK was never going to be the right author, any more than McMahon would ever be anything other than what he was: the archetypal solid, dependable British copper with a wife and bit of a weight problem. The salt of the earth, but not glamorous. Not thriller material.

'Ah well,' McMahon said, signalling a move to a less awkward subject. 'It'll all be over by the weekend.'

'You think?'

'I know,' he said. 'BK's only minding the place till Friday.'

Garrett's watch told her it was not even three o'clock, but already the day was starting to lose whatever vigour it had possessed. More cars and a taxi pulled into the yard within a few minutes of each other. The cast of BK's book most of them naively thinking they were here at the writing retreat for a poetry course – was beginning to assemble.

The first driver was a middle-aged man with a worried expression behind thick wire-rimmed glasses. McMahon's verdict was a noncommittal 'Hmm.'

His passenger, a woman of a similar age with a shaved head and numerous earrings, elicited another 'Hmm.'

While the man unloaded two bags from the boot, the woman squinted at her mobile phone, then held it up in the air and circled slowly round as if performing a ritual dance. Then she shook it and peered at the screen again. 'Bugger. No signal.'

'Good,' murmured McMahon. 'Always more tension when they can't call for help.'

Garrett looked at him askance. 'Whose side are you on?'

The woman told the man there was no bloody signal, as if he might not have heard her the first time, and the man slammed the boot shut and pointed out that there was supposed to be a land line.

'How am I going to get my emails with no Wi-fi?'

The man murmured something and she said, 'It's all right for you!'

'My money's on a strangling,' mused Garrett as man and woman each took a case and hauled it towards the front door. 'One of those two, by the other.'

McMahon was convinced that the woman with

a white perm and a stoop who arrived next by taxi was an amateur sleuth. 'I knew it,' he said. 'That's why we're in uniform. BK's starting a spin-off series. Miss Marple there will get all the interesting stuff from now on while we get demoted to being the hapless plods.'

Garrett, noticing the manila folder grasped firmly to the woman's chest, disagreed. If BK really were trying to bring her books up to date, she would hardly be writing a novel featuring a little old lady detective. This one was just a harmless poet, come to show her work to the tutor. Harmless, at least, on the surface. For all Garrett knew, BK might have written poisoned blow-darts into her handbag. Or a garrotte. Or a novel of sufficient weight to kill.

When a younger woman clambered out of a Mini, McMahon insisted to Garrett that his, 'Ah, that's better!' was neither sexist nor ageist. It was a compliment to BK's plotting skills. 'Two girls,' he said, 'You don't know which one's going to be the victim, see? Suspense.'

'Maybe it's neither of them,' she told him. 'That would be a nice change.'

'Maybe one of them murders the other,' said McMahon cheerfully as the young woman pulled a rucksack and a laptop case out of the boot. 'Maybe they both die. I reckon old BK's writing a serial killer.'

'God help us,' Garrett sighed. 'As if there aren't enough of them already.'

'Ah,' put in a voice from behind them, 'But they keep me in employment. And authors love them. Nothing sparks up a saggy plot like a fresh body.'

Garrett eyed the bulky, bearded figure in white overalls. He had appeared, she supposed, from behind one of the buildings. Or from BK's imagination, which was more or less the same thing and was a worrying sign that the author was already starting to gather her thoughts after the journey. 'It's a bit early for forensics,' she observed. 'Nobody's dead yet.'

The bearded figure shrugged. 'I can't be responsible for the order our dear author thinks us up in,' he said. 'I've always suspected she writes her scenes as soon as she has the idea, and then sorts out the joins later on.'

'Must make 'er an 'ell of a job to edit,' put in a man with a flat cap and green wellingtons who was tramping towards them from the barn across the yard.

'Oh arr,' agreed a plump middle-aged woman. The country-fair apron looked out of place on a figure with a claw hammer clutched in one hand and a fistful of six-inch nails in the other. Garrett tried not to think about crucifixion.

'Don't mind me and the wife,' said the farmer, tugging a strand of orange baler twine from one pocket and tying it around a broken hinge on a gate. 'We'm the local colour. Oh arr.' He sliced off a frayed end of twine with a Stanley knife. 'Tis a strange and lonely place, this. Noises in the night. Peculiar goings-on at the–'

'You don't have to start yet,' Garrett snapped. 'And you'll have to get a better accent than that. You sound like extras from *The Archers.*'

'That we be,' agreed the farmer.

Garrett sighed once more.

The forensics man was eyeing the barn and sniffing the air, and for the first time Garrett noticed the tang of cow manure. BK was definitely getting into the mood.

'Shame it's not summer,' the forensics man observed. 'You'll have a good number of flies here when it's hot. Do you keep pigs?'

'There won't be time for maggots to hatch,' McMahon told him. 'It'll all be over by Friday.'

'Pity,' observed the forensics man. 'I like a good maggot. It's the nearest we get to excitement in my trade.' He turned to the farmers. 'It's not like you see on the television, you know,' he said. 'Results at the click of a finger, limitless budgets, forensic investigators out chasing down villains, and not a notebook in sight.'

'Farming's not all it's cracked up to be, neither,' observed the wife, following her husband back into the barn. 'Mike! How much petrol you got in that chainsaw?'

At that moment there were raised voices from the house. It seemed Jaz did not believe Nat was here for a poetry course, and Nat was insulted by his lack of faith in her.

'Of course they're real,' she was insisting. 'They've got radios and everything!'

His reply came in a lower tone, and it was hard to distinguish the words. Garrett glanced at McMahon and the forensics man. 'We need to get out of the way. We aren't supposed to be here yet.'

'It's not our fault,' McMahon pointed out. 'We're stock characters, we always turn up first.'

'Yes, but the others aren't supposed to see us

till after the–' She stopped and glanced across to the barn. 'Maybe you're right: she's not doing the usual. Maybe she's moving out of Police Procedurals and into thrillers. Maybe this time the victim is...'

'Nah,' McMahon told her. 'Not one of us. She can't do that.'

'Why not? We could have a tragically heroic end. One of you two could save me and sacrifice yourself.'

'Not me,' said the forensics man, retreating towards the lane.

'You can't kill the detective,' McMahon insisted, turning back to argue with his partner. 'Look what happened to Sherlock Holmes. Conan Doyle had to bring him back. And so did the BBC.'

'Holmes was popular,' Garrett pointed out. 'BK is a midlist author who's selling fewer with every book. Who'd miss us?'

The silence that followed was broken only by the sound of Nat telling Jaz it wasn't her fault he had come all this way. She hadn't asked him.

Garrett went to the Fiesta and peered in through the open window. 'You never see a window winder these days, do you? Everything's electric.'

McMahon said, 'If we're not needed, we could go off and hunt down a cream tea. Sod the diet.'

'We ought to shut this first.'

'We're miles from anywhere,' McMahon reminded her. 'Nobody's going to nick it out here. Come on. I bet there's a village with a teashop.'

'Ever heard of Rural Crime?' Garrett withdrew from the front of the car and shaded her eyes with one hand, trying to see into the back. 'He's got a toolbox in the footwell.'

'Always put your valuables out of sight,' quoted McMahon. 'Throw it in the boot for him if you're worried about Rural Crime.'

But Garrett dared not move it. For all she knew, BK had written the toolbox in there as a clue. Or as a heavy rectangular red herring. There were some things a character could not interfere with, even when the author wasn't looking.

That was just as well, since she would have looked even more guilty if Jaz had caught her moving his property when he stormed down the path and demanded to know what they were snooping round his car for, if they weren't proper cops.

They were halfway to the gate when he called, 'Wait!'

His hands were held out in a gesture of openness. 'Listen. I was out of order just now. Could you two do me a favour? Go back in there and tell Nat what you told me?'

Garrett swallowed. This was turning out to be far more complicated than usual. If only she had insisted on staying out of sight. But as soon as McMahon had spotted the girl with the flowery suitcase, he had been unable to resist making an unscripted interference. And being McMahon, and being solid rather than sharp, he had no idea how to think up a second lie to cover the first one. *Any fool can tell the first lie,* a barrister had once told Garrett in a thriller about city fraud. *It's being able to follow through that counts.*

So when they were seated round the kitchen table, McMahon abandoned any attempt to stick to the pretence of the Murder Mystery Weekend.

What he did say seemed even less likely than anything Jaz or Nat had been willing to believe before. Understandably, Jaz greeted it with, 'That's bollocks!' followed by an appeal to Garrett. 'What's really going on?'

But Garrett was feeling a curious sense of relief at not having to hide the truth any more. 'He's right,' she said. 'All of us. All except for BK. We're all only fictional. We only exist briefly, while she's working on the book.'

'Out, brief candle,' intoned McMahon. Seeing the expression on Garrett's face he added, 'We do have Shakespeare in Peckham, you know.'

'I promise we'll find out who did it,' put in Garrett, offering what consolation she could. 'We always do. That's how BK works. After eighty-five thousand words of blundering about, we rise from a trough of despair to an exciting finish and justice is done.'

'You'll be famous,' said McMahon.

Jaz said, 'I've never heard of this BK Henshawe woman.'

'Moderately famous,' conceded McMahon. 'Amongst readers with conservative tastes.'

Nat was still looking frightened. 'BK is the one in the purple boots?'

'That's her,' McMahon said. *'A bright new talent in crime fiction. The Times.'*

Garrett reflected that they had been splashing *A bright talent!* across BK's book covers for ten years now. There had been nothing since to surpass it. *'A reliable exponent of the genre – the Independent'* didn't have the same ring about it.

The bookshops no longer displayed her work with the covers facing the front. Now, unless BK had slipped into the crime section and done a little rearranging, readers were obliged to turn their heads sideways and hunt for her name along alphabetical rows of spines.

Nat said, 'She didn't look nasty.'

'You'd be amazed,' McMahon told her. 'You can't guess what goes on in people's heads from looking at them. Think of all the dear old grannies who used to watch the wrestling so they could yell at Giant Haystacks.'

'I don't want to die!' cried Nat, who was far too young to remember Giant Haystacks. 'I knew I should never have left Streatham!'

'Take no notice, babe,' said Jaz. 'It's all bollocks. It's a wind-up.'

'What if it isn't?'

He draped a tattooed arm around her shoulders. 'I'll look after you.' He turned to the police officers. 'Piss off, the pair of you. You're upsetting my girl.'

Neither of them stopped to argue. Garrett suspected BK had written Jaz a military background. To her relief, BK had also written them a Vauxhall Astra and a village with a pub that did decent evening meals. That was one good thing about BK: even if her backgrounds were inconsistent from book to book, you could rely on her to think them through for each story. Some authors forgot to feed you for days. Once Garrett – under the name of Simpson, or was it Samson? – had been left on a lone stakeout for twenty-seven hours with a big Thermos of coffee and nowhere to wee.

But as she settled under the duvet in her anonymous flat in a nearby un-named town, Garrett was uneasy. She had never warned a victim before. McMahon, his head turned by those high heels and the silly suitcase, had gone even further. It was deeply unprofessional to mention the author. Now the girl was confused and scared, and explaining that it would all be over by Friday hadn't been much comfort. Jaz's words, shouted after them as they hurried away down the path, echoed in her mind. 'What sort of police are you, then, hanging around waiting for someone to get murdered? Why don't you stop it happening?'

There was an answer to that, of course, but Garrett knew Jaz wouldn't want to hear it.

By now Nat and Jaz might be speeding away up the M5 in the Ford Fiesta, safe from BK Henshawe's murderous intentions. But BK would not be thwarted for long. Perhaps forgetting Nat had ever existed, she would turn her attention to the girl with the laptop. Or the woman with lots of piercings and no signal, or her partner, or the little old lady with the folder of poems, or...

'Ungth.' McMahon's voice sounded flat, as if his throat was responding but his mouth was still asleep.

'I've had enough,' Garrett told him.

'I'll pick you up in five minutes.'

'Wha?'

'Ten, then. Give you time to clean your teeth.'

Garrett pressed the 'end call' icon and the screen faded to black. Then she clicked on the bedside light. The laminate felt cold under her feet, and when she pulled on yesterday's socks they felt faintly clammy. No matter. *Why don't you stop it?*

'Because we're fictional characters,' grumbled McMahon. 'It's not our – bloody hell, woman, slow down! What if there's a tractor round the corner?'

'At four in the morning in November?' But she slowed down anyway. If they ended up in a ditch, they would have a lot of explaining to do to BK. Although since BK had dreamed up a car with no bumps and scrapes, was that how the Astra would still look when it appeared in her story? Garrett didn't know. Just like she didn't know the answer to most of the questions a bad-tempered McMahon was now posing, such as, 'How can we make anything happen if BK doesn't want it to?'

'She's *asleep*,' Garrett pointed out. 'She's not concentrating on anybody. She's not moving the pieces around the chessboard.'

'Then how do they bloody move at all?'

'How should I know? How is it you're still able to complain? All I know is, police officers are supposed to prevent crime. That's what we're here for.' She stamped on the brakes as the headlights caught a stone-covered bank dead ahead of them, and hauled the wheel left to follow the potholed tarmac of the lane.

McMahon was saying something about being there to solve murders, not stop them happening. 'Old Pathology Pete is right. We'd all be out of a job. BK included.'

Garrett chose to concentrate on the road.

She flicked off the lights and crawled the car

halfway up the drive before cutting the engine for fear BK would be woken by the noise. As they picked their way towards the house in the dark, McMahon said, 'I hope you've got a plan.'

Garrett nudged him and pointed. 'The Fiesta's still here.'

'Perhaps the murderer's done for both of them. Young lovers found in each other's arms. Death under the duvet. How's that for a title?'

But when they crept into the kitchen (the lock was, in McMahon's professional opinion, a joke) they found Jaz very much alive. Finally he accepted that they meant no harm, lowered the knife he had been holding at Garrett's throat (she had been right about the military training), and told them what had happened so far.

Guessing that the murder was supposed to take place at the writers' retreat itself, Jaz had driven Nat to what he called a 'safe house' and then returned to make a full recce of the site. Now that reinforcements had arrived, he suggested they hold a briefing around the kitchen table.

Garrett and McMahon exchanged a glance. In their absence, Jaz seemed to have taken it into his head to become a major character. But what sort? Was he the suspicious interfering vigilante who would turn out to be a red herring, or was his offer of help a cover for his wicked intentions? They only had his word for it that Nat was safely tucked up in an un-named bed-and-breakfast in Great Torrington. For all they knew, BK had spent her evening writing a scene where Jaz had murdered his girlfriend in a fit of jealous rage. Now, caught on the brink of a getaway, he could be trying to throw them off the scent. The absence of bloodstains or any signs of a struggle on his person meant nothing. Jaz was a trained killer.

It occurred to Garrett that plots were even more complicated without an author. At least when BK was in charge you usually knew which crime you were investigating, even if BK had no more idea than you about where the story was going, or who had done the murder, until the book was nearly finished. This crime prevention fiction was like chasing fog.

'Keep up, will you?' McMahon voice cut into her thoughts. 'This was your idea. We're not doing all the work while you have a kip on the kitchen table.'

Both the men seemed to think the three of them were working as a team. Jaz was saying something about perhaps being too late already. Nat was safe, but there were other likely victims.

'Didn't I tell you?' demanded McMahon, who seemed thoroughly awake now. 'I told you BK was improving. She's got us so we don't know where to look.'

'Wonderful,' said Garrett.

'What I reckon we need to do,' McMahon continued, 'Is to delay the body turning up. Nobody's going to be calling the police until there's a body. Until the body turns up, BK will be busy thinking about where all her suspects are. Me and Garrett can pretty much–'

'But that's not the point!' Sometimes Garrett wondered how McMahon got any work at all. 'We don't want there to be a body. We want to stop the murder happening in the first place.'

'I don't see how,' said McMahon. 'We've got one potential victim out of harm's way, but what about the others? What about the girl with the laptop?'

'Sound asleep ten minutes ago,' Jaz told him. 'But even the three of us can't patrol the whole place. There's only one way to stop these murders.'

Garrett said, 'And that is?'

'Kill BK,' replied Jaz calmly, as if he had been waiting for them to catch up.

'We can't do that!' said McMahon.

'We're the police, Jaz,' Garrett explained. 'This isn't the 1970s. Committing one murder in order to prevent another is against national guidelines.'

Jar shrugged. 'Suit yourselves. It's BK, or some innocent poetry-scribbler. And I bet she won't stop with one.'

Garrett felt suddenly cold. It was true that authors murdered a shocking number of people. But to do away with an author – worse, for a police officer to be involved – was something she had never dared consider. 'It seems so ... ungrateful,' she murmured. 'Especially when there are writers who murder lots more people than she does.'

'Sod gratitude,' said McMahon. 'And sod the guidelines. I'm sick of being messed about. She's given me a diet and a family in Peckham I didn't even know about, and I've never forgiven her for the drink problem. But we can't kill her.'

Jaz said, 'Why not?'

'Because,' Garrett explained patiently, 'a bunch of fictional characters can't murder a real person.'

'We can't?' Evidently Jaz had not considered this.

'We can look,' said McMahon, 'but we can't touch. We can't even warn her off, because as soon as she's thinking about us, she's in charge of what we do.'

'We could try acting out the ending first,' Garrett mused. 'You know, like Agatha Christie. Call a meeting while BK's asleep, and accuse everybody until someone breaks down and confesses, then lock them up and that's the end of the plot.'

'But if whoever it is hasn't done it yet,' said Jaz, 'what are they going to confess?'

Garrett realised her scene order was becoming as muddled as BK's own. She supposed it was inevitable, since it was theoretically impossible for any character to be more intelligent than her author.

'Besides,' put in McMahon, 'if BK hasn't made her mind up who it is yet, the murderer won't know they've got murderous intentions anyway.'

'There must be something we can do.' Jaz looked from one to the other as if waiting for one of them to admit they were only teasing him. 'Surely?'

Garrett stared at a long crack in the wooden table. If they had been in a proper plot, this would be the moment at which someone would have a bright idea, so that the others could tell them it was too dangerous and probably wouldn't work anyway. Then the person with the bright idea – it was usually her – would ask if anyone had any better suggestions, and of course nobody would have, so then she would insist on going ahead and McMahon would reluctantly agree to back her up.

'It has to be our own idea,' she mused. 'And it can't be a coincidence. Readers don't like coincidences. Or *deus ex machina.* Readers think that's cheating.'

'Or what?' said Jaz.

'An unexpected rescuer from outside,' McMahon put in. 'So if you're thinking of calling in some mates from the SAS or whatever, forget it.'

Jaz scratched one ear. 'Funny. I know I must have some, but I can't remember any of their names.'

'That's because they're only background,' Garrett explained. 'They don't have any part in the plot. There has to be a limited number of characters and they all have to do something in the story, otherwise readers get confused and bored and lose interest.'

'And BK gets in a mess too,' McMahon put in. 'Too much to think about at once and she starts putting people on unnecessary diets, and forgetting where they come from.'

Garrett thumped a fist on the table. 'That's it!' she exclaimed.

Finally McMahon said, 'Will you be telling us, or do we have to guess?'

She looked up to find the other two staring at her. 'Sorry. I was thinking. But have you noticed how there are never more than three or four of us in a scene at any one time?'

McMahon said, 'So?'

'She can't control lots of characters at once.'

'What about when she had us chasing round

the stands at the football match?' demanded McMahon. 'And the shooting with the tourists outside Exeter cathedral? And the lost child with all those families on the beach?'

'But they're all background,' Garrett insisted. 'Scenery. She's not concentrating on what everyone's doing. She sets them in motion so the reader knows they're there and then she forgets about them while she's focusing on the main characters. If we get everyone together and we all do different things – ask questions, get into danger, argue with each other so we don't fade into the background–'

'How would that kill her?' asked Jaz.

Garrett smiled. 'We don't need to kill her,' she said. 'We just need to stop her killing one of us.'

BK Henshawe had downed plenty of Sainsbury's Cabernet before, but it had never left her feeling like this. It wasn't that she felt ill, exactly. She just didn't seem to be able to concentrate this morning. It was only eleven o'clock and already she had consigned three unfinished scenes to the 'dump' file on the desktop. Perhaps she was distracted by the unfamiliar silence of the surroundings. Perhaps she was still recovering from yesterday's long drive. Perhaps just a small glass of – no, not before six. She was a professional. That was the rule.

The chair scraped back across the stone floor as she stood, stretched and wandered over to the kettle. Coffee.

No, not coffee. She was feeling jumpy already.

She returned to the table with a steaming mug

of camomile tea. Staring at the stained insides of the mug through the thin liquid, she wondered if she should get up and fetch a saucer for the teabag.

'Concentrate!' She was glad there was nobody to hear her talking to herself. She paused, listening for the sounds of the countryside, and was rewarded with the roar of a chainsaw. She flipped over the page of her notepad and wrote the heading 'Background' and then 'CHAINSAW?' below it, then returned to the screen and scanned through the text, hunting for a suitable place to insert a note. Failing to find one, she returned to the pad and ran a yellow highlighter over the word 'CHAINSAW?' adding, 'put in later' above it. Then she drew a ring around 'put in later'.

She had covered several pages with scribbled notes. They were decorated with circles, arrows and asterisks, but on screen, where it mattered, she was making no progress at all. It was baffling. She had come here with plenty of ideas, all ready to be spliced together into a classic country-house murder mystery. There was no problem about motivation. She had long relished the fantasy of bumping off a couple of her more successful competitors – in the guise of poets, of course, rather than crime writers, so they couldn't sue. But somehow every time she settled down with a fresh coffee to start a scene, extraneous characters and ideas kept popping into her mind and distracting her.

What were the names of Jaz's comrades in the SAS, or was it the Marines? Could she use them as part of the plot? In fact, could he have been in and out of the Marines at the age of twenty-five, or should she make him older? She reached for the mouse and then remembered, for the umpteenth time that morning.

No internet.

She took a pencil and added, 'Age of Marines/SAS veterans' to a list of questions that included, 'Ford Fiesta window winders' and 'Slurry pit on sheep farm?' and 'Distance to tea shops?' and 'Tractor overturns,' and 'Listen to Devon accents,' and 'Crushed by stampeding ewes' and 'Do Police drive Astras?' and 'Poetry competitions' and 'Rural taxis' and 'Real forensics officers have note-books,' and 'Chain saws – diesel?'. This last had been scribbled out and the word, 'No!' written beside it.

BK sighed heavily, turned over to a new page, and wrote, PLAN in big letters at the top. Then she added the word FINAL in front, and under-lined them both, all the time wondering whether the girl with the laptop might be an undercover reporter on the trail of a serial killer in wire-framed glasses who left one of his poems on each body.

The warble of the house phone startled her into guilt, reminding her of the world she had come here to escape: the world of agents and deadlines and messages from Facebook telling her fewer people liked her this week than had liked her last week.

'No, everything's fine,' she found herself assur-ing one of the absent centre managers, who then of course asked the question she was dreading.

'Oh, the writing's fine,' she lied. 'Just pulling

some ideas together. You know. Making the most of the time.'

The manager took the hint, said they would be back by teatime on Friday and would try not to disturb her again.

BK Henshawe put the phone down and found herself willing it to ring again. Anything but to have to go back to that laptop: to the teeming ideas that wouldn't arrange themselves, and the words that wouldn't come.

A walk, a failed attempt at meditation, several guilt-ridden games of Freecell and a bottle of Cabernet later, BK told herself she must pull herself together. She was a professional. Time was passing. She would take the advice of the creative writing gurus and write something – anything at all, just to get herself moving. She reached for the pad and began.

The managers returned on Friday afternoon as agreed. To their surprise they did not find BK Henshawe seated in front of her laptop, but behind the barn, damp and mud-splattered, swinging an axe down to split a large log into two raw-faced chunks. They waited until she had put the axe down before asking – somewhat tentatively, since they had met plenty of writers – how the work had gone. BK smiled vaguely and said, 'Oh, fine. Lots of ideas. It's just a case of pulling them all together. You know.'

After she had driven away, narrowly missing the gatepost, they found three A4 pads crammed into the kitchen bin. They were covered in writing. Not a new novel, but some scrappy notes and then pages and pages of the same sentence, scrawled over and over again in increasingly erratic handwriting.

'There is NO SUCH THING as writer's block.'

As the managers of the writing retreat stood appalled, the minor characters who had only been invented for BK's latest book faded forever into the Devon drizzle. The stock characters drifted away too, still needed by other authors, but bearing a new secret with them. This was only the beginning. As they were called upon to work in new settings, the story of their success at distraction would spread.

Writers tucked away in the seclusion of their studies would be such easy targets. Murder rates – especially in Oxford, Cambridge, and the once-peaceful hamlet of Midsomer Norton – would tumble. It occurred to the police officer once known as Garrett, or Simpson, or Samson, or none of the above, that some of her time-travelling comrades in crime prevention could prevent the build-up of historical murders, too. The hideous flow of ink creating more and more Victorian murder victims could be stopped. The expansion plans of Medieval killers could be thwarted. Countless Tudors and Romans might be saved from being created merely to be tortured and cruelly done away with.

Garrett, already insubstantial, could just make out McMahon's grin as they waved goodbye to each other at the gate. Nobody would ever hear of them by those names again, but in the hidden world that characters inhabit when they are not on duty, she was pretty sure they were destined to become the greatest crime-fighting duo in the history of fiction.

The Guest List
by Stella Duffy

There is a stillness, settled on the room, the house. It is calm, and beautiful in that calm. A light, soft, fine, falling through the bedroom window on to her cool, smooth skin. He reaches out to touch her and then draws his hand back. No, not yet. It's not yet time. There is a path to clear first, a past to clear.

The Bride Groom

If anyone had told Ed it was going to feel like this, he'd have laughed at them, smacked them on the back if they were a man, chucked her under the chin if it were one of his girl friends, and said, as everyone expected Ed to say, as Ed Malone always said, 'I know what I'm doing, don't you worry about me.'

No-one told Ed it was going to feel like this – this big, this real, this true – because no-one has worried about what Ed might feel for years. No-one has had to worry about Ed's feelings. When you're as fortunate as Ed Malone, what could there ever be to worry about? Ed is the loving, loved, warm-hearted, smart-witted, clever, affable, great looking, good guy and no-one has seriously worried about Ed since he came home from school, a month or so before his twelfth birthday, and announced,

'I'm Ed now. I'm almost a man. I don't think you should call me Eddie any more.'

Sure, as Eddie there might have been times when he'd sloped through the back door with a cut lip from over-active games with his friends, or bruised knees and scraped shins from climbing trees, but once those games progressed to the kind a boy plays with a girl, and once the climbing became first hills, then rock walls, then mountains, actual mountains, once Eddie became Ed, no-one needed to worry about him any more.

Ed had it all. Classic good looks, a great job with a good firm that valued him but knew he was never going to be one of those guys married to the job, and maybe even valued him more for that. He was well-liked, well-considered, a good friend, and a great date. Edward – call me Ed – Malone was one of those guys. Easy-going but able to let loose every now and then, ready to push himself while carrying you on his back if you needed him. Everyone loved Ed, and Ed liked everyone. Kept them all a little at bay, kept himself just a little distant. Only one or two thought he was actually aloof, the rest assumed it was something about being golden, too much contact with ordinary folk might rub away some of that glow. Not that Ed ever behaved as if he were better than anyone else, not at all, but he had to know, on some level. Everyone else could see that he was loved deeper, prized higher, befriended more readily, surely Ed must feel it too? While he gave no indication of thinking he was different, still, Ed kept to himself, ever such a little. Which, of course, only made him more of an attraction to that kind of woman, and a few of those kinds of men. The ones who set their caps at the unattainable, who are so golden themselves that they cannot believe anyone might not want them as much as everyone else does.

But Ed did not want them as much as everyone else did.

And then, at thirty-two, he met her. The One. His match.

The Bride

She was, of course, the girl equivalent of Ed. Impossible to be a golden couple, unless both are equally golden. And she did shine. Emily Gordon, of the three Gordon girls, Charlotte, Anne and Emily, the brother Charlie Junior leading them in everything. Their parents might have had half the state's money behind them, a senator in each family as great-uncles, and Charles Gordon Senior could trace his people right back to the founding fathers, but the Gordons liked people to know they had a sense of humour as well. As well as wealth, privilege, power and a well-developed artistic side. Those four children were born with silver spoons in each of their mouths and the sun shining wherever they went. Charlie and Charlotte were twins, charming, cool, relaxed and, even in their youth, at one with privilege. Anne, the middle child, took after her mother in good looks, her father in intelligence, and the twins in everything else. All three had the ease associated with long-held wealth, the comfort in any surroundings, an ability to speak with every rank of person and make them feel they were the only person in the room. But it was in Emily that the Gordon shine really came into its own. She was beautiful, that was a given. She was terribly bright and had the charm to know when to show it and when to hold back. She was great fun to be with, excelled at sailing, swimming and skiing, she sang with both gusto and perfect pitch. Emily was everything a good family could want from its youngest child. The Gordons were the kind of people bred to sit on boards, lead trusts, head governments – though not necessarily as leader itself, that would be vulgar, something quieter, a bit more back-room, one of those roles that truly wield power. Emily was the first girl in her class to have a serious romance, and the last to lose her virginity. She was the first in her group to have a crush on another girl, and the only one to act on it. Emily Gordon had all of the family elegance and the best of her generation's passion, and she was also just a little bit bad. Of course, it was the wild that made her really shine.

Not nasty-wild, never mean-wild. But ... wild.

It was the wild that made the wedding the truly perfect day that both of them had been longing for.

Ed Malone and Emily Gordon request the pleasure of your company at their could-have-been-you shindig. No need to bring booze, we know your usual.

Only Emily would have hand-written nine invitations and used the word shindig with shame.

Only Emily would have dared could-have-been-you.

The Guests

Mitchell Dawson, Ted Lanes, Joseph Marquand, Tom Ellison, Caro Dawson.

Emily's ex-lovers. Mitchell and Caro were brother and sister.

Jenifer Hodges, Maggie Whyte, Sarah Goodall, Trudi Amundsen, Caro Dawson.

Ed's ex-lovers.

Yes, Caro had slept with both Emily and Ed. Not at the same time. Emily might have had her wildness but, no doubt because she'd grown up as the youngest and loveliest of her siblings, she wasn't keen on sharing.

Some of the Guests knew each other, Mitchell and Caro, obviously. Ted Lanes and Sarah Goodall had been an item since Ted stole Sarah from Ed, or rather, Ed let Ted think he'd stolen Sarah, when actually he and Emily had begun their affair six weeks earlier, and neither Ed nor Emily wanted to be thought of as the bad guys. After an obligatory two months of getting over it, and another month dating Trudi (rebound) in order to prove he was ready for another relationship, Ed emerged with Emily on his arm and the golden couple was formed. Anyone who paid very close attention to their behaviour might have noticed that they weren't behaving like a couple who'd only just started dating, more like one that had been together for a few months at least, but people rarely paid very close attention to Ed and Emily. They thought they did, they listened to the stories, laughed at the jokes, but there was always so much going on around Ed and Emily, so much to do, that actually paying close attention to them was difficult, hard to see the truth through the glow. Ed and Emily were an event, a feast, an exploration of pleasure in the form of fun, friendship and constant frolicking. It is blinding to look at the sun.

After a while, when it was time to be friends again, to nostalgically look back on the old days, wryly smiling, Ed and Emily asked Ted and Sarah to join them at the lake. The Malone's lake. (The Gordons had the education, the business and the big, big house, the Malones had the new farm, the old farm, the older forest, and the very old lake. Of course Ed and Emily were a love match, no one doubted that, but it didn't hurt that their families were also balanced in title deeds and land registrations.) There was a slightly awkward start to the day, when Sarah didn't quite know how to greet Ed, after all, the last time she'd seen him he had been leaning over her in the bedroom, insisting she spit out every dirty little detail of the interaction she had just confessed to having with Ted. Sarah, being a good girl, and having only gone as far but no further, sobbed and confessed, blow by blow. She was so in thrall to her own shame, a mortification she would later share with Ted, her sister and her girlfriends – nothing confirms a young lady as a good girl quite so much as sincere humiliation – that she failed to notice that Ed was lapping up her squirming shame. If she had, perhaps she wouldn't have agreed to that day at the lake. Or the shindig. But agree she did, as did Ted, and it was Emily's smiling welcome, her outstretched arms, her sisterly hug that made it fine for Sarah to turn to Ed, look up to him (a good foot taller) and smile bashfully, 'Nice to see you again, Ed.'

Ed winked at Sarah, Emily kissed Ted right on the lips – as, it must be noted, she did with every man, loving the slight tremor it invariably created in the more traditional of their men friends – Ed smacked Ted on the back, one of the two men opened a nice cold bottle of champagne, and then everything was fine, easy.

The long and lovely brunch slid into a walk and a swim, then a picnic and slowly back to the lakehouse, early afternoon sun sharp through the heady pines. There was another bottle of champagne for afternoon tea and finally a light supper to help Ted sober up before the drive home.

'Remarkably adult' was how Sarah described the day as she snuggled up to Ted in the front of the car on the way home, Ed and Emily waving from the lakehouse verandah.

'Fucking whore' was Ted's eventual response when, after twenty minutes of silence, Sarah pleading and begging him to speak, he dropped her at the crossroads, two miles walk back into town in a summer frock and strappy sandals, fury and incomprehension her only companions on the old lake road.

Back at the lakehouse Ed stretched out on the daybed in the evening sun, his face aching from the grin he'd been suppressing all day, lapping up Emily's recounted whispers, one after the other, tiny little whispers she'd offered up to Ted as gifts throughout the day. A 'Do you worry about Sarah?' here, a 'Did you see how Ed looked at her?' there, all through the day, until Ted was seeing Sarah with brand new eyes. And then, the final straw, just as Sarah was kissing Ed goodbye, Ed's hand that little bit too firm on her lower back, just as Sarah was getting into Ted's car, Emily hugged Ted fiercely and this time she had no question in her tone at all, 'I heard them, when they took the dishes to the kitchen, they are still fucking.'

The way Emily bit her lip as she pulled back from him, the way she frowned her fine brow, shook her pretty head (so her honey-blonde hair fell more beautifully across her tanned shoulders), it was all Ted could do not to scoop her up and save her then and there. Well, he couldn't save Emily, but he could certainly dump Sarah.

Ed almost made himself sick with laughing.

And so, The Guests

Sarah arrived alone, of course, returning to the lakehouse, hands shaking as she drove the long stretch out to the scene of a crime she didn't commit. She parked the car alongside three others and followed the trail of balloons past the lakehouse itself and up round the back to the dancing room, installed for the Malone children when they were in their teens, hardly used since, but a perfect spot for a party, even more distant than the house itself, quiet, secluded, yet with stunning views from the glass doors and windows forming three of the four walls. Windows that Mr Malone had had double-glazed long before it was the fashion, not wanting any of his youngsters' wild music to float down the hill and disturb his peaceful fishing.

Sarah stopped at the door, stock still when she saw Ted was in the room ahead of her. Emily watched, there was a moment when Sarah considered leaving, when she thought the better part of chagrin would be to run, and then a sigh, a shake of the head, a stiffening of the backbone, and she threw back her head, pulled open the door, and made straight for the drinks table. Emily was there before her and already pouring a strong, cool and clear martini.

'You look like you might need this.'

Then a girly hug, enveloping her with soft skin, softer hair and a sweet-sour perfume that was almost wrong and simultaneously delicious.

Ted didn't see Sarah at first, and when he did he made sure she saw him smiling as winningly as possible at Jenifer Hodges as they both knocked back the perfectly-chilled champagne.

Jenifer who was still a little in love with Ed, even though she was now married to Mitchell.

Mitchell who was Caro's brother.

Caro who had been the lover of both Ed and Emily and was now living with Joseph Marquand.

And finally Maggie, Ed's first love, Emily's best friend from high school, her family the link between the Gordons and the Malones, her parents the ones who first sat the Gordons opposite the Malones at a dinner table, in many ways the reason for the love between Ed and Emily.

Maggie. The first to go.

The Deaths

Maggie always had been a bit of a lush. She'd arrived at the dancing room, complaining already that she'd had to trek further than the house and she hadn't worn the shoes for anything but lounging on a deck, air-kissed Emily, lip-kissed Ed, and then quickly downed the one, two, three Manhattans that Ed expertly mixed for her. One glass and she was a little woozy, a second glass and she thought perhaps she should have eaten breakfast that day, all very well wanting to be as thin as possible when she saw Emily and Ed, Ed who she had never stopped loving, wanting, but maybe food would have been a better stomach-lining than three cups of black coffee. And then, after a few conversations and the dawning realization that there would be no other guests, and there was no-one here she might go home with, a third drink, because oh fuck it, why not, she always coped better when she was a little gone.

Maggie, well and truly gone. No amount of Sarah screaming, or Ted running around the now-locked room looking for a telephone – no telephone, four walls, three of them glass, all sound-proofed – or Caro standing over Maggie, sobbing and shaking between bouts of trying to bring her back to life with inept mouth-to-mouth made any difference. Maggie, the first to go.

The one door locked, no in, no out, windows soldered shut. Ed did always love his power tools. Ted banging round the room knocking into things, gasping, gasping for breath as if there is no air in the room. No air in Ted. And then, Ted knocked out, knocked over. Running flailing one minute and down the next. A hand clutching his heart and – done. Night night, Teddy.

Then, in quick succession, together almost, as they'd maybe have wanted it, maybe not how Jenifer wanted it, Jenifer and Mitchell – beer drinker Mitchell, 'amber stuff only, thanks' Mitchell – both suddenly dizzy, overcome, and then, gasping for breath, a thin breath, not ... enough ... oxygen ... in ... the ... air, hands clawing at throats, gasping, gasping, gasped. Last gasp. Gone.

Sarah next. Sarah who didn't drink, not these days, not any more, not since she drove her car into that young boy just stepping off the curb and God knows she might have killed him, did enough damage, bones and spleen and bruising, so much bruising, and it was only the family money that saved her from jail, the whole town knew that, but money talked louder even than the gossips, and now the boy's family had a new car and a great vacation and the boy had a college fund too, so, well ... their choice, understandable, no-one to judge. Emily and Ed to judge.

Sarah clutching her glass of water so tight, sipping at it slowly to calm her down, calm her nerves, this had to be a dream, it couldn't be real, not Ted, her Ted, her Teddy dead – no matter that he hadn't spoken to her in months – and Ed, smiling, grinning over her, asking her if she wanted a refill.

Sparkling water, fresh and cool, and Sarah suddenly throwing it over herself, throwing it in her own face, 'What the ... how did that how...', legs jerking, arms jerking, sp ... sp ... spasms, convulsions, down now and spinning on the highly polished, so polished, deeply polished parquet dancefloor. Whirling dervish Sarah. Stopped.

Joseph Marquand, not really a friend, not a friend of either family, just the live-in boyfriend of Caro. Live-in, how modern, how uncouth. Emily and Ed were waiting until they were wed. Ed thought Caro clinging, Emily assumed Joseph suffocating, either way, Joseph had insisted on accompanying Caro and so here he was, paying the price. Another beer drinker. They'd checked.

And then Caro. Libertine Caro. Wild party-girl Caro, drinking-til-she-falls-Caro. Sleep with anyone, value no-one, Caro. She stood in the room, looking around her. Sarah, Ted, Jenifer, Mitchell, Joseph, Maggie.

'How did you do it?'

They smiled.

'Us?' one said.

'How?'

'That would be telling,' the other answered.

They held hands. They moved closer.

Caro didn't look so strong now, so passionate, so free. Something of the party had left her.

The party had left her. She slipped, slid, slumped against the drinks table, and then she fell.

Emily and Ed turned to each other and kissed.

The cleanest, clearest kiss they'd kissed since they had The Idea. They had done it, they were free.

The Idea

I don't want to marry you knowing there are other people you have loved, I have loved.

We won't invite them.

They might turn up.

Like the wicked fairy in Sleeping Beauty?

Yes. And then there will be that moment…

…the hold your peace moment?

Yes. And I will wonder...

So will I...

So…

I don't want them to be able to come to the wedding. I want it to be impossible for them to come to the wedding.

OK.

I love you.

I love you.

The Rest of Their Lives

The lakehouse was closed up. More power tool action, strong Ed, manly Ed. It was the end of summer and no-one ever went there the rest of the year. They'd tried, when Ed was younger, the whole family had spent one dank and dripping Thanksgiving looking out at the rain and the cold, cold lake. It was always just too sad to look at the water and not swim, the trees around here did not turn to red, yellow and gold, they stayed green, pretending summer, while heaven turned to a lowered grey and it rained for almost six months of the year. How it rained. Anyway, there were other houses to go to when summer was done. So the lakehouse sat quiet and still.

Of course The Guests were noted missing. But not immediately. None of them had been invited to The Wedding after all. And so, in the ceremony, when it came time to 'speak now or forever after hold your peace', peace was held. And when it came time to demand that no man put asunder, Ed and Emily turned to each other in the full knowledge that now there was neither man, nor woman, to put them asunder. Knowing that their pasts had been wiped as clean as the future, there was just this moment, just the two of them, this moment and always.

And by the time The Guests were noticed missing, by the time the connections were made, slow slow slow then quick quick quick quick, by the time the bodies were finally found – the lakehouse would never be the same again – Emily and Ed were long gone. The honeymoon that was extended, the postcards that turned out not to have been posted by the happy couple at all, sent from first Venice, Florence, Milan, then London, Paris, and back to Rome for the romantic hope of Italy again, posted instead by the three young would-be travellers Ed and Emily had picked up hitchhiking two, four, five months before the wedding, trusting each one with a wad of cash and the postcards they'd bought, last summer in Europe, when The Idea first came to them. By the time the romantic honeymoon was discovered to have been a fraud, they had spent several weeks in the Swiss clinic and had flown on to Split to recuperate, then Istanbul, Goa, Australia, all the way round again to Venezuela, and now they had new faces, new haircuts, new bodies. They were both that little bit less beautiful, less golden, less likely to stand out. They were both that little bit more the other's. They would never fall out, because they could never fall out, and they would never part, because they could not, because the secret was stronger than a gold ring.

The Future

If and when children come, if and when Ed and Emily allow children into their couple – unlikely they think, but they know chance will always play a part – the children will believe the stories they are told. Children always do, not least because children are only really interested in themselves, where they fit into the picture. If they are told that life before them did not count, they will readily believe it. If they are told they are the centre of the universe, they will believe it – Ed and Emily did. Ed and Emily do. For now they are all there is for each other and that is plenty, has been plenty for them all this time – they had assumed, their families had understood this to be true – and now they know for sure. Any child who might arrive would easily believe there was never much of a past, just some people, once, who did not live long. Just a small town, once, that was no longer worth remembering.

Because none of it is worth remembering, none of it worth remarking. There is no past, and what future there is, is only Ed and Emily. For ever and ever, amen.

Now it is time.

There is a stillness, settled on the room. A soft light, fine, falls on to her cool, smooth skin. He reaches out to touch her

You may kiss the bride.

Lucky Liam
by Martin Edwards

Better to be born lucky than rich. The phrase had stuck in Liam North's mind ever since he'd first heard it as a child, during a family get-together at a pub on the front in Seaton Carew. His mother's brother had been talking about a distant cousin, who had announced her engagement to a banker whom she'd met at university. Uncle Graeme didn't have two pennies to rub together, and he wasn't lucky himself – a tree surgeon, he'd been killed six months later, in an unfortunate accident while felling a Lombardy poplar a mile outside Hartlepool – but it seemed to Liam that his philosophy was spot on. Money comes and goes, but if you're born lucky, in the long run, you'll get pretty much everything you could possibly wish for.

Liam's family was far from rich, but he did like to think he'd been born lucky. An affable manner and a love of words that endowed him with the gift of the gab helped him ease through childhood and the teenage years without ever suffering the consequences of his incurable indolence. He loved reading, and the way he surrounded himself with books gave everyone the impression of a likeable but studious young chap who was destined to go far. In examinations at school and university, his fluent way with words did not compensate fully for his lethargic attitude to revision, but ensured that his grades were borderline respectable. Good enough, as far as Liam was concerned, and when he blamed his failure to do better on recurrent migraines, everyone sympathised. People liked Liam, and were usually willing to give him the benefit of any doubt.

After a few inconsequential schoolboy romances, he met a fellow English student at the University of Sunderland during his first week on the campus. Sally was blonde and stunningly attractive, and she loved books just as much as Liam. She confided on their first date that she dreamed of becoming a writer, and during their student years, a stream of poems, plays, short stories and fragments of novels flooded from her laptop. None achieved paid-for publication, but words of encouragement never failed Liam. He wasn't convinced that Sally possessed literary talent, but never mind. One day, she might drop lucky.

They married three months after taking their degrees. Sally took an Upper Second, but Liam had to make do with a Third, even though she'd helped him with his course work, to the extent of writing most of it. She felt guilty about her own success because he'd suffered migraines during the whole of finals, and dismayed because the job market in the North East didn't offer much for inadequately qualified English graduates. The tricky question of how to make a living demanded an answer. Sally, keen, energetic, and a self-proclaimed 'people person', soon started climbing the greasy pole in human resources, but Liam drifted from job to job, working in bars and restaurants while he tried to write the Great North East England Novel. He seldom made it past chapter one.

Reading other people's books was less like hard work than writing his own, and he was taken on by an elderly fellow called Gidman who owned a second hand bookshop on the Headland at Hartlepool. The building reeked of musty old tomes, and its out-of-the-way location, on a road meandering between the Spion Kop Cemetery and the lighthouse, meant that customers were few and far between. The peace and quiet suited Liam perfectly. More opportunities for reading, less scope for anyone to stop him pleasing himself about how he spent his time. Gidman suffered from emphysema, and had taken Liam simply because he wanted to keep the business afloat. Earning only the minimum wage didn't worry Liam. Sally was picking up good money, and at least they didn't have any extra mouths to feed.

Sally proved unable to have children, the result of some sort of rare genetic condition. When the medical advice was finally confirmed, she wept throughout one long, long night. Nobody could have comforted her more assiduously than Liam. He kept repeating that it didn't matter, it really didn't matter. Sally, inconsolable, feared that he was simply being kind, but he was speaking nothing less than the truth. Kids would take a lot of looking after, and he preferred being the centre of Sally's universe. Thanks to her salary, they'd been able to put down a deposit on a tiny house in Seaton Carew, a stone's throw from where Liam had grown up. From the upstairs bedrooms, you could glimpse the sea. Life was good, who could want more? *If it ain't broke, why fix it?* That was another of Uncle Graeme's favourite philosophies, though it may have contributed to his inadequate maintenance of the circular saw responsible for his premature demise.

His idea for cheering her up was brilliant in its simplicity. She loved books too, so she could help out in the bookshop at week-ends, and assist with cataloguing and stuff on the evenings when they didn't have anything better to do. It wasn't reasonable to expect Gidman to cough up any more money, given the paltry takings, but it was a way of taking her mind off babies.

Sally proved agreeable, and for a while things went well. She'd developed an entrepreneurial streak, and soon she came up with several ideas to boost footfall, including occasional author visits. Inviting real life authors to sign their latest books in a second hand shop, where dog-eared copies of their earlier work were on sale for a pittance seemed counter-intuitive to Liam, but Sally was extremely persuasive, and before long, she'd lined up a series of events featuring the North East's more prominent literary figures.

Liam congratulated himself. Sally was kept fully occupied, and he was free to devote more of his own time during business hours to reading and daydreaming. One or two of his fantasies were inspired by what Sally told him about her oldest friend, a talkative, seriously overweight woman who had been abandoned by her husband, who had waited until twelve months after their wedding to discover that he was gay. Maxine was generous and good-natured, always doing good deeds for others, but she never had much luck. The poor woman was as plain as the back end of a bus, and didn't care for books. Nevertheless, she was legendary for her sex drive, and according to Sally, her maxim was *try anything once*. Physically, she repelled him, but he couldn't help wishing that Sally was equally adventurous. Some of the spark had gone out of their love-making, he couldn't deny it. If only she were less consumed with ambition – especially ambition for him. She wanted him to take over the shop once old Gidman died, and 'make a proper go of it'. All Liam wanted was for her to leave him to his own devices except in bed, of course. Once or twice, he noticed Maxine giving him a longing glance, but he pretended not to notice. He only had eyes for his wife. Life with Sally might not be perfect, but he couldn't deny that he'd dropped lucky with her. The very idea of sleeping with Maxine made him break out in a cold sweat, and even if it hadn't, he certainly couldn't contemplate the kerfuffle associated with divorce. *If it ain't broke...*

He didn't suspect that their marriage might be in the process of breaking until Sally invited Heath Morrison back to Headland Books for the second time in six months to conduct a workshop for wannabe writers. Morrison came from South Shields, and eighteen months earlier, his third novel, an introspective character study of a priapic coal miner, had been long-listed for the Man Booker Prize. Liam found Morrison's bleak worldview depressing on the page, and his cocksure manner – over-compensation, people reckoned, for a depressive streak – irritating when encountered in person. But Sally was smitten with his work, and eventually it crossed Liam's mind that she might also be smitten with the man himself. Morrison had a formidable reputation as a philanderer, and had once spent six months in jail after beating up a lover's boyfriend after a violent row in a Gateshead bar.

At first, Liam tried to shrug off the jealousy that she provoked whenever she harped on about the poetry of Morrison's prose. But she kept harping on about it, and when she mentioned that he'd offered her some advice on how to sharpen up her own writing, he made the mistake of blurting out that Morrison was an arrogant shit who ought to mind his own business.

'Liam!' Her cheeks were pink with outrage. 'That's a disgusting thing to say. I thought you liked Heath.'

He hadn't meant to let the mask slip. 'I only meant that you've as much talent as he has,' he improvised. 'You can't deny that Heath Morrison is a nasty piece of work.'

'Rubbish!' He took a step back, as if she'd slapped his cheek. Surely he hadn't lost his knack of mollifying her with a few well-chosen compliments? 'Heath is a true artist. You may not realise it, but he's tormented by self-doubt. People who say he's violent and arrogant don't have a clue what he's really like.'

She stomped off so angrily that he couldn't be confident that she would set about making their evening meal. In the end, he had to ring for pizzas to be delivered to their door.

Liam began to fret. He suspected that the only doubt tormenting Heath Morrison was whether he could add Sally's name to his list of conquests. How fortunate he was to be able to depend on her loyalty. All the same, it was a mistake to be complacent. Better keep an eye on things. Check her mobile phone account, that sort of stuff.

He was shocked to discover that his luck was about to run out. Sally and Morrison exchanged calls and texts with startling regularity, far more often than was justified by making arrangements for readings at the Headland Bookshop. On a Saturday morning at the end of May, he eavesdropped on one of their conversations, and confirmed his worst fears.

'I'm in the shop on Bank Holiday Monday,' Sally murmured. 'Liam asked me to help out while he visits this old bloke who wants to sell his books ... yes, we can lock the door as soon as you arrive. We're opening up, on the off-chance a few trippers come to visit the gun battery, and get caught in a downpour. I've said I'll get stuck into some overdue tidying, and that's enough for Liam to make himself scarce. He's such a bloody idle sod. Whatever the weather, there's no way I'll be rushed off my feet by customers ... no, I don't want anyone to watch us, thanks very much, I'm a highly respectable woman, I'll have you know ... honestly, Heath, you are the limit. Just as well you're so gorgeous, huh?'

The conversation subsided into a long, helpless giggle. Crouched in his hiding place, behind a bookcase full of battered self-help books, Liam barely managed to suppress a howl of pain. At lunchtime, when she went out to buy ingredients for their evening meal, he checked out the loft space at the top of the building. She'd starting using it for storage – but why would she want to store half a dozen luxurious velvet cushions? He had no difficulty in guessing their intended purpose.

Later that evening, as they ate together, he noticed that Sally was distracted, and realised that she'd not had much to say to him for quite a while. He'd simply not noticed her increasingly perfunctory replies to his remarks, or that so often nowadays – in the shop, in the kitchen, and most of all in bed – her mind seemed to be elsewhere. Now he understood where her thoughts were roaming, and a rage consumed him that felt unlike anything he'd ever experienced before.

Would Sally pack her bags, and leave him high and dry? The financial and practical consequences hardly bore thinking about. What if Morrison dumped her? She was evidently far from content with her marriage, and in time some other literary Casanova would seduce her. She was no longer the innocent girl he'd married. Things could never be the same again.

While brushing his teeth, he remembered that her firm had recently bestowed upon her a new perk, to supplement a measly rise in pay.

Life insurance for employees. What a pity Sally couldn't have an accident. Frankly, it would serve her right.

It occurred to him as he shaved the next morning that of course, accidents did happen. All the time. Why couldn't one happen to Sally? And to Morrison too, come to that? Killing two birds with a single stone was always attractive; economy of effort combined with maximum achievement.

Thinking furiously, he made an excuse to pop out to the shop, even though it was closed, and set about putting his plan into practice. He was acutely conscious that it wasn't a perfect plan. A good deal could go wrong. But then, you constantly read about supposedly perfect crimes that unravelled because of one piece of bad luck. Might as well trust to fortune, as he'd always done.

'What time will you be back?' she asked, as he dropped her off at the shop the next morning.

'Not quite sure. You know what Ernie's like.' He was off to see an elderly chap, one of Gidman's long-time customers. He was getting on, and had started rambling about selling his book collection. 'He'll insist on a good long natter, and it will take me ages to price up all the titles. I'll pop out to get us some fish and chips for lunch. I might be able to get back by mid-afternoon to give you a hand.'

'Really?' The flash of alarm in her eyes gave him intense pleasure, and it confirmed his belief that he was doing the right thing. The only thing. 'There's no need. The weather's so nice, I don't expect we'll get many people in. Everyone will have better things to do than bother about books.'

Everyone, including you and Heath Morrison, Liam thought savagely. 'Yeah, I suppose you're right. I may as well go straight home.'

She smiled, her relief as visible as face paint. 'Good idea. Would you mind picking up some salmon from Sainsbury's on the way back? I'll bake it in white wine for you.'

His favourite meal. She was trying, in her crude way, to atone for her betrayal. He patted her hand. 'Marvellous. I'll see you later.'

She waved happily as he drove off. Ernie Cobb lived just outside Hart, in a quiet cottage with a vast wilderness of a garden. Somehow he still managed to live on his own. He was in his eighties, and his memory was failing. Liam was sure he was in the early stages of dementia. Carers came in twice a day to look after him. Except on Bank Holidays, that is, when as Liam gathered, they only turned up once, at tea-time. It took Liam five minutes to reach the cottage, and five more to greet old Ernie and ask how he was, before making a vague excuse and nipping out of the house. Less than twenty minutes after dropping Sally at the shop, he parked behind a small auto centre that had gone bankrupt the previous winter. He satisfied himself that the spot wasn't overlooked before striding along the alley that ran behind the bookshop, a disused pub, and a semi-derelict warehouse. A gate gave on to a small yard. He undid the padlock, and scrambled up the rickety iron fire escape, right to the top. Nobody could see him. Stepping on to a railed walkway, he pushed open the skylight that he had left unlocked. The loft was dusty and cramped, the only means of exit a small trapdoor. He opened the trapdoor, and contemplated the long, narrow wooden ladder which led to the floor below. Bending double under the sloping roof, he steeled himself to wait in silence until the time came to do the necessary.

And it *was* necessary. Whichever way you looked at things, he really had no choice. True, he was taking a huge risk. Would his luck hold?

Distant noises came from downstairs, as Sally moved around at street level, three floors below. There were rooms crammed with books on the ground, first and second floors. On the second floor was a small office, and, immediately below the loft, an open space accommodating stacked chairs. Sally had come up with the idea of turning this into a compact venue for some of their author events. Liam remembered her saying that it was perfect for an intimate occasion. He'd never guessed what sort of intimate occasion she had in mind.

Ten minutes crept by before he heard the light clatter of her footsteps on the stairs. Coming to retrieve the cushions, at last. He'd wondered if she might have done so as soon as she'd arrived at the shop, so that by the time of his return, she'd already have had her accident, but he'd guessed that her first priority would have been to glam up for her lover. Putting on her make-up was a job she never rushed. On balance, he was glad nothing had happened yet. What if she'd had a slice of luck in his absence, and escaped with a few cuts and bruises? He slid the trapdoor shut, and waited.

He'd sawn through the ladder in three places, before putting it back together so that, at first sight, you'd never guess he'd tampered with it. Certainly, Sally didn't have a clue. Her crash and scream were simultaneous. When he peeked out through the trapdoor, it looked as though she were unconscious, but still breathing. There was no carpet on the floor, and she'd had a hard landing.

He'd fixed a length of rope to a rusty old hook in the roof cavity. It would be a bitter irony if in the absence of the ladder, the hook gave way and he broke his own neck, but he made it down safely. In his imagination, he'd pictured Sally opening her eyes as he crouched over her, and experiencing a terrible moment of realisation about what was to happen. He'd taken the precaution of carrying a short length of wood to club her into silence if the need arose. Thankfully, she didn't stir. As he'd expected, she'd heaped on mascara and her favourite purple eye-shadow, although the blood oozing from her cracked skull ruined the impression of loveliness.

The bell that rang when someone opened the shop door tinkled from downstairs. Liam was sure it was Heath Morrison, even before the bastard called Sally's name. When there was no reply, he could be heard springing up the stairs, taking the steps to the first floor two at a time.

'Sally! Where are you?' Morrison chortled. 'Playing hard to get? A bit late for that, sweetie.'

Liam decided to risk mimicking Sally's high-pitched giggle. He practised endlessly, but in the excitement of the moment, his impression left a good deal to be desired.

'Sally?' Morrison sounded suddenly wary. 'Is that you?'

The stairs to the second floor turned at a right

angle near the top. Liam stationed himself out of sight, behind a tall stack of books. He was sure that Morrison would only have eyes for Sally's prone body. People were so predictable.

'Sally, are you playing hide and seek?' The wheedling note in Morrison's voice was truly odious. He deserved his fate, no question. 'Okay. Coming, ready or not!'

Once again, he raced up the staircase, but his first glimpse of Sally, stretched out on the floor, halted him in his tracks. He had a book in his hand, but Liam had his club. No contest. Liam swung wildly, miscalculating the angle of his strike, and caught Morrison a glancing blow on the forehead. To his infinite relief, it was enough, combined with the shock of seeing Sally's body, to send the novelist tumbling backwards down the steps with a strangled cry of pain and horror. Liam leapt after him, kicking Morrison down as he fell, before hitting him a second time as they landed on the floor below. The other man groaned, but did not stir. Like Sally, he wasn't dead, but he wouldn't be getting up any time soon. So far, so good.

Liam picked up the book Morrison had dropped, before checking to make sure that the writer was, as usual, carrying a packet of Player's and a box of Swan Vestas in the pockets of his jeans. The man smoked eighty a day; filthy habit, he'd have died young anyway. Liam eased both boxes on to the floor with a handkerchief, because you couldn't be sure what might survive in a fire, and he worried vaguely about fingerprints. He'd never smoked in his life, but he'd nicked an identical box of matches from Ernie's sideboard when the old man wasn't looking, and he lit a couple. The first set alight a stack of *Book Collector* magazines he'd left on the floor close to Morrison, creating a merry little blaze. Going back upstairs, he put the second match to a heap of old newspapers. The results were quicker and more impressive than he'd expected. Both fires took hold, and started to spread. Within seconds, the smoke was bringing tears to his eyes, even as he hauled himself back up to the loft, and detached the rope from the hook. He didn't venture a last look at Sally, as the flames danced around her. It was a shame, but he couldn't afford to be sentimental. Destroying the books was an equally dreadful business, come to that.

By the time he wriggled out through the skylight, still clutching the book that Morrison had brought, the building was ablaze. There was so much tinder in a second hand bookshop. He stumbled down the fire escape, desperate to make good his escape before anyone saw him, and almost fell down the last flight of steps. Would it have served him right to break his neck after committing two murders and destroying Gidman's business? Liam didn't believe so for a minute. More of Uncle Graeme's words of wisdom came to mind. *You can't make an omelette without breaking a few eggs.*

Nobody saw him running down the alleyway, or jumping into his car. He heard the fire engine's siren when he was a mile away from the bookshop, and for a moment he wondered if, against all the odds, Sally and Morrison might be rescued. But no, it was unthinkable, so he didn't devote any more thought to such a nightmarish possibility.

'Shall I go to the chippy and get us each a cod and chips with mushy peas?' he asked Ernie a few minutes later. The old man nodded absently, and Liam wasn't sure that he understood the question. Going downhill rapidly, sad to say, but he was supplying a pretty much unbreakable alibi. Later, Liam would leave him a cheque for a box of books, and load them into his car. Ernie would swear blind that he'd been there all the time, but even if he didn't, that was Liam's story, and he meant to stick to it.

The police rang when he was on his way back from the chip shop. He hadn't expected them to track down his number so quickly – it turned out that they'd got hold of poor Gidman within minutes of arriving at Headland Books – but it didn't matter. He expressed just the right amount of horror at the news of the fire.

'But my wife...'

'What's that?' A sharp intake of breath from the young woman officer. 'You're not saying there's anyone inside the shop? On a Bank Holiday?'

'But yes – she was doing some tidying up. And a friend of ours was supposed to be coming over to lend a hand...'

'A friend?'

'Yes, Heath's a writer.' Liam clutched the phone tightly in a hand greased by the chip wrappings. 'Nice chap, no airs and graces, always willing to help a chum. But my God, you're not telling me – you have got the two of them out of there, haven't you?'

By the time he arrived back at the shop, it was a smouldering ruin, but still too dangerous for a serious rescue mission to be mounted. Liam did his best to be brave, but he couldn't help crying. To think of all those lovely books, burnt to a cinder.

In the days and weeks that followed, there was universal agreement that the place was a death-trap, and the wretched Gidman was only saved from serious trouble with the Health and Safety people by a fatal heart attack. Liam was fairly sure that one or two of the superficially sympathetic police officers had their doubts about the cause of the fire, but its intensity had, as he hoped, disposed of the evidence of the sawn-off ladder and the rope, and there was no forensic evidence to prove that Sally and Morrison had been attacked, or that anyone else had been in the shop when the fire broke out. Morrison was notorious for his heavy smoking, and he proved a splendid scapegoat. One rumour had it that Sally had resisted his advances, and he'd set fire to the shop in a fit of unthinking fury.

The police questioned him closely about Morrison, but he insisted (while taking care not to protest too much) that the author was a really good sort, his pal at least as much as Sally's, with no airs and graces despite his fame. He'd known that Morrison was at the shop on the day in question, and had meant to return there himself as soon as he left Ernie's. Even the more suspicious detectives seemed to conclude that, even if Liam had been cuckolded, he was to be pitied rather than suspected. Crucially, the investigation was led by someone on the verge of retirement who only wanted a quiet life. Liam played the part of the bereaved loser to perfection. All in all, he was asked fewer tough questions than he'd expected.

Everyone was very kind. His crime may not have been perfect, but what mattered was to be lucky, and he'd made his own luck. Naturally, he took care not to make a claim on the life insurance until the inquest was out of the way, and waited for Sally's firm to raise the matter with him. He explained that she'd never mentioned the perk.

At Sally's funeral, Maxine made a great fuss of him. Warm-hearted as ever, she'd insisted on popping round on a daily basis after the fire, to make sure he was all right, and although he much preferred to be alone with his books, he could hardly object. And then one day, when he was reminiscing sadly about Sally, she took him by surprise.

'Yes, she was lovely. Pity she was such a tart.'

'What?' Liam blinked hard.

'I mean, the way she carried on with that awful man Morrison, for instance. And he wasn't the first, not by a long chalk, I'm sure you know. She loved telling me about her flings, you know, she practically gloated over them. And over me, since there was no way I'd ever pick up handsome men the way she did. I never said anything, but I really loathed her for it. She was always the lucky one, I was poor old Maxine. As for the way she treated you, it turned my stomach.' She stretched out her hand, and brushed his. 'I'm so glad you did it.'

'Did ... what?'

'Got away with murder, of course.' She squeezed his arm playfully, making him wince. 'Let's not beat about the bush. I'm impressed, to be honest. Never thought you'd have it in you to try to sort things out. Let alone that you'd pull it off.'

He swallowed. 'I haven't the faintest idea what you're talking about.'

Maxine sighed. 'Liam, I was in Ernie's back garden that morning. He was my godfather, you know, and I always felt guilty that I don't do enough for him. I popped over to do a bit of weeding and such-like, the garden was like a jungle. Not that I'm really keen on gardening, but to be honest, he'd mentioned that you were coming over, and I thought it might be nice for us to have a bit of a chat, just the two of us, while Ernie had a good zizz after lunch. A chance for us to get to know each other better, eh?'

She gave him a meaningful wink. Liam couldn't manage to utter a word.

'Anyhow, imagine my surprise when you dashed off in your car again, five minutes after you came, without buying a single book. It confused me, never mind Ernie. I was so fed up, I gave up on the garden and went home. It was only afterwards that it all began to make sense, when I heard that you said you'd been at Ernie's all along, except when you went out to the chippy. But that was later, wasn't it?'

'You're making a terrible mistake,' Liam said.

'Believe me, I know what I'm doing.' Maxine beamed. 'I did wonder about the fire, remembering what Sally told me about her insurance. Kind of me not to mention that to the police, wasn't it? I insisted how happy you and Sally were together. To be honest, I can't find it in my heart to blame you for what you did. I reckon she and that nutcase Morrison drove you to it. You're a gentle soul, you just need the right sort of person to care for you. As for what happened, I wasn't absolutely sure until yesterday, when I took a look around your study. Guess what I found?'

She flourished in front of his eyes a fat paper-bound book marked *Advance Proof Copy.* Heath Morrison's new novel, a pretentious finale to an over-hyped career. Even before she turned to the title page, Liam knew what she'd spotted. The graphically phrased inscription to Sally, bearing the date of Bank Holiday Monday, the last day of the lovers' lives.

'I've taken a photocopy,' she said. 'Another sort of insurance policy, you see – against the risk that I might suffer an accident, like Sally. It's in safe hands with my solicitor.'

Liam glared at her. *It's a bluff,* he was thinking. *You don't have a solicitor.*

'Tristram acted for me in my divorce.' For God's sake, the woman was a mind-reader. 'We had something going for a few weeks, but I suppose he couldn't stand the pace. I can't deny, I'm a very demanding woman.'

Liam's throat was dry. 'What...?' he began.

'Don't worry,' she said. 'You can cope with my demands, I'm positive. I'm looking forward to showing you how. We'll have a quiet wedding, obviously. Something flashy wouldn't be right, when we're still coming to terms with the grief. Our shared loss. That insurance money will be really handy, while you're looking round for another job. In a library, perhaps? I know you love books, though personally, I've never seen the point of fiction. What's so good about something made up? Real life is what matters, if you ask me. Anyway, I'm not expecting you to kill yourself. Or me either, come to that. We can both work a couple of days a week, and spend the rest of our time together.'

Her face shone with happiness as she took his hand. He shut his eyes, trying not to show his revulsion at being touched by her damp, flabby flesh. To his horror, she mistook this as an invitation to force her slithery tongue between his lips.

'It will be lovely, promise,' she said a couple of minutes later, as he gasped desperately for breath. 'Sally wasn't right for you, under-sexed and indiscreet. Very different from me in every way, Liam. I reckon that at last, after all these years, I've finally dropped lucky. Just like you, dearest.'

The Enemy Within
by Ruth Dudley Edwards

'BASTARDS!!!!!!!!!!!!!!!!!!!!!!!!!!!!!!!!!' was the shakily-written message attached to the brick that had crashed through the window of Heffers. Holding it up gingerly between finger and thumb, Constable Bugg placed it in front of the bespectacled bookseller. 'What do you make of this, Mr Reynolds?'

'Not very much, Officer. It's clear, of course, that the writer is literate but almost certainly physically impaired, drunk or deranged. The paper is standard A4, but the rubber band looks like official Royal Mail issue, which suggests he or she may be in receipt of a great deal of post and...'

Bugg was damned if he was going to admit that all this was news to him and allow this smart-ass to lord it over him any further, so he interrupted importantly. 'Hardly a "she", sir. I mean you don't usually get ladies hurling bricks around the streets, now do you?'

'You don't usually get anyone hurling bricks through bookshop windows, come to that. Don't you remember that in the Clapham riots the only shop left unlooted was a bookshop?'

'But in Cambridge that'd be different, wouldn't it, sir? I mean these uni people like books, don't they?'

'Many of them do indeed, but in my long career, although I've known readers to shoplift, I have yet to come across an academic who tried to acquire books with the help of a blunt instrument.'

'With the country in the state it's in, sir, nothing would surprise me.'

'That is as may be, Officer, but a) from what I can see, no books are missing, b) the gentlemen who kindly boarded up the window in the middle of the night assure us that no one could have effected entry without shedding blood, c) there is no blood and d) in any case an intruder would have had no way of getting out of the shop without breaking another window.'

Bugg was a man notoriously reluctant to let go of a theory, but having chewed resentfully over Reynolds's objections he realised he was in a cul-de-sac. 'So what are you suggesting?'

Richard Reynolds was a patient man, and, besides, he was well aware from his reading of crime fiction that policemen were often thick. So, trying hard not to sound patronising, he said, 'It would seem possible that someone had a grudge against us, don't you think?'

'What kind of grudge?'

'I find it hard to think of anything. We run an honest business and we are considerate to our customers.'

'Do you screw your creditors?'

'I beg your pardon?'

'Come down hard on people that owe you money?'

'I understood your vernacular. I was just surprised that you should think Heffers would behave like that. It is not our style.'

'Well, why should anyone have a grudge, then?'

'I don't know, Officer. I'm merely trying to come up with suggestions.'

'Any others?'

Reynolds wondered if he was going to be stuck with this half-wit for the entire morning. 'I don't know. Maybe he found something about our window display objectionable?'

'Dirty books, do you mean?'

'I doubt any of them could come into such a category,' said Reynolds stiffly. 'We were aiming at the tourist market with an attractive selection of books about Cambridge – history, architecture, fiction and so on. I can't think of any that even the most delicately-minded could find offensive. Now unless you have more questions, I really should get back to work.'

Constable Bugg returned to HQ and was relieved when his sergeant said he shouldn't waste any more time on an apparently random act of violence. So he was aggrieved a couple of weeks later to be sent to investigate an attack on the Silver Street window of Ede & Ravenscroft, purveyors of academic dress, and university and college memorabilia. 'It's a copycat attack, Sarge. Same kind of brick, same message, even same kind of rubber band.'

'Anything stolen?'

'No. And they've no more idea than had Heffers who could have a grudge against them.'

'Why would anyone do a bookshop and an outfitters?'

Bugg had a rare moment of inspiration. 'Someone with a grudge against Cambridge so he went for books and stuff about it?'

'If I had a grudge against Cambridge I reckon I'd be more likely to set fire to the Guildhall or chuck paint over that horrible blob beside it that passes for a statue.'

'I guess you think bigger than this guy, Sarge.'

The sergeant shrugged. 'Well, all we can do is tell the troops to keep an eye out for some bloody flutter roaming the streets in the middle of the night carrying a brick with intent to chuck.'

Oddly enough, it was as a pair of constables strolled past Heffers after midnight a week or so later that they heard the distant sound of breaking glass. They took to their heels at a smart pace, but by the time they had found that the King's College official gift shop had a smashed window, the perpetrator had escaped.

'So it was the same ingredients again,' said Constable Bugg when he dropped in on Richard Reynolds. 'And the same message.'

'And a similar target?'

'Yep. It was The Shop at King's, which is stuffed with college souvenirs.'

'I don't want to interfere, Officer, but have you had any success in locating the source of the bricks?'

'We haven't got time to do that kind of thing,

sir. What with the cuts and all we haven't the resources to be making complicated enquiries. It'd take forever. What's more,' he added importantly, 'we have to be cognisant that this kind of thing is pretty small beer compared with most of the crimes that face us every day.'

He had left the shop before Reynolds could think of a polite way of telling him he was a jerk.

The Mistress of St Martha's, Baroness Troutbeck, had no such inhibitions when they discussed the brick that had come through the dining-room window of her college the night before. 'Good grief, Constable Buggins, are you seriously telling me that this loony's been running round Cambridge for weeks throwing bricks through every second window and you haven't got hold of him yet? What are we paying our taxes for?'

'It's Constable Bugg, not Constable Buggins.'

'Don't be pedantic. I'm asking why you haven't stopped this crime wave.'

'It's only happened three times before to my knowledge,' muttered Bugg defensively.

'I'm supposed to find that reassuring?'

'We are doing everything we can to apprehend the villain, your ladyship.'

'Everything you can do has clearly not been enough. You'd better tell me about the other outrages and let's see if I can sort it out.'

'Do you realise, Richard, that the cretin hadn't even investigated the source of the bricks?'

Reynolds, who was sitting comfortably in the

baroness's second-best armchair, took another sip of his champagne. 'I do indeed, Jack, but he seemed to think such activity beneath him.'

The baroness drew deeply on her pipe. 'We need to take control then. I agree with you about the handwriting.' She blew out a fierce column of smoke which briefly enveloped Reynolds, who began to cough. 'I hope you're not coming down with something, Richard. That sounds nasty. Vitamin C's the thing. Eat more oranges. Oh, and drink more whisky. Always does the trick for me.'

She waited with her foot tapping until his paroxysm ended and his eyes ceased weeping. 'As I was saying, I agree about the handwriting. This isn't some young townie oik engaged in the time-honoured pastime of gownie-bashing. Uneven though it is, the quality of lettering of "BITCHES" calls to mind a calligrapher who's been on the sauce.'

'I wonder why "bitches"? After all, these days you're a mixed college.'

'That is one of the many questions we must address over dinner, my dear Richard. You've just time for a refill before we have to go in. I've put you beside our stone-deaf Fellow so we can speak freely.'

'I have a headache,' Richard told Sally over breakfast next day. 'But worse is the state of my lungs from all the cigar smoke after dinner.'

'Doesn't the smoking ban apply to colleges?'

'She's found some way round it for her quarters, I think. Or she's merrily breaking the law. However, on the positive side, we made a lot of progress. Our reasoning is that our brick-thrower is subject to unplanned psychotic or drunken episodes of violence...'

'Or somnambulism?'

'Possible but slightly far-fetched, but whichever it is, he's almost certainly impulsively using bricks that are close at hand. So Jack's giving an interview today to the *Cambridge News,* flashing a photo of the brick and asking anyone who knows of a handy pile of similar anywhere within or close to the city centre to give her a call. Anonymously if they wish.'

'Fingerprints?'

'Drunk, mad or asleep, he was cunning enough not to leave any.'

'And have you any suspects?'

'We thought about people with a pathological hatred of Cambridge and concluded that – while there could be plenty – we should look out particularly for recent arrivals who are having a hard time.'

'That'll keep you both busy,' said Sally rather tartly. 'Now are we going to continue playing private investigators or might we think of going to work?'

'Another triumph, if I may say so,' bragged the baroness over the phone to her old friend and ally Robert Amiss a week later. 'And I achieved it single-handed.'

'It wasn't single-handed. What about that nice bookseller?'

'Well, I admit he took on your Watsonian role

without complaint, if perhaps without alacrity.'

'I don't think anyone's ever taken on that role voluntarily. Press-ganging is what comes to mind.'

'Stop fussing. How one acquires a Watson is neither here nor there. What matters is that they are more intelligent than the original and just as obliging. Richard's a good chap with whom I've been shooting the breeze about books for several years, but mind you I did find him a bit rigid about staying in the shop rather than pursuing the inquiries I wanted pursued.'

'No sense of proportion, obviously.'

'Absolutely.'

'So what's the story?'

'My *cri-de-coeur* to the *Cambridge News* brought several responses, including a furious one from some stuffy inspector yammering about the potentially "deleterious consequences" of interfering in police "lines of enquiry". Pointing out that their constable had been true to his name by doing bugger-all, I saw him off in short order.'

'I'm sure you did.'

'But we rapidly struck gold, for two callers pointed me towards the crumbling wall of a front garden on Hills Road which has a plentiful supply of similar bricks.'

'That's hardly the main drag.'

'It's only a hop, skip and a jump from it and it's something anyone walking to the railway station might well have noticed. And my contention, Watson...'

'Only you,' said Amiss with a touch of bitterness, 'would presume to run two Watsons simultaneously.'

'I don't see why I shouldn't, but technically, I'm not. Richard and I have done our job and I have released him back into the wild, if that's a suitable description of Heffers.'

'Oh, get on with it.'

'The picture we'd built up together over dinner was of a lonely old academic incomer who might well try to escape the hated Cambridge from time to time and therefore knew the route to the station.'

'Why old?'

'We reckoned a youngster's language would have been a lot fruitier.'

'Why not a Gaudy Night-style outsider?'

'Cambridge may have been slow to change, but it no longer resembles the Oxbridge of the 1930s, Robert.'

'You could have fooled me.'

'That's quite enough Oxford snobbery. But it illustrates why an Oxford import might not take to Cambridge. Outsiders think we're the same, but we know that's an illusion.'

'It was certainly true when I had my few months at St Martha's that I thought every day how boring, introverted and humourless Cambridge was. I never decided whether it was to do with the Fens or the awful train service. No wonder they all became spies.'

'Robert, do you want me to let loose a torrent of insults about Oxford?'

'I was just trying to help.'

'As I was saying, my gut instinct was that we were dealing with a distressed Oxonian so I drew up a short-list of Oxford imports, one of whom, oddly enough, had been to High Table at St Martha's the night we were bricked. And following a discreet enquiry I found he'd also been entertained at King's just before their gift shop was attacked.'

'Was the port below standard, or something?'

'John Maynard Keynes may have been unsound on monetary policy, but no one can dispute that owing to his performance as bursar there is nothing to criticise about the King's wine cellar. However, their Fellows can be snooty. And I also have to admit that the prime suspect didn't have a great time the night he dined here. It may be that he values conviviality more than good browsing and sluicing.'

'Don't tell me. You didn't like him so you ignored him.'

'I didn't dislike him. Indeed, I think he wasn't unattractive. But I can't deny that I was focusing hard on a potential donor on my left and mostly left him to Emily Twigg, who these days wouldn't hear a bomb going off. And of course she got deaf too old to learn to lipread. You wouldn't have to be very touchy to decide you'd been ignored and neglected.'

'So who is this guy?'

'Patrick Grosvenor-Sturrock, a classicist who spent his entire career in Oxford until he was persuaded to become Master of St Gilbert's.'

'That dump?'

'It's only a dump because it's been run by malign imbeciles for years. It may be slightly off the beaten track, but there's nothing wrong with the buildings, the gardens or the cellar and there's plenty of rent coming in from all over the city. But Grosvenor-Sturrock was approaching retirement with no chance of becoming head of an Oxford college, so was seduced by the notion of having a fiefdom of his own.'

'Failed on the due diligence, did he?'

'Heard what he wanted to hear. He didn't realise that they were looking for a cat's-paw while – though mild-mannered and certainly no leftie – he's a reformer. All hell broke loose after he took up residence and told them that a college named after a saint who was notorious in the twelfth century for having founded an order for both sexes could not in all reason hold out against accepting women.'

'Oh, dear.'

'Oh, dear, indeed. And he'd burned his boats in Oxford. And being a widower, he was rattling around in a large master's lodge with no one to talk to and all the fellows hating him.'

'Poor sod. How did you nail him?'

'Richard had mentioned in passing that it's possible to trace the movements of a mobile phone retrospectively even when it's off, so I decided to confront Grosvenor-Sturrock and threaten him with that.'

'Good grief. Can they?'

'Probably. But Grosvenor-Sturrock was unlikely to question it. So I went to see him and got the truth.'

'He remembered what he'd done?'

'Hazily. He broke down and told me he was having terrible dreams about discovering he'd burned down St Gilbert's. One really bad night he woke up thinking he'd reduced the whole city to rubble. So when he was drunk he sometime set off to do something less drastic to relieve his feelings.'

'He's bonkers.'

'A bit. But nothing that can't be fixed. What he needs is a companion-in-arms and that's what he's now got. Vacation's coming up and he and I are going to take a little recuperative trip during which we will together work out how to do down the mouldering old parasites and take control of St Gilbert's.'

'What about the cops?'

'None of their business. What they don't know won't hurt them.'

'But he committed criminal damage, damn it.'

'Packages of cash with an anonymous apology will be delivered to Heffers, King's and St Martha's. I will announce publicly that bygones should be bygones and I can't imagine there will be much appetite for hunting down the perpetrator.'

'And Richard?'

'Even Holmes didn't tell Watson everything. I will be vague and leave him to draw his own conclusions. Since Heffers will have been handsomely compensated and the nuisance will prove to have been stopped, I expect that'll be good enough for him.'

She paused expectantly. 'Why aren't you congratulating me on my public-spiritedness in bringing calm and peace to this little city of mine?'

'Because you've got so much out of it. Aren't you off now to have a fling and then devise with your new swain a strategy to do down the fellowship of St Gilbert's.'

'No shit, Sherlock,' said Baroness Troutbeck.

The Good Thief's Guide to Book Selling
by Chris Ewan

'I'm so sorry,' the owner of the bookshop said, not for the first time. 'We had hoped for a lot more people.'

'It's no problem,' I told him.

Which was a lie. Because it was a problem for him, no question. And it was also a pretty sizeable problem for me.

It was a problem for him because he was in the business of selling books. Or at least, that was the theory. As it was, I'd been sitting at a table in his independent bookshop in the middle of a small town in the middle of England for well over an hour now, and I was yet to sign a single one of my novels to anyone besides the sister-in-law of the poor, embarrassed bookshop owner.

And it was a problem for me because I was in the business of writing books. Crime thrillers, to be exact, which for reasons that have to do with my being utterly shameless, I may as well tell you are published under my own name of Charlie Howard. And if I wanted to stay in that business – which I did – and if I had dreams of making it as a bestselling author one day – which I had – then this was unquestionably not the way to go about it.

But then, life can be like that sometimes. You work diligently at your trade, you refine your skills and try your absolute best, and events can still conspire to frustrate you.

Take my other profession by way of example. Let's not be coy here – I steal things. I happen to be very good at it. But I can't tell you how many thefts I've carefully planned over the years that have gone sideways for reasons that were beyond my control.

So I had a lot of sympathy for the owner of the bookshop, who'd certainly gone out of his way to publicise my event. And I had a reasonable amount of sympathy for myself. Today's no-show by the discerning readers of the local area was just one of those things. There was nothing to be done. We had no one to blame.

Unless…

'I'll tell you who's to blame,' said the owner of the bookshop.

His name was Rodney. He was short and round, with a balding head and a mighty impressive moustache. He was the type of guy who genuinely suited a cardigan – there aren't too many of them around. The cardigan he had on was a deep shade of burgundy. It complemented his cheeks.

'It's the Swooper.'

'Excuse me?'

'The Swooper. I call him that because he swoops in and steals my customers.' And with that, Rodney tucked his fatty chin into his chest, spread his arms at his sides and began to flap them up and down, as if he was a grossly inflated albatross.

'And what do other people call him?'

'Duncan.' Rodney grimaced, as if just the name itself should be enough to give me the measure of the man.

'And how does this Duncan steal your customers exactly?'

'He swoops.'

Oh, boy.

I held up a hand, cutting off Rodney's demonstration. It was a Saturday morning and the high street was respectably busy outside. If a potential book buyer did happen to glance through the window, the last thing I wanted was for them to be put off by Rodney's birdman routine.

'You'd better explain,' I said.

And so he did.

He told me that Duncan was the manager of a new branch of Media House that had opened on the nearby high street during the past year. I'm sure you've heard of Media House – it's the glitzy national chain with that cryptic slogan on all its advertising: 'Music, DVDs, Books & More'. Personally, I'm always bugged by what the '& More' might be, but it was the 'Books' part that was vexing Rodney.

According to him, as soon as the store had opened, Duncan had dropped by to introduce himself. He'd taken a good look around Rodney's shop. Then, within days, he'd gone on the attack.

'Attack?' I said. 'That sounds a bit dramatic. I know business is tough right now but you have to accept that Media House do some things pretty well. It's an economies of scale thing – you're bound to find it difficult to compete with them.'

‘True enough,’ Rodney said. ‘And if that’s all this was, then maybe I could accept it. But this guy – the Swooper...’ He shook his bloated head, as if there weren’t sufficient words to express his disgust for the man. ‘He steals my events.’

‘Excuse me?’

‘I’m known for putting on author events. Crime authors are a speciality. It’s my passion, really, and I’ve managed to secure some pretty big names over the years. Until recently, a lot of customers would travel from a long way away to get a book signed.’

I crossed my hands behind my back and tried to overlook the very empty bookshop that surrounded me. It was a very pleasant bookshop. It was well stocked and well catalogued and well cared for. But it was, well, empty.

‘But then a strange thing started to happen,’ Rodney continued. ‘Whenever I scheduled an event for one of the bigger crime authors, I’d get a call a few days later from their publicist. They’d tell me they were sorry but they had to cancel. The author only had a limited amount of time to tour and another opportunity had presented itself.’

‘That opportunity being Media House.’

‘Quite. Duncan was swooping in and stealing my events.’

‘Hmm,’ I said. ‘I’m never one to knock a good conspiracy theory, but it doesn’t sound like the type of thing most of the authors I know would allow to happen.’

‘Some did. Others were pretty decent about it. They turned Duncan down when he got in touch.’

'I'm glad to hear it.'

Seriously. People talk about honour among thieves, but in my experience, honour among crime writers is way more likely.

'So was I, to begin with.' Rodney smiled crookedly. 'But whenever an author stayed loyal to me, Duncan employed a new tactic. He'd order lots of copies of that author's latest book and feature them in a huge window display in the week leading up to my event. He'd offer a heavy discount too – more than I could afford to match if I wanted to make any kind of profit. When that happened, nearly all my customers would buy the author's book at Media House. Some of them even came in here with books they'd already bought from Duncan to try and get them signed.'

'Ouch.'

'I'm afraid I lost my temper at that. I shouted at people. Embarrassed authors. Word got around.' Rodney shrugged. 'Long story short, Duncan identified what my shop was best at and he swooped in and took it from me. Now he's taken nearly all of my customers, too. Another few months like this and I'm not going to have a business left to run.'

Rodney slumped down on to a stool behind his cash register (which did look awfully dusty, I had to admit). He clasped his hands to the top of his head and groaned.

And of course I felt bad for the poor chap. It was obvious that he was passionate about selling books. Even a cursory glance at his shop would tell you that. But hey, I'm a neurotic writer, and one thing in particular was bugging me about what Rodney had said.

'He didn't swoop for me.'

Rodney gazed up, his hands sliding down his face to tug at the pouched skin beneath his hang-dog eyes. 'Excuse me?'

'He didn't swoop for me. You said that when you book crime authors for an event, Duncan swoops in and tries to lure them away.'

'Well, not all of them.'

'Oh. Who else did he let you keep?'

Rodney stared at me for a long moment. He swallowed hard.

Blame my ego, I guess, but realisation was a little slow in dawning. 'Wait. Are you saying I'm the only one?'

Rodney squirmed. He looked like he'd rather be just about anywhere else right now.

'But I have a new book out.'

Which was true. *The Thief on the Run* was the latest volume in my series of thrillers about professional burglar Michael Faulks. It had only been published two weeks ago. And granted, it hadn't received a review in a national paper just yet, and the print run was somewhat less than I would have preferred, but since it was very possibly my best book so far, I was hoping it might find a reasonable audience. Hell, I was hoping it might find any kind of audience.

'Well, that's insulting,' I said.

'To be absolutely honest, inviting you here was a bit of a test. I wanted to know exactly how far Duncan would go.'

'No, my mistake. *That's* insulting.'

I set down my pen. I'd been holding on to it for

most of the past hour – twirling it between my fingers, throwing it into the air – ready to sign a book at a moment's notice. But right now I was ready for something altogether different.

'Where are you going?' Rodney asked.

'Just popping out for a short walk. If the book buying public shows up in vast numbers, tell them I'll be back soon.'

'Forgive me, Charlie. I didn't mean to upset you. I think you're a wonderful writer and I'm thrilled to have you here. It's just that I'm under a lot of pressure at the moment. I'm not thinking clearly.'

'It's fine,' I told him, half-in and half-out of his door. 'It's not you I'm annoyed by. I want to know why this Swooper didn't swoop.'

It got worse when I reached Media House. There was a huge display of books in the window for a just-published crime novel. But it wasn't my just-published crime novel. It was the latest international, best-selling, monster hit from a hugely successful American author.

The author was one of my favourite writers. He was also a friend. But for reasons that will become obvious, I'm afraid I can't tell you his name.

We'd first met, very late at night, at a hotel-based mystery convention in the United States. I was drunk at the time – that tends to happen at mystery conventions – and I was weaving along a hotel corridor in search of my room. I didn't find my room to begin with, but by way of consolation, I did find the writer in question. Alas, he was naked apart from his socks, standing knock-kneed in the middle of the corridor with his hands covering his crotch. He was also whispering in a rather urgent tone through the door of his hotel suite.

'Problem?' I slurred.

'Argument.' He smiled sheepishly. 'Been shut out of my own room. And since I don't have my pants on, I don't have my key.'

'Oh, I can easily fix that,' I told him.

And because I was tipsy, because I was keen to impress the guy, I whipped out my trusty spectacles case, removed my picking tools and nudged him to one side. Thirty seconds later I had the door unlocked. I pushed it open. And there, sitting on the end of the bed, clutching a sheet in front of her very naked body, was another famous mystery writer. Can't tell you her name, either.

Naturally, they were both married, though not to each other. But since that was none of my business, it had never struck me as something worth mentioning, and in the years that had followed, I'd formed good friendships with them both. Coincidentally enough – and for reasons that I swear are entirely unrelated – they'd each been willing to blurb quite a number of my books.

Now I found myself staring at my friend the famous American author again, only this time he was fully dressed and he was featured in a glossy poster that told me he would be appearing at Media House to sign copies of his new book on the following Saturday.

I was pleased for him. Naturally I was. But I can't pretend that I was immune to a fleeting stab of envy.

I walked into the store. It was vast and slick. A neon sign informed me that the books section was on the first floor and I took the elevator up and made my way over to the Crime and Mystery shelves. There were plenty of novels in stock. They were beautifully displayed. But there was not a single book by yours truly.

So maybe they'd sold out. That was always possible, right?

Only one way to be sure.

It took me several minutes before I tracked down Rodney's nemesis. He was standing over by a Customer Information booth, gripping a clipboard to his chest.

He had on a shiny grey suit over a light grey shirt and dark tie. His hair was gelled and spiked. A name badge pinned to his breast pocket read: DUNCAN MILLS. MANAGER. He looked, at first glance, much more suited to working in a mobile phone shop. Perhaps that was the mysterious '& More' Media House could offer its customers.

'Excuse me?' I said. 'I wonder if you can help me.'

I could wonder all I liked because Duncan ignored me to begin with. He was too busy looking over my head, flashing a smile at two teenage girls who were giggling over by a display of vampire romances.

'Hey.' I clicked my fingers before his eyes and he snapped out of it and gave me a look like I'd trodden dog crap on the carpet. 'I'm looking for a book.'

'Then you're in the right place, pal.'

'It's only just out. But I can't see it on any of your shelves.'

'Could be it hasn't come in yet.'

'I guess it could. But would you check for me?'

He rolled his eyes, then turned and vaulted the service counter as if he was a cop in a Hollywood movie sliding over the bonnet of a car. He nudged a computer mouse, waking a nearby terminal. 'Name?'

'The book is called *The Thief on the Run* by Charles E. Howard.'

'Nah.' He winced. 'Sorry, but we won't have that.'

'You haven't checked your computer.'

'Don't need to. We really only stock bestselling authors.'

I won't pretend that didn't hurt.

'How can you expect authors to become best sellers if you don't stock their books?'

'Not my problem, pal. They should write better stories.'

I gritted my teeth. 'Do you happen to know anywhere else where I might find a copy? A friend mentioned that there's a good independent book-shop nearby. He says it sometimes has signing events for crime authors.'

Duncan was already looking over my head again, back at the two girls. 'Nah,' he said. 'I don't know of anywhere like that. There was a place, but I think it went out of business.'

'Right,' I told Rodney, as I burst back inside his

shop. 'You're putting on an author event. Next Saturday morning.'

'I am?'

I paced the shop floor. It was a much smaller shop floor than the one I'd just vacated, but I absolutely preferred it.

'You are. It's going to be your most successful event ever. It'll put your shop back on the map.'

'No offence, Charlie, but even with more advertising – which I can't afford – I'm just not sure you're quite the draw we'd both like you to be.'

'Not me, you fool. We're talking about a world famous author.'

'We are? Who?'

I told him. He reared back, bumping into the shelf of hardbacks behind him.

'I can't get him,' he protested.

'Maybe you can't. But I can.'

'But isn't he already doing an event at Media House?'

'He was,' I said. 'Before we swooped in. Now get on the phone and order his latest book. Secure as many copies as possible.'

Rodney wrung his hands. 'I don't know, Charlie. I can't risk any mistakes right now. If I don't sell any–'

'Oh, you'll sell them,' I told him. 'I'm going to make certain of that.'

Just after nine o'clock on the following Friday evening, I backed a van up to the loading bay behind Media House. I'd chosen the time very carefully. In my experience, if someone spots you lurking at the back of a property after midnight, they're likely to think you're up to no good. But if they spot you before twelve, there's a reasonable enough chance they'll believe you have a right to be there. Especially if the van you've acquired for the night happens to be branded with the name of a local cleaning firm.

Of course, I didn't have any right to be behind Media House. And I certainly didn't have any right to remove my picking tools from my spectacles case and pop the lock on the loading bay doors. But then, it was a long time since the vagaries of right and wrong had taxed me unduly. Call me a crook, if you will, but at that particular moment all that really interested me was breaking in as quickly and as efficiently as possible.

I was wearing a black nylon jacket with the collar raised around my jaw and a baseball cap with a peaked neb angled down over my face. I made sure I didn't look up until I was through the door because I didn't want the security camera fitted above it to record my features.

There were more cameras inside, as well as an alarm system, but I can't pretend they had me quivering in my baseball shoes. The system that had been installed was comprehensive and cripplingly expensive, but it was also relatively simple to disable if you'd read the appropriate literature, rehearsed the appropriate moves and had the appropriate nerve.

My natural prudence encouraged me to take no more than thirty seconds to bypass the alarm and I permitted myself another half-minute to kill the cameras. I was done five seconds early so I took a short pause to stand in the middle of the silent stock room and luxuriate, for just a little while, in the pleasure of being in the middle of a space where I had absolutely no business being.

Well, no business except burglar business.

By ten o'clock the following morning, a very long queue had formed on the pavement outside Media House. There were a lot of passionate readers in the line. There were a great many fans of my friend the American author. But none of them were going to be buying copies of his latest best seller from Media House any time soon.

There were a couple of reasons for that.

Firstly, the queue of crime fans weren't the only people outside on the street. Duncan the Swooper was there, too. So were all his staff. And so was my good friend the American author, as well as Philippa, his young, pretty publicist. Philippa kept checking her phone and tutting loudly. I was pretty sure she was becoming concerned about whether her author would make his next event, scheduled for two o'clock in the afternoon, almost fifty miles away.

Because shockingly, it appeared that someone, somehow, had changed all the locks on every door into the store. And while a locksmith was currently working as fast as he could to overcome this unexpected obstacle, and while it wouldn't be too long before Duncan would be able to get inside, it also wouldn't be long until he discovered that the security code on his alarm system had been altered in a hugely destructive manner that would take even a highly skilled engineer many hours to resolve.

And secondly, every copy of the American author's latest book had completely vanished from the display at the front of the store. In fact, by the time Duncan did eventually get inside, he'd quickly discover (to the accompaniment of the screeching wail of his malfunctioning alarm system) that there wasn't a single copy to be found anywhere inside the premises.

Which was all thoroughly unpleasant for Duncan, no doubt, and probably accounted for the spitting rage he seemed to be in.

But it wasn't such a big problem for everyone else. Because luckily, I'd had the foresight to ask my friend the American author for the contact details of his UK publicist on the pretence of securing a free copy of his latest thriller. And even more fortunately, I was able to ring the lovely Philippa and suggest that she, and her author's long queue of fans, might wish to make good use of a very well stocked independent bookshop that happened to be located just a few streets away.

A shade under two hours later, I was sharing a glass of sparkling water with my friend the big shot American author, admiring the sight of Rodney gleefully processing his latest sale.

The two of us were sitting side by side behind a pair of fold out signing tables. And granted, the vast majority of people who'd come along had wanted to pick up a signed copy of my friend's new book and perhaps have their photo taken with him, but a respectable number had also decided to chance their arm on an autographed edition of *The Thief on the Run*. Which, I had to admit, was a pretty neat turn of events.

I yawned – I couldn't help myself since I hadn't had much sleep – and I raised the hand with my signing pen in it to cover my mouth.

'Fatigued?' my American colleague asked me.

'Just a little. It's all this unfamiliar signing business.' I shook my wrist. 'A seasoned pro like you gets used to all that wear and tear, I guess, but I'm still pretty green.'

'At this, maybe. But there's a lot I happen to know you're good at. Locks, for one thing I remember.'

He looked at me a beat too long. Then he grinned.

'That was a nice thing you did for your friend, the bookseller. Illegal, but nice.'

'I have no idea what you're talking about.'

'Sure you don't.' He stood from his chair, gathered up his jacket and signalled to Philippa. Then he leaned down to shake my hand. 'See you around, Charlie. I sure hope my books turn up again soon.'

He patted me on the shoulder and made his way over to the door. But really, he had nothing to worry about. I'd already arranged for the stock I'd taken from Media House to be returned later that afternoon. I had no doubt that the books would sell out fast and that Duncan would need to order plenty more copies in the coming weeks. And meantime, Media House hadn't been completely short changed, because as it turned out, some kind soul had arranged for a display of an alternative title to be placed in the window, completely free of charge. Two hundred mint copies of *The Thief on the Run*.

Remember My Name
by Christopher Fowler

Maddock swam with the same languor, the same sense of luxury he possessed out of the water, his tanned arms lifting and falling through the warm blue shadows. He was happiest at night on his own in swimming pools, or here in the calm morning gloom. Rolling onto his back, he studied the subterranean roof as he lazily drifted beneath it. He had already swum his thirty lengths; now he could relax in these last few minutes before heading to work.

The tight-fitting plastic goggles dyed his cool green world. Chlorine affected his vision adversely. More than ever he found himself wearing shaded lenses of some kind; his eyes were becoming increasingly sensitive to light. He considered buying photoreactive glasses, but wondered how they would affect his appearance.

He was forty one and in good shape, happy with his body, vain about his ability to maintain a flat stomach. He felt he still had his pick of the females, and his current girlfriend, an astonishingly athletic nineteen-year-old from Poland, watched him with a possessiveness that made every one of his friends feel bitter about themselves. His wife pretended everything was fine, and spent her days shopping with a personal assistant she had hired from a website. She seemed to be happier when not having to think about him, which suited both of them.

At this time of the morning there was usually no-one else in the swimming pool. The lane-ploughing high-flyers had showered and dressed, to disperse eastwards into the city, where they could hone their aggression on office colleagues. One other swimmer remained, a slender young woman with cropped blonde hair, seated motionless on the edge of the deep end. She was wearing a white bikini that was cut outrageously low. To be honest, he was surprised the club had allowed her in dressed like that. The bikini bottom slimmed to a single silver string at the sides and left very little to the imagination.

The girl leaned back, staring into the sharp mesh of light that filtered from an arabesque of glass bricks set in the side wall. Above the diving board, the light shafts were flying buttresses of bright air that fell and splintered into the refracting depths and were lost forever.

Maddock lowered his feet, reaching down to touch the sloping floor of the pool. He stood still and allowed the water to settle. Through his green lenses the woman looked confident and attractive. It could do no harm to swim up beside her, he thought. He took his time, windmilling slowly, kicking once in a while, then gliding to the tiled edge.

He wouldn't remove his goggles because his hair dripped chlorine into his eyes, and besides, they left oval rings on his face. Resting the soles of his feet against the wall of the deep end, he gripped the edge and flexed his muscular arms, looking up at her.

Fascinated by the strong slivers of light that pierced the pool and descended into pale helices, she seemed determined not to look his way.

'I know you,' he said finally. 'I'm sure we've met before somewhere.'

The girl allowed a moment to pass before she turned to him and smiled. 'Yes, I think we have,' she agreed pleasantly.

'Didn't we go out somewhere?' he asked.

'Yes, we did.'

'Was it a date?'

'Not really. But I felt like I got to know you.'

'How was I?'

'Oh, you were very funny.'

'When was this?'

'Mmm.' She thought for a moment. 'Four years ago.'

'Really? That long? Where did we go?'

'A restaurant in Soho with a French name. The food was wonderful. You ordered a dozen oysters.'

'Really?' That wasn't much of a clue. He always ordered a dozen oysters when he'd just met an attractive girl. He smiled back, intrigued.

'You insisted on paying for absolutely everything.'

'Now that doesn't sound like me at all,' he laughed. 'What did we do after?'

'We went to a nightclub and drank champagne.'

'And I paid again?'

She nodded slowly. 'Oh yes. I'm surprised you can't remember my name.'

'I'm not good with names. Faces and bodies,

though, I'm usually good with those.' The amusement faded slowly to a warmth between them, but the water started to feel cold on his back and thighs. He moved a little closer to her. 'So tell me,' he coaxed, 'where exactly did we meet?'

'I'm sure you'll remember if you put your mind to it,' she teased. 'You even paid for this bikini, in a roundabout way.'

'Now that's impossible. I only buy presents–'

'For your wife.'

He was growing a little uncomfortable. He liked to be in control.

'I told you I was married?'

'You even showed me her photograph. It was in your wallet.'

'You know what?' He wagged his finger at her. 'I think you're bluffing, you're making all this up. Lots of men like oysters, lots of men keep photos of their wives in their wallets.'

'To be fair, you were a little bit drunk when we met. You'd been celebrating a deal.'

He shrugged, shook his head. He was growing tired of this game. But then she shifted her position at the pool edge, opening her thighs slightly. Her bikini bottom was no bigger than a cocktail napkin folded in half. He felt himself harden.

'I give up, tell me.'

'Okay. Come here and I'll let you in on the secret.'

She said this very slowly. *She knows how to make a man listen,* he thought, *by talking with your eyes.*

She raised her hand and beckoned him closer,

and knew he would follow because she was attractive and he was intrigued.

A sixth sense told him that something was not right, but he pulled his broad arms up on the pool edge, intrigued, following the outline of her body, trying to fathom her motives.

As he did so, she brought her other hand around and closed the white plastic tag over his wrist in a swift, practised movement. He looked down in astonishment and found the tag locked in place, the unbreakable kind they put on packing crates with the small square lock that could be moved forward but not back, the kind his own factory workers had frequent cause to use.

The tag was looped through something that lay on the side of the pool. He recognised it as the grille of one of the oblong steel drain grates that sat in recessed trays around the pool's edge.

Knowing better than to pull on the tag, he snapped off the goggles with his free hand and took a good look at her.

'I remember you,' was all he could manage. 'You wouldn't come back with me to my hotel. Take this damned thing off.'

'You still don't remember my name, do you?' She smiled.

'No,' he admitted. 'I don't remember your name. But I remember who you are. You're the shopping woman.'

'That's right. Your wife hired me as her personal shopper. She doesn't really need someone to shop for her, she just needs someone to talk to. She's lonely and desperate to tell someone about her life.'

He remembered now – he had been buying a gift for his latest girlfriend at Harrods, and had bumped into his wife and her personal shopper. To cover his guilt, he had picked up his wife's bill.

'I've heard all about you. The endless insults and infidelities. Your wife is too scared of you to do anything about her situation.'

'You shouldn't listen to anything she says. She's got her art classes and cookery clubs and her clothing allowance, what more does she want? And anyway, what the hell has it got to do with you?' He tore at the strap, which tightened painfully, leaving a crimson mark on his wrist.

'You're right, it has nothing to do with me in my capacity as a personal shopper. But we offer other online services to women who are in pain, like Mrs Maddock.'

'What are you talking about? Who are you?' He pulled frantically at the strap but the heavy grating wouldn't budge. The plastic band was cutting his wrist, sending scarlet drops into the blue water.

'You don't need to know who I am. It's all on our site,' she said. 'It's called Getridofhim.com. You can buy anything on the internet. Even freedom. You really should try to remember my name.'

He panicked now. Lisa? Hannah? Sarah? Usually when he asked a woman her name he barely heard the answer. His mind rushed back to the moment in the department store and tried to recall the exact conversation between them. Something came.

'Amanda. It's Amanda.'

Turning from him, she dragged the heavy grating with some difficulty, and now she quickly pushed it forward, forcing him to move his hand with it. The steel block toppled into the pool with a bass splash, setting the surface in motion once more as it swiftly dragged him down to the bottom.

'Not even close,' she said as he sank.

His ears popped. The breath burned in his lungs. He fought against the weight of the water but in his panic he accidentally sucked the stinging chlorine into his throat. He coughed, choked and breathed in again, and now his fate was sealed. Something burst behind his eyes. The blue turned to red.

The building's brochure was proud to point out the attractive specifications of its amenities. In particular, it mentioned the swimming pool situated on the lower ground floor, and the fact that its deep end was a full twelve feet. Maddock was five feet ten inches tall. The block attached to his wrist weighed just over twenty kilos, far less than the bar she raised at the gym each morning on the floor above the pool. She was a lot stronger than she looked.

She stood by the edge of the pool's sky-cracked surface, staring into the glaucous corner of the water where Maddock's body thrashed, his brown limbs waving hopelessly beyond reach. He released a blast of air bubbles that rose to the top like silvered jellyfish, but it took several minutes for him to stop plucking at the grate and grow still, and for the pool to glaze over once more.

'Maybe you'll remember my name in your next life,' she told him, and turned to leave the swimming pool.

Flotsam and Jetsam
by Michael Gregorio

Some things, by their nature, float.

Others, by their nature, sink.

Some do both. Human bodies, for example. As any forensic pathologist will tell you, it's a question of how long they've been dead and in the water.

Charlie Aston was a great one for walking. 'Give me a pair of stout boots, a large-scale OS map, and I'll walk from here to Eternity,' he once declared. This was part of what drove Charlie Aston. The rest was fuelled by inherited money, and the search for fame.

He was on his seventh book. *On* is not, perhaps, the right word. *In* might be more appropriate. His pitch was this: he would pick a country, buy maps, fill a rucksack with fresh socks, underpants and t-shirts, then walk from A to Z, taking photos as he went, keeping notes of everything he saw along the way. Sometimes, he was obliged to take a tent. And you couldn't do without canned food or bottled water. Then there was a compass – a spare in case of accidents – his binoculars, sunglasses, sun-hat, sun-cream, and a gel to keep the midges away. The alpenstock was a must. Crampons, too, on occasion. Pullover, gloves. The list went on and on. And being a travel writer, pens and moleskin notepads were pretty high on the list. And a photographer couldn't do without a camera, though the digital era had been a lifesaver. Now, he could leave the heavy spare lenses at home. Even so, by the time you added a sleeping-bag and an inflatable pillow, there was a hell of a lot of stuff to carry on your back. As a rule, he stuck to mountain hostels, trekking from one bunk bed to the next in daily stages, anything to keep the weight down. Striped cotton pyjamas were only a tenth of the weight of a down-stuffed sleeping-bag.

His pride and joy – he had spent a lot of money on it – was his super-waterproof, super-airtight Austrian rucksack. It didn't let anything in, or anything out. *Unsinkable!* That was what the advert said.

The walk completed – it might take five days, five weeks, or he might go back to the same area again and again – the notes and pictures would be assembled as a guide to walking the particular trail that had attracted him. He'd been just about everywhere in the Alps, crossed the Pyrenees on foot, hiked from one end of Europe to the other, more or less, from Sicily to Stavanger. Once, he had even been to the United States. By QE2, first-class return, of course. Anything to avoid the plane. *'Rambling in the Rockies'* was now in its second edition. The first five hundred had gone like a bomb. A chap named Richard Reynolds had even posted a great review on Amazon.

Charlie was sitting in the departure lounge at Heathrow airport and his stomach was heaving.

It was his sixtieth birthday, and he was off to South America – Caracas first, then onward by local airline. It was time to walk the Andes, though getting there was the problem. He'd been putting it off for as long as he could remember. If you were travelling anywhere in Europe, you could jump on a train in London, then catch the ferry. Sooner or later, you'd get to wherever you wanted to go. He had particularly loved the Dover–Calais hovercraft before it went out of business: it floated high above the waves, and didn't depart if the sea was rough.

He recalled his first sea-trip to the Isle of Man at the age of six.

Mum had made him wear his new school uniform aboard *The Manx Queen*. She (Mum) was so proud of him, she said. Hitting choppy water off Birkenhead, ten minutes out to sea, his stomach had started rolling. Mum had lots of love, but little patience. 'If you're going to be ill, Charles,' she said, 'lean over the side and do it there.' He had done as he was told. The stiff northerly wind had eased off for a moment as he threw the contents of his stomach at the sea. Then the wind had picked up with a vengeance, and deposited the same foul stomach contents on his black school blazer.

'Mum wasn't happy,' he confided to a nun named Sister Gwendoline who was going home to Albuquerque. She had been in Rome for a conference, she said.

'A conference? That does sound interesting. What was it about?' asked Charlie.

'Silence,' the nun replied. It turned out that she belonged to a cloistered order.

'Nuns who never speak?' asked Charlie.

'That's right,' she said with a Texan twang that

would have knocked Tom Mix from the saddle.

'I hope you don't mind my asking?' Charlie felt a bit embarrassed, but there are questions that just have to be faced. 'Why are you talking now to me?'

'Are you a nun sworn to silence?' she asked.

'Well, no, of course, I am not,' said Charlie.

'That's it, ya see?' she said – the vowels were longer than a dog's hind leg. 'The other nuns don't talk back, so why waste precious time?'

He was shocked to hear this. 'So, you talk whenever you aren't inside a convent?'

'I am *never* long inside a convent,' Sister Gwendoline replied, tucking a finger inside her wimple, and giving it a tug. 'I avoid those places like the plague. I don't hold with these clothes, either. But I had to dress up, goin' over to the Vatican, an' all. They're pretty stiff on pro-to-call in there, I can tell ya.'

Charlie Aston felt a little bit out of his depth. It wasn't often that he chatted with a nun, especially one from a cloistered order, who didn't like wearing nuns' clothes, couldn't stand convents, and told him so. *Speaking,* that is, like a person who wasn't dressed like a nun.

'Isn't talking ... well, I mean to say, isn't it ... breaking the rules?'

Sister Gwendoline smiled at him. 'Too darn right. I never say a darn word when I'm forced to spend a night in there. It's like water off a duck's back, I'm jus' passin' through.'

She sounded, he thought, a bit like Dolly Parton. Quite nice once you got used to it, though the full-length black habit, the black cowl and the starched white bib and wimple would have looked out of place in Memphis, Tennessee.

She glanced at his bulky Austrian rucksack. 'So, where're y'all going with that big bag?'

Pretty soon he was telling her all about Peru, the Andes, all the walks that he had done, all the books that he had managed to publish. 'You mus' be very proud,' she said, 'though I don't know why you bother. They ain't hardly nuthin' left to see.'

Next thing, she was showing him photographs of all the places that he would be going to on a smart little gizmo that she called an 'Eye-phone.' Hundreds of pictures in fabulous colour. Jungles, rivers, waterfalls, mountain paths, mountain peaks. There were Peruvians dressed in wool that they had woven, brightly coloured pullovers they had knitted for themselves. There were people from the Amazon jungle wearing very little. In some cases, nothing at all. In others, a long bamboo pipe wedged over their willies.

'I been around,' Sister Gwendoline said. 'A day or two in Albuquerque, see my sis, then I'm off to Papua New Guinea. It'll proba'ly be as borin' as all the rest.'

It sounded a bit like 'been there, done that,' but Charlie didn't particularly care. Sister Gwendoline had an email. She had a portable computer, a sun-panel charger, and a satellite broadcasting-dish of some sort, too. 'People give you the most amazin' stuff,' she said. 'You'd be surprised. It's one of the perks o' being a missionary sister. They get these trinkets for Christmas, and they don't know what the heck to do with 'em.'

As they were exchanging email addresses, Sister Gwendoline's flight was called.

Caracas wasn't even up on the notice-board yet, and Charlie Aston was terrified of flying. That was why he'd come to Heathrow so early, hoping to bore himself beyond terror. That was why he had bought himself a costly first-class refundable ticket. Just in case he chickened out.

As Sister Gwendoline disappeared from sight, he stood up, slipped his arms inside the straps of his fabulous rucksack, and made his way to the airline company counter.

'May I help you, sir?'

'I chickened out,' Charlie said, slapping his ticket down on the formica top.

The clerk wasn't happy, but what choice did he have? The traveller had paid through the nose for the right to change his mind, and that was precisely what he had done.

'We cannot refund cash, I'm afraid,' the clerk said stiffly. 'You paid by credit card, I see. We have to go through them. It may take a week, it may take a month.'

'But it will come in the end?'

'I imagine it will, sir.'

'Not to worry, then,' Charlie said happily, as he headed for the exit and the Underground. He would catch the evening train to Dover, jump on a ferry, be in Paris by morning, then decide on his next move from his favourite hotel in the Latin quarter. He had seen the inside of an airport, so that was Chapter One wrapped up. Sister Gwendoline had promised him photos and her unpublished travel notes within a day or two.

Cobbling *Ambling in the Andes* together in, say, Switzerland – yes, that's where he would go – a couple of weeks on the sundeck of the *Palais Leman* in Lausanne – would be a stroll, a lark. In a word, it would be fun.

'Ah, the wonders of technology!' he enthused as he left the airport behind him. He could have arrived in Paris in no time if he had cared to test the wonders of the Channel Tunnel, but planes and tunnels have one thing in common, something that Charlie Aston couldn't abide. They were long claustrophobic tubes with no way out. Once the trip started, you were there for the ride.

And so, the ferry.

It was the first one to go down in fifty years, they said on *Channel 4* the next day.

Then somebody remembered a similar incident when they had forgotten to close the car-boarding ramp in the prow. Nobody remarked much on the historical precedents. It was the loss of life that captured the popular imagination. Especially the story of the man in massive steel-tipped walking boots who had thrown his unsinkable rucksack into the water, jumped in after it, and gone straight to the bottom before he could swim a single stroke.

'There was flotsam and jetsam all over the sea.'

The newsreader didn't seem to appreciate the difference.

The Photocopy Murders
by Susanna Gregory and Simon Beaufort

About six months ago, old James Barton died. It wasn't unexpected, as he must have been at least eighty, and was of the red-faced, fidgety kind of disposition that made a fatal heart attack inevitable. He had been the managing director of Grafton Investments – the company I work for – more than forty years, and his death meant that someone else would be promoted to take his place. There were three contenders for the honour, each convinced that the post was rightfully his, and all believing themselves so superior to the rest of us that they insisted on being called 'Mister' – as in Mr Arbury, Mr Lensfield, and Mr Downing.

My name is Alice, I'm sixty-six years old, unmarried, and my job at Grafton Investments – simply 'Grafton' to those of us on the inside – is the photocopiers and scanners. I operate them, clean them, refill the paper trays, push, pull and twist levers to clear misfeeds, and contact the engineers when all else fails. There are five machines, and no one knows them like I do. I look after them as though they were my children, and everyone knows better than to tamper in my domain. I've been Senior Technical Operator (which is Grafton's fancy title for the work I do) for thirty years, and, although it might not sound like much, I like my job. You'd be amazed at the things you learn when you're photocopying other people's documents.

Anyway, suffice to say that I know more about what happens at Grafton than anyone else who works there. There aren't many people I really like at the company, if the truth be told, but I have long had two good friends there. The first is the cleaner, Rose. She was born and bred in Cambridge, where Grafton is located, and she loves the city dearly. Although she's the same age as me, and obligatory retirement looms for both of us horribly soon, she's a lively soul. She attends Cambridge United football games with her grandsons, passionately supports the light blue at the Boat Race, would do anything for the University's Botanic Gardens, and says her job keeps her young. She has dyed-black hair and talks too much, but she's a good soul.

My other friend is Bill Hughes. Like Rose and me, Bill has been at Grafton for years – not like Mr Arbury, Mr Lensfield and Mr Downing, ambitious newcomers who only joined the company because they saw old man Barton would soon either die or retire, leaving the post of MD open. Bill is a kindly man with a bald head, who for years was in charge of office management. This meant he ranked below the other three, and – unfortunately for Grafton – apparently didn't stand a chance of becoming MD.

Like me, Bill and Rose have always been early birds. We usually arrived at seven in the morning, when Rose would make tea, after which we would sit in her little cubby-hole of cleaning equipment, chatting until about seven-thirty, when we started work. Rose did most of the talking, largely because she had more to say than Bill and me. All three of us were devoted to Grafton in our own ways, but Rose was the most vocal. In the weeks following the death of old Mr Barton, we talked about little other than who would win the cherished post of MD, with its company car, huge salary, and wide-ranging powers. We were all nervous, afraid that the successful candidate might start 'stream-lining'– which we all know means sacking people. Or worse yet, order a 'procedural review,' which means looking for excuses to sack people. It was an unsettling time.

Then everything at Grafton changed. It began on a cold Monday morning in November, when the city streets glistened with dampness and a halo of fog hung around the orange street lights as dawn fought its way through the clouds. I live in Newnham, whereas the company office is located in a beautiful Georgian house adjacent to Midsummer Common, a marvellous expanse of grass and trees arcing around parts of Jesus College. That day I walked north along the Backs, the green, picturesque region where some of the older College's gardens run down to the River Cam. Then I crossed the river and plodded along Garret Hostel Lane, between Trinity College and Gonville & Caius; passed Heffers Bookshop, my favourite place to browse and shop in the whole city; slipped along All Saints Passage; and headed down Jesus Lane.

Rose was already at the office, shrugging off her raincoat, which was limp with the dampness outside. Bill arrived soon after, putting his old-fashioned hat on the stand in the hallway. Dear Bill. His hats had resided on that stand for more years than I could remember, and I hoped with all my heart that the new MD wouldn't oust him just because he was quiet and careful, and didn't possess much of the self-centred aggression that seems to be a necessary part of business these days. We drank our tea listening to Rose's colourful account of a football game she'd seen that weekend, then started work.

My machines were on the first floor, in a small room near the suites occupied by the three divisional managers. The secretaries were on the ground level, while the rest of the staff were in an open-plan office on the floor above. The photocopy room had been positioned for the convenience of the managers, although it would have made more sense to have them near the secretaries, as they were the ones who did most of the work. But I wasn't complaining. I liked being near the centre of power, and in a position to overhear secret conversations muttered in the corridor outside.

I hung my coat on the back of the door, and switched my machines on one by one, still smiling at a remark Rose had made about one of the Cambridge United strikers. It was then that I noticed something odd. Someone had been using my machines over the weekend, when I wasn't there.

At first, I was angry. There was no note of apology for intruding into my domain, and the lid of the Hewlett-Packard felt wrong, as though someone had wrenched it carelessly. There were also dirty brown spots on the glass surface, which really annoyed me – I always kept my machines spotless. No one at Grafton ever has mysterious smears or nasty dots on the documents that *I* copy. Then I saw some wastepaper in the bin, where someone had obviously made a mistake in copying. This was also irritating – if people were careful and read the instructions, they wouldn't make mistakes, nor would they waste paper and ink.

I snatched the ball out of the bin and straightened it out. At first, the image told me nothing. It was one that had been made while the lid had been left up – something else about which I have very strong ideas. It wastes the carbon in the cartridges, something I never allow to happen. Anyway, someone had done it that weekend. The image caught by my Hewlett-Packard was that of a man, and he had been leaning forward with both hands on my glass when the machine had copied him. I recognised the hands immediately. They belonged to Mr Arbury – I knew because I recognised the horrible jewelled ring he always wore on his little finger. I decided to have words with him when he came in, prospective MD or no.

But Mr Arbury didn't come in that day, or the next. We were all mystified, because missing work at such a crucial time would seriously damage his chances of snagging the big job. I discussed it with Rose and Bill on Wednesday morning.

'Maybe he's realised he's not good enough,' said Rose, slurping her tea. 'He's decided to give up the race before he embarrasses himself.'

'That doesn't sound like Arbury to me,' said Bill doubtfully. 'I was under the impression that he thought himself by far the best of the three.'

I agreed with Bill. Everything about Mr Arbury suggested that he thought he would make an excellent MD, and that anyone who thought otherwise was mistaken.

'Well, it's between Mr Lensfield and Mr Downing now,' said Rose. 'Mr Arbury's little holiday has ruined *his* chances of promotion.'

Neither prospect filled me with pleasure. Mr Lensfield was tall, cadaverous, menacing, and cold – it would be like having Darth Vader in charge. Mr Downing was short, fat, and untruthful, telling people different stories depending on his mood. We began to talk about where Mr Arbury might have gone, laughing at Rose's suggestion of a mini-break in Geneva, learning how to make cuckoo clocks. Then I remembered the spoiled photocopy I'd rescued from the bin. I dragged the others upstairs and showed it to them.

'Look at his hands,' said Bill, sounding puzzled. 'They're clawed – like he was fighting or something.'

'They are,' agreed Rose. 'And look at that shadow behind. It's as if someone came up and made him jump.'

They were right: it did appear as though Mr Arbury had been using the photocopier when someone had startled him by appearing behind him. I suppose he'd pushed the green button by mistake, catching his surprise for posterity. And then he'd gone missing. I remembered the dark spots on the glass, and told the others about them.

'Blood,' declared Rose salaciously. 'It goes brown when you leave it for a day or two.'

Of course, I'd cleaned it off the glass, but Bill helped me pull the Hewlett-Packard away from the wall, and, to our horror, we saw there were more dark marks down the back. They were definitely splashes of some sticky, viscous liquid, and it slowly dawned on me that Rose was right. I got down on my hands and knees and inspected the carpet. There was a faint odour of pine, as though disinfectant had been used on it, and there was a pale patch where some of the colour had leached out.

We all looked at each other in horror, and it was Rose who finally broke the silence by stating the obvious.

'Blood was spilled here, and someone cleaned it up – although not very well. Whoever it was missed a lot of the mess, and using disinfectant was stupid. Everyone knows that bleach is the only thing for those kinds of stains.'

I didn't know it, and I suspected Rose didn't either, but had gleaned her knowledge from watching *CSI* on telly. Not the most accurate source of forensic information, perhaps, but one that she believed.

'There's only one explanation,' said Bill grimly, looking first at me and then at Rose. 'Arbury has been murdered! Someone did away with him over the weekend, while he was using the photocopier.'

'Then the culprit is either Mr Lensfield or Mr Downing,' said Rose quietly. 'They're the ones who would gain from Mr Arbury being gone.'

'What should we do?' I asked, alarmed by what they were saying. 'Call the police?'

Bill gestured to the splashes and the photocopy. 'This isn't enough to go bandying that kind of accusation around. They'd think we were mad!'

'I agree,' said Rose. 'Let's just wait and see if anything else happens. We'll keep that paper and leave those spots, though. Then we'll have them to show the police if need be.'

By Thursday, Mr Arbury's wife had reported him missing, and the police came to Grafton to ask if any of us had seen him since the previous Friday. I had a brief, muttered conversation with Rose and Bill, and we agreed that we should pass them our 'evidence' and suspicions. Rose offered to go with me while I told them, but Bill declined. He said he shouldn't be involved, although I didn't really understand why, and was a little annoyed with him for not standing with us. Still, Rose was more than enough support. She marched into the room where the police were drinking tea and informed them that we had all the evidence they needed to arrest Mr Lensfield or Mr Downing for murder.

Of course, the police were a little more circumspect. They put our photocopy in a plastic bag, and spent some time poking at the brown spots behind the Hewlett-Packard. Then they left, without telling us what they planned to do.

The following morning, I sat with Bill and Rose among the brushes and disinfectants, and we discussed the case.

'Mr Arbury is dead,' said Rose with authority. 'And Mr Lensfield or Mr Downing did it. Murder, that's what it is. With a garrotte.'

'How do you know it was with a garrotte?' I asked, startled.

'You could tell from the photocopy,' she explained. 'Someone came up behind him, threw a piece of wire around his neck, and strangled him with it. There was a bit of blood as the wire cut into his neck, but not as much as there would have been if his throat had been cut.'

'She's right,' said Bill. 'Don't forget the way his hands were clawed.'

I wasn't sure whether I agreed with their conclusions – I always thought people's hands went to their throats when they were strangled, to try to loosen what was cutting off their breath. But I didn't have a better explanation, so I didn't argue. Perhaps Rose's affection for *CSI* had taught her something about the art of murder after all.

'So where's the body?' I asked. 'Still here, on the premises?'

'Probably in those big rubbish bins out the back,' replied Bill. His words emerged with a nervous giggle. 'Arbury was a large man, and you wouldn't want to carry him far.'

'Shall we look then?' I suggested.

'It's raining,' said Rose, cupping her hands around her hot tea. 'We'll check later, when it's not so wet. So which of them did it, do you think? The sour Mr Lensfield or the deceitful Mr Downing?'

'Lensfield would be my bet,' averred Bill. 'I don't think Downing has the nerve, despite his arrogant bluster. I think Lensfield is by far the nastier of the two.'

'Oh, no,' argued Rose. 'Mr Downing is much more unpleasant. He's such an accomplished liar and probably imagines he can run circles around the police, confusing them with his sly tongue.'

'What would happen if they all murdered each other?' I asked curiously. 'Who'd be in line to take over the company? Or would someone from outside be appointed?'

'I don't think we'll get an outsider,' replied Rose with cool conviction. 'After all, the last time the shareholders looked elsewhere, we ended up with Mr Arbury, Mr Lensfield, and Mr Downing. I think they'll want to play it safe, and have someone they know.'

'Who?' I pressed.

Rose looked at Bill. 'Someone with a lot of experience with the company, who's loyal, good at his job, and who's liked by employees.'

'Me?' Bill sounded startled when she fixed him with her beady gaze. 'I don't think I'm in the same league as Lensfield and Downing.'

'Exactly,' said Rose. 'And that's why you'd make such a good MD.'

Bill blushed modestly. 'Do you really think so?'

Bill and I arrived at the same time the following Monday, and I waited while he fumbled with his keys to open the door. Rose was hurrying across the Common towards us, her raincoat billowing and her hair protected from the elements by an old-fashioned headscarf. It was another grey morning, with wet, brown leaves moving in listless eddies in the wind, and the grass of the Common was soggy underfoot. I could hear the low roar of cars and lorries pouring into the city. Cambridge has the most awful traffic, which starts to choke its streets ever earlier in the morning. Lights already gleamed from the windows of many offices, and some people had even started to put up Christmas decorations.

'Blimey!' said Rose when she reached us. She pulled off her scarf and shook out the flattened hair underneath as she followed us inside. 'What a miserable morning! It's a good thing it wasn't like this yesterday – we had a sponsored activity day at the Botanic Gardens to make money for a glasshouse for tropical plants.'

She chattered on while Bill flipped the switch on the hall light. It failed to come on, and he clicked it on and off several times before conceding defeat.

'Light bulb,' he muttered. 'I'll change it before anyone else arrives. We don't want Lensfield or Downing falling over the carpet and breaking their necks, do we.'

'Let them,' said Rose carelessly. She walked to the end of the hall and fiddled with the stair light. That was out, too.

'Something must have tripped the mains,' said Bill, testing other switches with the same result. 'I'll fix it now, because we can't have a cup of tea until the electricity is back on.'

I went upstairs while he descended to the basement, because I was carrying a bag of library books that I wanted to leave there. I opened the door to my little kingdom, and when I saw what was there I gave a piercing shriek that sounded deafening even to my own ears. Mr Lensfield lay on his back next to the Canon copier, his eyes wide open and an expression of stark surprise on his skeletal face. Even from where I stood, I could see his burned fingertips and the scent of singed flesh was still in the air. I could only assume that he had been electrocuted.

I can't recall the exact details of that morning. Bill and Rose came racing to find me when I screamed, and Rose's hands flew to her mouth, so I thought she was going to be sick. Bill was more practical, and quickly shepherded us both out of the room. Rose made tea, pushing a cup of the over-sweetened liquid into my trembling hands, while Bill called the police. Eventually, my shaking stopped, and I began to think rationally about what I had seen.

'It was probably an accident,' Bill was saying. He was standing in the hall, so that he would be able to see the police when they arrived, and let them in. 'These old houses have notoriously ancient wiring, and I've lost count of the times that I've suggested an electrical overhaul to the powers that be.'

'It *is* dangerous,' agreed Rose. 'Do you remember when I got that shock off my Hoover last year? I complained about the electrics then, but Mr Barton said there was nothing wrong with them. He claimed that there was just a fault in that one plug, and he got Bill to fix it.'

'I remember,' said Bill. 'There was no earth, and it could have killed you.'

'I suppose Mr Downing will be MD now,' said Rose glumly. 'Pity. I asked him to sponsor an event at the Botanic Gardens, and he refused. I don't want anyone *mean* to take over the company. Even old Barton, who wasn't generous, helped out with occasional donations. Mr Downing won't.'

'No, he won't,' agreed Bill.

The police arrived, and spent a long time charging up and down the stairs and poking about in my domain before removing the body. When they finally left, and I had the room to myself again, it was covered in fine silver dust. Rose said it was something to do with fingerprints, but it took a long time for the two of us to wipe it all away. I was relieved that Mr Lensfield's corpse was no longer in the building, although I fancied I could still smell the odour of his charred fingers.

The police told us that old wiring *was* the cause of Mr Lensfield's death, and said it was a tragic accident. Then they warned me not to use my machines until a qualified electrician had come to look over them. However, I wasn't convinced that Mr Lensfield's death *was* a 'tragic accident' – not considering the evidence we'd uncovered about the fate of Mr Arbury, and I told them so.

'I can see why you're worried,' a sergeant said kindly to Rose and me. 'You've had a nasty shock...' He trailed off, stricken at the faux pas, then hurried on. 'But there really isn't anything to make us suspect foul play. Look: you can see where the wires have crossed, and there's no earth. That's dangerous, and it's no wonder someone was killed.'

'That's what happened to my Hoover last year,'

said Rose, bending forward to peer at the mangled plug the policeman held in a little plastic bag. 'It didn't kill *me*, though.'

'Perhaps Mr Lensfield had a weak heart,' suggested the sergeant. 'We'll know after the post mortem. We'll keep you informed.'

And then he was gone. I could see what he thought: that Rose and I were a pair of fussing old grannies with overactive imaginations who'd been reading too many whodunits from the mystery section over at Heffers Bookshop. I imagine my bag of books – all crime fiction – waiting to be returned to the library didn't help, either. I wished I'd hidden them, because then he might have listened to me. Because I *knew* Mr Lensfield's death wasn't an accident, and I was *sure* what we found on my Hewlett-Packard had something to do with the disappearance of Mr Arbury, too.

There wasn't much for me to do as long as the photocopiers were out of action. I was restless and unsettled, and wandered listlessly about the building, helping Rose with a little dusting here and there. Bill said I should go home, but I didn't want to be on my own with memories of Mr Lensfield's staring eyes and yellow teeth fixed so clearly in my mind. I wanted to stay at Grafton, with Bill and Rose.

At ten o'clock Mr Downing arrived. I studied him carefully, and could see from his smugly arrogant face that he was delighted by what had happened: the path was now clear for him to be MD. I followed him around a bit that afternoon, watching the way he eyed the various offices and spoke to certain people. I could tell he was making plans for when he was in charge. For example, it was obvious that he intended to take the nice Constable reproduction from the hall and put it up in his own room. And I was fearful for Bill. Mr Downing spoke very rudely to him about some stupid, minor matter. After the reprimand, Bill walked away, his cheeks burning. It was clear that he would be sacked if – when – Mr Downing became MD. Then Mr Downing turned and glowered at me, and I had the sense that I might not be long in following. And Rose. None of the managers liked her cheerfully outspoken manner.

Eventually, I went out for a walk. I strolled around the city centre, and stared despondently into garishly decorated shop windows in Petty Cury. Then I sat for a while in the Round Church, thinking about the deaths of Mr Arbury and Mr Lensfield. It was obvious that Mr Downing had had a hand in both, so why could the police not see it? I considered the facts carefully, analysing what had happened logically, like the protagonists in the crime novels I so loved. I soon knew exactly what had happened.

Mr Downing had ambushed and garrotted Mr Arbury two weekends before, while Mr Arbury had been using the Hewlett-Packard. Then he had tampered with the Canon's plug, which had electrocuted Mr Lensfield. But I was missing a body. I realised then that I needed to find Mr Arbury if I wanted the police to take me seriously. I recalled Bill suggesting that we look in the rubbish bins for the body, but Rose had demurred because it had been raining. Well, it wasn't raining now, I thought.

I marched back to the office with grim determination, and headed straight for the two huge blue wheelie bins that were stationed in the dingy little yard at the rear. But of course, they had been emptied since Mr Arbury had gone missing, and there was nothing in either except something from the kitchen that stank of stale milk. Disheartened – but also vaguely relieved – I reconsidered. Where else could a corpse be hidden? The basement!

Rose was cleaning the hall when I went inside, and I persuaded her to come with me. She was immediately game, and led the way down the stone steps to the two fairly large rooms that were used for storage. There were numerous old filing cabinets there, most of them rusty, because the cellars were damp, as old buildings often are. There were also the mains switch boxes, which the police had taped closed to prevent anyone touching them before the electrician had declared them safe. Rose had a torch, so we were able to see fairly well.

There weren't many places to hide a body, so it didn't take long for us to see that Mr Arbury wasn't there. We slumped in defeat, but then Rose suddenly gave a cry of excitement before bending down to pick something up from the floor. It was a ring. Not just any old ring, but Mr Arbury's ring – the one he always wore on his little finger, and that had been caught by the Hewlett-Packard before he had gone missing.

'What are you two doing?' Bill's voice so close behind made us both jump out of our skin.

'We've found Mr Arbury's ring.' Rose sounded

pleased with herself as she held it up for Bill to see. 'Now the police will *have* to suspect foul play. He had no reason to come down here, and he liked this ring – if it had dropped off while he was alive, he would have picked it up. Besides, just think about the image that was caught on the photocopier – he was certainly wearing it when something odd happened to him.'

'I'm not sure about this,' said Bill, shaking his head. 'The police already think the pair of you are mad. I think you should leave matters well alone.'

'I won't,' I declared stoutly. 'Mr Downing has murdered his rivals, and I, for one, don't want a killer as MD of the company that I have served for so many years.'

'Nor me,' said Rose, and we both stamped away, leaving Bill alone in the cellar.

Tuesday was a glorious day, and Rose and I were heroines. We had taken Mr Arbury's ring to the police and they'd thanked us politely. They put it in one of their see-through plastic bags and showed it to Mrs Arbury, who wept bitterly and said her husband would never have allowed it to leave his finger voluntarily. She was convinced that it being in the basement meant something untoward had happened to him, and because she was close friends with the Chief Constable's wife, her suspicions were taken seriously.

The police evacuated Grafton and began a systematic search for a body, which they eventually found in – believe it or not – the little bathroom that was attached to Mr Downing's office. We heard later that it was wrapped in several layers of thick plastic and then shoved in a cupboard, which explained why no one had noticed the smell when they had visited Mr Downing's office.

Although most people had gone home when the police closed the building, Rose, Bill and I stayed, watching the comings and goings of men in white overalls and elasticated dusters over their shoes. Mr Downing stayed too, but not because he wanted to. He was acting MD and the police wanted him on hand to answer any questions. Or so they said. Personally I thought that the police had taken our accusations seriously at last, and wanted Mr Downing where they could see him. A little later, after Mr Arbury's body had been found, we saw Mr Downing being led out of the building in handcuffs.

'I knew it!' I exclaimed. 'He killed them both!'

'I thought Lensfield seemed a more likely candidate, personally,' mused Bill. 'He always seemed more menacing than the other two.'

'I always suspected Mr Downing,' said Rose confidently. 'He was by far the worst of the three. Everyone who's ever met him knows him for a liar – virtually everyone at Grafton has been misled by him at some point or another. The police will soon learn not to believe a word he says.'

I realised she was right, and that all of us had first-hand experience of Mr Downing's almost pathological reluctance to tell the truth.

'I didn't kill him,' we heard him bleat. A white van was waiting to take him away, but he stopped walking abruptly, reluctant to get inside it, probably because he knew he'd never be free again. 'I never use that bathroom, because the plumbing leaks. I never go in there!'

'Is that true?' I whispered to Rose. As the cleaner, she was intimately acquainted with all the offices and their occupants' habits and foibles.

She shook her head. 'I've never had any trouble with the plumbing, and the loo and sink certainly needed scrubbing weekly, so someone was using them on a regular basis. And as no one else can get into the place without going through his office...'

'Then why didn't you see the body?' asked Bill curiously. 'Arbury died last weekend, so he must have been in there all that time.'

'It's been locked,' explained Rose. 'And now we know why. I just assumed that either Mr Downing was in it, or he didn't want it cleaned. I should have opened it anyway.'

'It's a good thing you didn't,' said Bill with a shudder. 'He killed two men in cold blood, and I'm sure he wouldn't have thought twice about adding a cleaner to his list. Thank God you aren't the kind of person to pry!'

'He's still declaring his innocence,' I said, turning back to the unedifying spectacle of Mr Downing continuing to resist arrest. 'He's saying that he never uses that loo, so never bothers to look in it.'

'So would I, if I were in his situation,' said Bill. 'He's been caught red-handed and he knows it. He'll need to use every lying skill at his disposal if he wants to evade a life sentence.'

'He won't get away with it,' said Rose. 'He's

"banged to rights" as my grandsons would say.' She turned to Bill. 'Maybe we should have a celebratory drink.'

'To celebrate what?' I asked, a little snappishly. 'It wouldn't be very seemly to gloat over two deaths and an arrest for murder.'

'To celebrate our new MD,' replied Rose. She smiled at Bill. 'The shareholders will appoint you now.'

'Yes,' said Bill, with a serene smile. 'I suppose they will.'

Life at Grafton was calm, peaceful and enjoyable once the looming spectres of Mr Arbury, Mr Lensfield, and Mr Downing had been eliminated. Bill was a patient, understanding MD, and people gave him their best because he made them feel important. His employees were happy in their work, and, although he wasn't the kind of man to set the world on fire with innovative ideas and far-sighted policies, we plodded along very nicely, and the shareholders were more than content.

Bill was a good friend to the Botanic Gardens, too, and Grafton became one of its major benefactors. Meanwhile, Mr Downing protested his innocence even after the judge had sentenced him to life for the murder of his two colleagues, but no one took any notice. Justice had been done, his nasty plan had been thwarted, and we had someone good and decent at the helm of the company we loved.

Yet a couple of things Mr Downing said at his trial nagged at my sense of order – one or two facts that didn't quite add up.

First, Mr Downing was shorter than Mr Arbury, which would have made it difficult to garrotte him – but the prosecution said 'difficult' didn't mean impossible, and the jury accepted that point.

Second, Mr Downing had alibis for most of the weekend when Mr Arbury had died, although there were odd hours where his movements were unverifiable. The defence claimed that he wouldn't have had time to commit the crime, but the prosecution argued that it didn't take long to throttle someone and shove the body in a toilet cupboard. Again, the jury elected to believe the prosecution.

And third, I thought that Mr Downing might actually be telling the truth when he claimed to have no idea how to fix an appliance so it would electrocute someone. Even his wife, who seemed relieved to be rid of her husband and kept fluttering her eyelashes at his solicitor, said he was hopeless with anything electrical or mechanical.

All this got me to thinking. We'd assumed that Mr Downing was the one who had the most to gain from the deaths of Mr Arbury and Mr Lensfield. This was true. However, someone else benefited from all three men being out of the picture – namely Bill. My stomach churned when I remembered him saying that he'd spent most of the weekend Mr Arbury was murdered watching TV alone. He had no alibi. And Bill was tall – the perfect height to garrotte Mr Arbury. Then I thought about what happened to Mr Lensfield. It was Bill who had mended the plug on Rose's Hoover. He was practical and mechanically minded: he would certainly know how to electrocute someone.

Everything was suddenly very clear. Bill – dear, sweet, kindly Bill – had murdered Mr Arbury and Mr Lensfield, and had cunningly set up Mr Downing to take the blame. It had worked perfectly, largely due to Rose and me, and our dogged determination to find bodies and evidence. What should I do? Ethically, I knew I should go to the police. But then Bill would be arrested, and Mr Downing would almost certainly be compensated by being made MD. It would be the end of our pleasant, happy company, and Rose and I would be out of work.

But the affair nagged at me, and I felt I had to talk to someone. Obviously, I couldn't approach Bill, even though his promotion hadn't stopped him from enjoying early morning tea with the photocopy-machine operator and the cleaning lady. I decided to confide in Rose.

I caught her as she was putting on her coat to leave. It was lunchtime, and most people had already gone out, taking the opportunity to enjoy a rare day of sunshine. Bill was out, too, at some business meeting or other. The hall was deserted.

'I think Bill killed Mr Arbury and Mr Lensfield,' I blurted. 'And then he arranged for Mr Downing to be blamed.'

Rose looked startled. 'What on Earth are you talking about?'

Quickly, I told her what I'd reasoned, and as I repeated it, I was more than ever convinced that I was right to question the court's verdict. Why would Mr Downing resort to murder to get what he wanted, when his forte was lying? And why would he store the body in his own bathroom? Why not someone else's, so that they would be blamed? In fact, why leave the corpse in Grafton at all, when it would have been much more sensible to dispose of it elsewhere? After all, Mr Arbury had been killed at a weekend, when the building had been empty, so why risk storing it in his own loo? When all was said and done, Mr Downing was not a fool, and I was sure he would have shown more innate cunning had he been the culprit. There was only one conclusion: Bill was the killer.

'Bill could never have come up with a plot as clever as that,' said Rose dismissively. 'Nor would he have been willing to take such a risk.'

'But he did take the risk,' I argued. 'And it paid off. Beautifully.'

'Yes, it did,' agreed Rose with a satisfied grin. 'Better than even *I* predicted. But Bill is no killer so don't you go accusing him. And it has all worked out for the best. I couldn't have planned it any better, even if I do say so myself.'

Castles in the Air
by Elly Griffiths

I got this job because I hate books. At least that's what the bookshop manager, Mr McGuire, said. I didn't think I had a chance, to be honest. There aren't many jobs in this town and I knew there'd be loads of applicants. My A levels were in DT, IT and PE. My mum said that I'd picked them because I prefer initials to real words and she had a point. Anyway, my grades weren't that good and I thought you might need English to work in a bookshop. I also thought that it might be a bit of a girl's job. But Mr McGuire said that he was fed up with all these girls bleating on about how they absolutely *loved* books, books were their *life*, they'd just *die* if they didn't have a book by their side every second of the day. 'They might love books,' he said on my first day in the shop, 'but could they stack boxes or organise a spreadsheet? Can they make a good cappuccino? Believe me, boy, that's the future of bookshops. Cappuccinos.'

Mr McGuire is building a coffee shop on the second floor. It's going to take up the whole of the travel and biography sections. He's going to have me trained to make proper Italian coffee.

'I'm going to be a barista,' I told mum.

'I'm so proud,' she said. 'I always wanted you to do law.' Mum likes to think she's funny. It's because she reads *Private Eye*. She's an artist and, when I was younger, I used to get embarrassed because she didn't dress like other mothers. She'd turn up to collect me from school in a smock covered with paint or a short skirt and crazily patterned tights. I bought her a tracksuit for her fortieth and she never wore it once. Now I'm quite proud of her for being different. She's brought up my brother and me on her own (my dad left when I was ten) and she hasn't done too bad a job. My brother's dead clever, he's only fourteen but he's the school chess champion and he's grade eight on the French Horn. And he reads all the time. 'It's just you, Dylan,' says Mum, 'who thinks books are the enemy.'

When people hear that my name's Dylan they think that it's after Bob Dylan or that Welsh poet. But, no, trust mum. It's after some dozy rabbit in a children's TV programme that was on about a million years ago. It was called *The Magic Roundabout* and Mr McGuire says it was really all about drugs. That doesn't surprise me. I think Mum was pretty wild in her art school days. My brother's called Ozzie which doesn't sound so bad until you find out that it's after a poem called Ozymandias. Poor kid.

I don't know quite when my battle against books started. I think I used to read when I was Ozzie's age or younger. There were these cool books about Vikings that I really liked. Then, I don't know, books started to get longer and more boring. I got a Nintendo DS and spent most of my time playing on that. The final straw was having to do *Of Mice and Men* for GCSE. I hated that book. Lenny was obviously a homicidal maniac with a rabbit fixation and George wasn't much better. It was only set for the lower stream because it was short (and they probably thought we'd identify with Lenny). When I finished it I swore I'd never read a novel again. By the time I was eighteen, I hadn't read a book for nearly two years.

Mum used to try to get me to read (exciting looking parcels under the tree that turned out to be – gee thanks – a book) but she gave up in the end. Even so I think she was quite proud of me for getting the job in the bookshop. She was a bit worried when I didn't want to go to college. Although my A Levels weren't up to much but I would probably have got in to read PE somewhere. But just the word 'read' put me off. More books, even when you're doing PE? No thanks. But working in a bookshop was quite a respectable job. Best of all, it was *interesting.* Mum's highest term of praise.

It was on an interesting morning in early September that I met her. I spotted her immediately because she was standing by the poetry shelves reading a book. We don't get many Readers, as Mr McGuire calls them. 'Readers aren't Buyers,' he says, 'so we don't want to encourage them. No chairs or sofas or cosy corners where they can curl up and forget the world. Overhead lighting and wipe-clean surfaces. That's what keeps the Readers away.'

But the overhead lighting didn't seem to have deterred this girl. She was leaning against the wall, apparently absorbed in her book. That was the first thing I noticed. The second thing was her hair. She had this long reddish-brown plait that fell below her waist. I remember thinking that it was like a rope, that if you were drowning you could grab onto it and save your life. God know why that went through my mind. I'm not the sort of person to fantasise about drowning or about girls for that matter. Oh, I like girls, don't get me wrong. It's just that so far my relationships had been more the 'wanna go out?' 'don't mind' variety. In fact 'relationship' seemed too big a word for them. Those bookish girls have *relationships;* the rest of us just go out.

'Go and ask her if she's buying that book,' Mr McGuire hissed. 'She can't just stand around reading all day.'

I was a bit nervous but he was the boss and I'd only been working there a few weeks. So I sidled over carrying a pile of George RR Martins.

'Areyougoingtobuythatbook?'

I didn't mean it to come out quite like that but she turned and smiled.

'I don't know,' she said. 'I was just reading it. I don't know much about Gerard Manley Hopkins, do you?'

'No,' I said. It was safe to say that I'd never heard of him.

'It's extraordinary some of the things he does with words. It feels quite modern but he died in 1889.'

'Oh,' I said. Was she actually trying to have a booky conversation with me?

She must have seen my face because she laughed and said, 'Don't you like poetry?'

I was on safer ground here. 'No,' I said.

‘I haven’t read as much poetry as I should,’ she says. ‘But I’m off to uni soon and I want to get lots of reading done before I go.’

My argument against university in a nutshell. But she was smiling at me so I didn’t want to be rude. She was pretty really although you didn’t notice it at first. She had these wide apart eyes that were a strange colour, somewhere between grey and blue. When she was talking she looked right at you, which not many people do. It made me feel nervous.

‘I need to put these on the shelves,’ I said, indicating the Georges.

‘I haven’t even got started on *Game of Thrones* yet,’ she said. She sounded genuinely worried. ‘So many books, so little time.’

When I came back from the fantasy section she was at the till. Mr McGuire was wrong. She was a Buyer as well as Reader. She bought the Gerard Manley Hopkins book and she put another in front of me.

‘Try that,’ she said. ‘You might like it.’

After she’d gone I looked at the book. It was by TS Eliot and it was all about cats. I put it back on the shelf.

She was back the next day. This time she was looking at the history shelves.

‘I want to find out about the Spanish Civil War,’ she said.

‘Are you reading history at university?’ I asked. I was quite proud at the way it came out, ‘reading’ and everything. I sounded like one of those people from *University Challenge* (Mum and

Ozzie's favourite programme).

'No,' she said. 'English. But I've just read this great book about the Spanish Civil War and I wanted to know a bit more about it.'

That was another thing I hated about English. You finish a book, hooray, let's tick that one off, and the teacher's saying that you should really read another book just to get the historical *back-ground* or for the *contrast* or whatever. But this girl looked absolutely thrilled at the thought of more reading.

'Modern history's over there,' I said.

Instead of moving she held out her hand to me. 'Joanna,' she said.

I find hand-shaking embarrassing but I managed it. 'Dylan,' I mumbled.

'Cool,' she said. 'Like...'

'No,' I interrupted. 'Like the rabbit in *The Magic Roundabout.*'

She laughed. 'Do you have a lunch break, Dylan? Fancy getting a sandwich in the mall? It's a lovely day.'

God knows why but I said yes. I think it was partly just to get rid of her. Sometimes now I wish I'd said no but that's not how life works, is it? It's not like a book. It only goes forwards, you don't get flashbacks.

She was right. It was a lovely day. We bought sandwiches and ate them in the little square of green opposite the 99p shop. It's funny, normally I would have felt nervous, having lunch with a girl I didn't know, but she made it seem all right. I think it was because she was so normal. She wasn't flirting or coming on to me. She was just chatting. Like we were friends.

She told me that she was eighteen and going to university in October. She was going to Cambridge, a place I'd only heard about in *University Challenge*.

'Are you really clever then?' I asked.

'No,' she said seriously. 'I just worked hard. I'm not naturally clever but I love reading and that helps with English. What about you?'

I told her about the acronym A Levels.

'What's your favourite sport?' she asked. I liked the way that she didn't ask about grades or any of that stuff. Even so, I felt a bit embarrassed. You see I've never much liked football, which was a big problem at my school. You were nothing if you weren't in the football team. My sport was pretty low down in the pecking order.

'Running,' I said. 'I liked long distance running.' All the other kids used to moan about cross-country running but I loved it. Getting into the zone, running almost in a trance, the only sound your feet pounding on the grass or the tarmac or whatever. I used to train in the early mornings and even this crappy town looked good then, the mist rising from the river, the roads empty, the smell of grass and fresh, clean air.

'You used the past tense,' she said. 'Do you still run?'

'Only for the bus,' I said. 'You stop doing sport when you leave school, don't you?'

'That's like saying you stop reading when you leave school.'

'Yeah well I did that too,' I said.

Joanna was at St Faiths, the private girls' school

out by the golf course. I knew her family must be posh, I knew it by her voice, but this just confirmed it.

'I got a scholarship,' she said, rather defensively. 'My sisters did too.'

'How many sisters have you got?'

'Three. Two.'

We said goodbye because I had to get back to work and she wanted to go to the library (natch). All afternoon I wondered about someone who didn't know how many sisters they had. Maybe she's terrible at Maths (one of the annoying things about those bookish girls is how they all hate Maths) but even so. About an hour before closing time she was back, holding out a book to me.

I looked at the front. It was called *The Loneliness of the Long Distance Runner.*

'I had to get it from the library,' she said. 'I didn't think you'd have it here. Don't tell your boss.'

I'd told her a bit about Mr McGuire. You won't be surprised to hear that he hates libraries.

'It's a short story,' she carried on. 'By Alan Sillitoe. I thought you might like it.'

'How long have I got to read it?'

'Three weeks.' She said it like it was an unimaginable stretch of time. It had taken me a whole term to read *Of Mice and Men* and that's only about a hundred pages long.

There was a pause and then she said. 'My sister died. That's why I said I had three sisters at first. I hate saying two. It feels like I'm disowning Elizabeth. She was ill for a long time but I wasn't prepared for her to die. It's so final, death. Not like reading a book. If someone dies in a book, they're alive again every time you read it.'

What could I say to that? 'I'm sorry,' I said at last.

'Read the book,' she said.

After that we met every day. It was a really hot September, better than August had been. We'd have lunch on the green and, after work, we'd walk down to the river. We'd sit there with our feet in the water and we'd talk. I've never talked so much in my life. My mates and I, we don't talk much. We'll meet at someone's house, play a few computer games and watch TV. We'll only talk about what's happening on screen at that particular moment. The past and the future doesn't come into it. I used to talk to mum but, as I've got older, it's embarrassing somehow. Ozzie still chats away to her – what superpower he'd have if he could choose, what he'd like for dinner, his favourite French Horn music – but mostly I just listen.

Sometimes it would get dark and we'd still be talking. Then we'd walk back into town, get some chips and maybe a couple of beers and go back to the river. The water had this strange green light sometimes, phosphorescence she called it, and we'd sit there with this glow on our faces, like aliens. Once I took a photo of her and her hair was all electric, standing up round her head like a halo. That was the only time I ever saw her hair loose.

Mum saw me with Joanna one lunchtime and

was convinced that something was going on. She kept talking about my girlfriend, 'you know, the one with the lovely long hair.' 'She's not my girlfriend, Mum,' I'd tell her patiently. 'She's just a friend.' And that was true. It was the 'just' that was a lie.

We told each other everything. I told her how upset I'd been when dad left. I even told her that I'd wet the bed for months. She told me how awful it had been when Elizabeth died. 'I thought I couldn't show any emotion because I've always been the strong one in the family.' She wasn't the oldest though. She had an elder sister who was married and a younger sister who was a bit of an airhead. 'Give me her number,' I said. 'I love airheads.' 'I'll give you her number when I go to university,' she said. 'You can take her out then. But this is our time.'

Sometimes, at night, I used to look at her facebook profile. It was the usual thing: lots of girls fooling about in funny hats, a few pictures of her with her family and her dog (Scrabble), a few posts about books and films. It was funny though, when I looked at her facebook page I felt that I didn't know her at all. But, when we talked by the river, I felt that I knew her better than I knew anyone. Better than Mum or Ozzie or Tom, who's been my best mate since Year Three. It almost felt like we were the same person.

I read the book she lent me. It was actually quite good. It's about this boy who's at Borstal. He starts running to forget about being locked up, to escape inside himself. Then he gets offered a place at a posh school. All he has to do is win a race. He's miles ahead but he stops just before the finish line. It's meant to show that he's his own person but I thought it was a bit stupid, to be honest.

'So if I'd won the county championship I could have gone to St Faiths,' I said.

'Except it's a girls' school,' said Joanna.

'All the same,' I said. 'I could have been a contender.' I meant it to be funny but it came out wrong. I sounded bitter and sarcastic.

'Dylan,' she leant forward so that her face was only a few inches from mine. Her hair was tickling my face. 'You are a contender. Not because of where you went to school but because of *you*. You're clever and funny and sweet. You've just got to believe in yourself.'

But it was enough that she believed in me.

September was endless but then it was over in a flash. One day Joanna came into the shop and started buying all these pens and notepads and things.

'Stocking up?' I said.

'Yes,' she said. 'I'm off on Saturday.'

Saturday. It was three days away. Mr McGuire came over, all happy because she was buying stationery. He thinks that's the sort of thing the shop should be selling. 'A notepad's used up in a week,' he'd say. 'And then they buy another. But a book can last forever.' He made it sound like something disgusting. *Forever.*

'We'll miss you,' he said to Joanna. 'I've never known a Reader buy so many books.'

'We'll have to have a farewell party,' Joanna said

to me later. 'Friday night, down by the river. I'll bring some wine.'

On Friday I wore my best green top and told Mum I'd be home late. 'Going somewhere nice with your girlfriend?' she said. 'Have fun.' But I didn't think I'd ever have fun again. I'd bought Joanna a present, a bicycle bell because she told me that everyone cycled in Cambridge. It had Dylan from *The Magic Roundabout* on it. I hoped it would remind her of me. I wondered how I'd cope, stuck in this stupid town with no-one to talk to. Maybe I should go away, try to get into college somewhere. The night before I'd even downloaded some prospectuses.

'Excuse me,' said the girl at the counter. 'Have you got a book called "Grumpy Git in a Green Shirt"? I think it's by Charles Dickens.'

I looked up. I didn't recognise her at first, even though she was staring at me with those wide-apart grey eyes. It was Joanna but instead of her long plait, the rope that was going to save me from drowning, her hair was cut short and dyed bright red.

'You've cut your hair,' I said stupidly.

'Yes,' she said. 'Thought it was time for a new look. Do you like it?'

'Yes,' I said.

I hated it.

We went down to the river and we sat on the bank and drank the wine. I gave her the bicycle bell and she gave me this bag that she'd made herself with big fabric stars on it. I could tell immediately that it was full of books. I have to admit that I was a bit disappointed. Joanna had done nothing else but give me books and lend me books since we'd met. I'd hoped that her leaving present would be something more personal.

She saw my face. 'It's not just a bag of books, Dylan. Each of these books is special to me. I'm in all of them. You're in all of them. That way we'll never lose each other. Just start to read and you'll see.'

She leant towards me and, just for a second, I thought about kissing her. Then a couple of drunks came staggering along the tow path and the moment was lost.

When I got home I opened the bag. Some of the books were new from the shop but some were her old books, ones she'd had as a child. She'd written her name in them. Joanna M, England, Great Britain, Europe, The World, The Universe. The first one I opened had a hideous cover showing four girls sitting in a garden.

Little Women. Well, I wouldn't find Jo in that. But it was a place to start.

The Stain
by Jenna Hawkins

Life leaves a stain. I already know that. Seth's empty paving slab is a different colour to the rest. Darker, smoother. Stained by his years there.

The university buildings and pollution-washed churches are still and silent. Only the traffic seems to have woken. Delivery trucks sit on krrbs and cyclists stream past. The flavour of baking bread is on the air.

Alice Glynn digs her chin deep into her scarf. She fixes my new colleague with a worried glare. 'He's a person. Like you. Like me.'

Trelford nods, robotic and automatic, as if he has heard this argument too many times to count. 'Miss Glynn, yes he is. But unfortunately we need a little more to go on.'

I look back down towards the dusty slab of pavement. I wonder about the man who usually sits here.

'What makes you think that something has happened to him?' I ask.

Trelford throws me an irritated look.

Alice straightens. 'Unlike most of the people in this town I actually talk to the homeless.' A cleft appears between her eyebrows. 'He's been here outside my shop for years. Every day. Without fail. Something's happened to him.'

'Well, you say he's been gone for three days.

Maybe he just moved elsewhere?' My words sound pathetic and convey none of the optimism I intended.

'Maybe he's dead!' she fires back.

Trelford squares his shoulders. 'Look, Miss Glynn. We appreciate your concern, but to report someone missing there needs to be something concrete. A name–'

'His name is Seth.'

'A full name.'

Her eyes probe mine – maybe she thinks that because I'm a woman I'll be more understanding. My eyes don't give her the answer she is looking for. She nods defeatedly.

For the rest of the day, I feel guilty. I have failed before I've even begun.

Unlike Sidney Street yesterday, East Road is roaring in the early morning. On my way to Parkside Station, I hesitate at the doorway of the homeless shelter. There are two men and a woman perched on the steps, behind a veil of cigarette smoke and the smell of beer.

'No trouble, officer,' one of the men – the older of the two – says. He gives me a toothy grin.

'Do you know a man named Seth?' I fasten my uniform at the neck.

The woman laughs and lifts a beer can to her lips. Her skin is dry and lined, although she can't be much older than me.

The younger man shrugs. 'Maybe.'

'A homeless man. He usually sits out on Sidney Street during the day. I'm just trying to find him.'

The younger man holds his wrists together.

'Cuff me, officer. I know nothin'.'

'I just want to make sure that he's okay. So if you've seen him–'

'Not seen him for three days,' the older man says.

Something inside me fires up. Like a bolt of warm light that shoots right through my solar plexus. 'Three days?' My voice sounds instantly sharper.

'Three days.' He nods slowly. The skin around his eyes is dark and loose. His hair is patchy on top. He breathes out a cloud of cigarette smoke.

'What do you know about him? – Seth.'

'He's quiet,' the woman says. 'Doesn't talk much.' She takes another swill of beer. 'We're all sad here. But, well, some of us deal with it better than others.' She grins at her beer can. 'Seth ... he's always sad.'

'I really need to find him. Do you know anyone–'

'Ask Charlotte,' the older man says.

'Charlotte?'

'She's his friend.'

'Is she here?'

He looks around, as if he has forgotten who is sharing the steps with him. 'Nah. You'll find her though. She's around. She's always around.'

I try not to let my frustration seep through my voice. 'How will I know her?'

He smiles. A joke that I don't get. 'You'll know her. When you see her, you'll know her.'

'So, Kate, I hear you wiped the floor with the other lads in training.' Trelford places his tray next to mine and sits down.

My insides are thrumming with the idea of finding Seth, but I still feel the glow of satisfaction at this new information. I try to sound casual. 'Where did you hear that?'

He taps the side of his nose. 'Over-achiever, are you?'

I place my cutlery carefully on my plate and turn to face him. 'What's that supposed to mean?'

'Nothing.' He holds up a harmless palm.

A pause.

'Do you know if there is a homeless woman around town named Charlotte?'

His eyes narrow. 'Why do you want to know?'

'I just thought that–'

'You're not still harping on about that bloke who's supposedly missing? Look Kate, we did our bit.'

'I checked. The incident has been closed already. No-one is doing anything.'

'What can we do? Deviation from routine does not a missing person make. There was nothing to suggest a crime had taken place. You're going to have to get used to disappointment.'

I pick my fork up and use it to absently shuffle my peas.

'Why do you even care so much?'

'Why should we only care about people who have got family members to miss them?'

'Look, Kate, take it from me. I've got seventeen years on job–'

I don't look at him as I say, 'It's fine. Forget about it.'

Part of me accepts it then. There's nothing I can do. But later on the beat, I see her, huddled against the black iron railings of The Church of St Andrew the Great alongside a ratty Labrador. The man at the shelter said I'd know her when I saw her.

He was right.

'Excuse me? Are you Charlotte?'

The girl looks up. So does the dog. The girl has a thin face that might have been pretty before the streets took their toll. Her hair is scraped back into a fountain of dreadlocks and her earlobes are swamped by a tangle of silver hoops and a row of studs. I used to envy self-assured girls like her.

She eyes me sceptically. 'So what? I've not done nothing.' In front of her is an upturned cap with a few pennies inside. She tugs it closer to her.

'I know. I just wanted to ask you about Seth.'

Half of her mouth quirks. 'Don't bother. He's gone.'

I chance a glance over my shoulder to where Trelford is waiting for me. An elderly man has approached him and is gesturing to the road, where cyclists are slaloming around taxis. It looks like he is complaining. Hopefully he'll buy me a few minutes.

I squat down so that I can look her in the eye. 'I know. I want to find him.'

'He's dead.'

I feel my spine stiffen. 'What do you mean?'

'I mean he's dead.' She sniffs the air and dabs a finger to her studded nostril. 'He must be.'

'Why do you say that?'

'I was with him. A few days ago.'

'At his regular spot on Sidney Street?'

Charlotte gives me a puzzled, slightly indignant look. 'Anyway. We're just chatting and suddenly Seth goes white.' She laughs thinly. 'Whiter than usual, I mean. Like he's freaking out.' She hesitates and reaches for the Labrador, and rubs its ear. 'Seth was so great. He'd always save some food for Rusty.'

'Rusty?'

Charlotte nods towards the dog. 'He had nothing, and he was still generous. I already miss him. I'll miss him forever.'

'How long had he been on the streets?'

'I dunno. Ten years? Way longer than me.'

'Why? What happened to his home?'

Charlotte shrugs, losing interest.

'You said he freaked out the other day. Why?'

'He saw someone. Someone he knew. Someone he wasn't expecting to see.'

I glance over my shoulder. Trelford is on his way over, his expression impatient, his stride wider than usual.

'Who?'

'I don't know. A man. He was wearing a suit. Looked posh. He walked past. Didn't even see Seth, but Seth saw him.'

'Go on.'

'Seth starts mumbling, like he's frightened or something. Saying he's in trouble. Saying he's in danger.' She blinks away the memory. 'Please. Can't you do something?'

Trelford's footfalls grow louder.

'Quick. Tell me about the man he saw.'

'He was walking up the hill, towards the river ... you know, Magdalene Bridge. He had a briefcase.' The effort of memory brings tension to her face.

'What then? What did Seth do?'

'He said he needed to get away. Before something bad happened to him.'

Trelford arrives at my side and sighs loudly.

'Where would he hide?' I say.

Charlotte stares at me, and doesn't reply.

A man is screaming. My gut tells me it's Seth even before we get dispatched.

I'm not used to the siren yet. My heart flutters frenetically all the way to Blinco Grove.

We can hear the screaming the moment we get out of the car. I've never heard screams like these. Ragged and endless. The sound of agony. Agony I hardly dare to contemplate. This is a family street. No-one should scream like that here. All I can think about is how I need to make the screams stop.

Trelford is already radioing for back-up. 'Kate! Wait!'

But I am running up the front path. There is stained glass in the front door. I press the doorbell and then hammer a fist against the glass.

Abruptly, the screaming stops.

I hammer again. 'Police! Open up!'

Trelford arrives at my side, breathing angrily.

A shadow moves on the other side of the glass. With an elongated groan, a narrow gap appears.

'We've had a report of a disturbance,' Trelford says easily. 'Mind if we come in for a chat?'

He starts to step inside, but I stand still, glued to the doorstep.

'Trelford,' I say. My voice is a hoarse whisper.

He doesn't hear me. 'Who was screaming?'

I fumble my baton from my belt. My fingers find the pepper spray. I follow Trelford into a narrow hall and down to the kitchen.

I see the man first, tied to a chair. His chin is low against his collar bones. And then I see the woman, slumped on the floor like she's just been dropped there. My eyes find the man in the chair again, and the glistening lines of scarlet which run from the side of his neck. I know that they are both dead.

Tears mist my vision. 'Why did you do it, Seth?'

Seth stares back at me, the blood-smeared knife dangling at his side. He is so thin. The thinnest part of him is his throat. I can see cartilage, jutting from hollow caverns. He pants, agitated. 'He killed my family.'

I look back at the dead man. At the pinstripe suit trousers and the loose tie around his neck.

'Three years, he was given,' Seth says brokenly. 'Three tiny years for the life of my wife and my two children. And now he's living and working like nothing happened. He took everything from me. He should have been given life. He should have rotted in that jail. There's ... there's a car outside. They still let him drive. After ... after he killed my family.' Sobs sound in his thin throat.

And then he moves. Suddenly, Trelford is on the floor, and Seth has his arm wrapped around my neck. I kick back at him, wriggling and fighting.

A scarlet pool spreads beneath Trelford's body.

I scream. The back of my mouth hurts with it.

I fire the pepper spray, but it hits the air. For a moment I paw clumsily at his grip, reeling in his smell – the unwashed skin, the sour reek of old sweat, and the salt of his tears which seem to be in every pore. Then I strike him on the shin with my baton.

He grunts and buckles.

I lurch out of his grip and stumble.

The world tilts dizzily, and grows hazy.

I can feel warm liquid on my skin. My hand clamps instinctively around my throat as my knees hit the ground.

Seth watches, eyes drowning in an emotion too complex to identify.

I fold to the floor. The room is shrinking away into darkness, and all I can see is the blood that seeps into the tiles, staining them with bands of burgundy. The light shimmers in its surface.

My life's stain.

Life leaves a stain. I knew that. But I never imagined that it would look so beautiful.

The Storytellers
by Suzette A. Hill

'They were holding hands,' the boy said, *'and* sharing a chocolate ice-cream.'

'What nonsense you talk,' reproved his mother, 'as if Mr Higgs and Cecily Jones would be doing anything like that. Really, Charlie, you do tell the most fearful whoppers! Besides, you were in the dark. How do you know they were sharing an ice?'

'Because old Higgs was in front of me in the queue at the interval and took the last one, the one *I* wanted,' Charlie explained. 'And I heard him say to the usherette, "Oh that's all right, we don't like vanilla so we'll make do with this one between us".' The boy gave a disgruntled sigh, evidently still piqued by his loss, and returned to revving his Dinky car. Brrrm-Brrrm!

Mrs Penrose studied him sceptically, but after a pause said, 'So what about your friend Mickie, did he see them?'

Charlie shrugged. 'Dunno. Shouldn't think so, he'd gone for a pee.'

'I've told you before not to use that term, it's vulgar. What you mean is that Mickie had gone to spend a penny.'

'Hmm.' (Brrrm-Brrrm!)

His mother sniffed and left the room saying nothing.

Later that evening, however, she did have a few words to say. 'Do you think they really were in the cinema together, Arthur?'

'Unlikely,' her husband replied, 'I know for a fact that Higgs hates cowboy films, particularly those with Ronald Reagan. He told me once that the only American star of that ilk he could stand was Roy Rogers and that was only because of the horse Trigger. The boy is pulling your leg.'

'Why should he do that? And why would he invent Cecily Jones? After all, she's just the typist there.'

'Ah, so it would be a slicker tale if it were Mrs Smithers from Brook Court would it?'

'Not in the one-and-ninepennies it wouldn't,' his wife rejoined tartly.

'Well I shouldn't bother your head about it. If Ted Higgs wants to take his secretary to the flicks does it really matter? With a wife like that I'm not surprised he craves chocolate ice-cream and a cuddle. But in any case the whole thing is bound to be academic – I've told you before, the boy's an inveterate liar. Gets it from your brother.'

The shaft delivered, Arthur returned to his crossword and smugly filled in a two-part clue of sixteen letters: Magdalene College.

Mrs Penrose glowered, struggled for a reply and then tittered. 'But you have to admit it would be funny if there was something in it. I mean to say...!' She left the remainder unspoken and instead went to the door and called up the stairs. 'Charlie! Come down here a moment would you dear, your father wants to speak to you, and we've got some nice toffees.'

'I do not want to speak to him,' her husband expostulated, jettisoning his newspaper, 'but I wouldn't mind a couple of those jaw-breakers. Come on, hand them over.'

'Only if you ask Charlie a few tactful questions.'

'So you liked the film then, did you?' enquired Arthur jovially.

His son nodded, mouth stuffed with toffee.

'Many people there, were there?'

Another nod.

'Oh bound to have been,' interjected Mrs Penrose, 'westerns are always popular. Why, I think you said that even Mr Higgs was there – in the row in front of you wasn't he?' She shot a meaningful glance at her husband who dutifully took his cue.

'Er, with a friend was he?'

'I think so,' replied Charlie vaguely, 'that pretty blonde lady, Cecily something.' He eyed the toffees speculatively.

'And did they say hello or wave to you?' enquired his father.

'No, they were busy talking.'

'Ah ... talking about the film I daresay.'

'Didn't sound like it. She kept laughing; and then I heard him say something about that if the plan worked they would soon have something really big to celebrate.' He frowned, and then added, 'I wish grown-ups wouldn't do that.'

'Do what dear?' asked his mother.

'Sit with their heads so close that you can't see the screen. I mean just when Ronald Reagan was sneaking up on the rustler with his gun all ready they had to shove their faces together so tight that I missed the best part. The rustler got away. He had played some trick I think, and I didn't see what; and I couldn't ask Mickie because he was still having a – er, spending a penny.' Cheated of the film's best moment, the boy made a compensatory move in the direction of the toffee tin.

'All very sad, I'm sure,' observed his father, 'but that's life, old son: things happen just when you don't want them to and people get in the way. You'll learn that soon enough.' He pre-empted the boy's outstretched hand and took the last toffee.

'And then what happened?' Charlie asked eagerly.

'Then,' said Miss Jenner with maximum emphasis, 'then they formed a gang and called themselves the Cambridge Cut-throats.'

'Cor,' exclaimed Mickie appreciatively, 'that's a good name.'

'What's a cut-throat?' Charlie asked.

Miss Jenner explained in lavish detail.

'From ear to ear?' Charlie repeated wonderingly.

'Oh yes, always from ear to ear,' Miss Jenner assured him. She smiled, amused by their rapt faces and glad of a chance to tell a tale rather than catalogue the books. Books were all very well, she thought, or at least the stories they contained; but filing the damn things and doing inventories was an awful bore. The boys were a pleasing distraction and she warmed to her theme: 'And then you see, just as the man was staring into the Cam wondering what he was going to have for his tea, a punt glided out of the mist, and in it sat three corpses bolt upright – all headless.' She paused, and then for better effect added, 'And two of them had no arms either...'

A brusque voice interrupted. 'Now Miss Jenner, if those children have come to buy something kindly sell it to them and send them off. We can't have people just hanging about: this is a bookshop not King's Cross station!' Mrs Higgs eyed the boys with distaste.

Miss Jenner grimaced. 'Yes Mrs Higgs, they are just going.' And giving her listeners a broad wink she nodded towards the door.

'I don't think I like that lady,' announced Charlie as they scuttled round the corner into Market Street. 'My mum says she is too big for her boots.'

'Yes, and her boots are pretty big anyway,' sniggered Mickie, 'size nine I shouldn't wonder.' He emphasised the point by turning out his feet and galumphing theatrically into the gutter – a move that nearly dislodged a passing don from his bicycle.

'But the thin one's all right,' Charlie continued. 'Do you think that bit about the headless bodies was true?'

''Course not,' Mickie laughed scornfully, 'but it was good though, wasn't it!'

Charlie nodded. 'I bet I could write a story about a dead body – *and* with its throat cut from ear to ear.'

'So could I,' said Mickie carelessly.

'Not as good as mine.'

'Oh no?'

'Not nearly.'

'The lad's being very quiet tonight,' observed Mr Penrose, 'must be that Meccano set I gave him for his birthday.'

'He is writing,' explained his wife.

'Writing? He never writes – except for his homework and that's always a rush job at the last minute.'

'Well he is writing *now.* He asked me to buy him a special exercise book and a propelling pencil.'

'A propelling pencil! What's wrong with an ordinary one? Who does he think he is – Charles Dickens?'

Mrs Penrose gave a pained sigh and took out her knitting. After a few stitches she cast it aside, the sludge-grey sock failing to stir her imagination ... whereas the thought of Ted Higgs and Cecily Jones sharing an ice-cream did. 'Arthur,' she said, 'do you think Mrs Higgs knows?'

'Knows what?'

'About those two of course.'

Her husband rolled his eyes. 'Are you still harping on about Ted and that typist? I should have thought you'd got better things to think about.'

'Like mending your collars you mean?'

'No I do not mean. I mean like ... well, like...' He scanned the room for inspiration, but finding none blew his nose instead and shifted the coalscuttle.

'Of course we don't know for certain,' she mused, 'but all the same–'

'All the same you would *like* it to be so.' He snorted. 'I don't know – you women, you're all the same, can't live without a bit of gossip.' Then after a pause he added, 'Er, was that what Charlie said – that they were talking about a celebration?'

'Exactly,' cried Mrs Penrose eagerly, 'that's what struck me as odd too!'

'I did not say it was *odd.* I was merely voicing my surprise that the boy should use that term; he's only ten and I can't say that I've noticed an especially wide vocabulary.' He picked up the crossword and carefully entered the word 'supercilious'.

Mrs Penrose's left eyebrow rose fractionally.

Later, when with a mug of Horlicks she went upstairs to coax the boy into bed, she found him hunched over the new exercise book. 'I am writing a story,' he announced proudly, 'and it's jolly good.'

'Well that's nice,' she remarked, and setting down the mug looked over his shoulder. The scrawled paragraph was indecipherable but the heading was clear enough: MERDER IN THE POSH BOKESHOP.

'Oh ... I don't think that sounds very pleasant,' she said doubtfully, 'wouldn't it be more fun to write about a family of squirrels?'

'Don't like squirrels, they're soppy.'

'Gnomes?' she suggested brightly. There was a pointed silence as he continued with the propelling pencil.

Returning to the living room she informed her husband of their son's literary endeavours.

'Well he's right about the posh bookshop,' Arthur observed. 'He obviously means Ted's. With

Mrs H swaggering about with her airs and graces it couldn't be anywhere else! I went in the other day and asked for a book on car maintenance. Anyone would think I'd made an improper suggestion: "Oh Mr Penrose," my lady sneered, "I am afraid we don't stock *that* sort of thing, ours is a quality firm. I suggest you try one of the market stalls." Stuck up old bat! No wonder her hubby's having it off with that blonde bit.'

'Ah, so you *do* think something's going on then?' asked his wife in triumph. (She chose to ignore the verbal coarseness for fear of spoiling his train of thought.)

'Well,' he conceded casually, 'on the face of it I suppose it's possible ... the nipper might have got it right this time.'

Taking that as a clear consensus his wife returned happily to the sock.

'It's nearly finished,' exclaimed Charlie excitedly. 'Shall I read you the best bit?'

'If you like,' his friend replied.

The boy cleared his throat and frowning in concentration started to read: 'And then when the big policeman peeped behind the bookcase he saw an awful sight. "Bless my soul," he said, "that is a dead body, and what is more its throat is cut *from ear to ear* and there is heaps and heaps of blood everywhere. Look, it is dripping all down the shelves and making a mess of that very nice carpet."'

Charlie paused for dramatic effect, while Mickie looked suitably impressed. He continued. '"I wonder who that can be?" said Miss Jenner.

She looked a bit surprised.

'"Anyone can see who it is," said the big policeman, "that is Mrs Higgs. You can tell from the hairs and braces."'

'Tell from what?' Mickie asked.

Charlie raised his voice and repeated the words precisely.

Mickie looked puzzled. 'What braces?'

'*I* don't know,' the author replied impatiently, 'but that's what my dad says. "With all those hairs and braces – that Mrs H, she deserves to come a blooming cropper"... Now shut up and let me get on!' The story continued to unfold.

In Mrs Penrose's considered opinion Bene't Street's new tea shop was very nice, very nice indeed. The girls were polite, the scones tasty, the tea properly brewed and you met the right class of person... Not that she was a snob of course (not like that Ted Higgs's snooty wife!) but one did have *standards.* She had tried to explain this to the two men in her life, her husband and son, but neither seemed entirely receptive. Too late for Arthur no doubt, but there was still hope for little Charlie. She vaguely recalled something those Jesuits used to say, 'Give me a child till he's seven and I have the man.' Well, Charlie was ten now but still time for him to acquire a few social graces, or (as she had recently read in the etiquette column of *Home Chat*) to gain a 'sound *savoir faire.*' She gave a wistful sigh, and carefully crooking a little finger took up her tea cup and gazed out of the window contemplating her son's future and her husband's dullness.

What she saw in the street inspired mild disapproval coupled with rampant curiosity. Cecily Jones, the bookshop typist, was clicking past on those absurd heels and flaunting her plastic handbag as if it had come straight from Paris. The blonde perm was far too tight (the watcher considered), and those were definitely dark roots showing at the crown; and as for that silly bit of nylon fur on the coat-cuffs, ridiculous!... The girl was in a hurry (late for work?) and had soon passed out of sight; but it was glimpse enough to set Mrs Penrose's mind racing and for her thoughts to continue from where they had left off the previous evening.

Was Ted Higgs really carrying on with his employee? Of course he was! After all, what man shares his ice-cream with a woman not his wife and then puts his head so close to hers that the little boy behind can't see the screen? The answer could be only one thing: a *philanderer!* 'Disgraceful,' Mrs Penrose breathed with satisfaction.

She pictured the pair of them locked in ardent embraces in dark corners, holding furtive hands at twilight in Parker's Piece, exchanging yearning looks beneath the portico of St Mary's or under the hawk-like glare of Mrs Higgs; kissing and scuttling awkwardly among the bookshelves... Scuttling? No. On the whole, she reflected, Ted Higgs did not scuttle: lunge or lumber perhaps, but not scuttle – far too solid. Ugly too now she came to think of it... Still, people had funny tastes and doubtless the girl was only in it for what she could get; a flighty piece that one and no mistake! She ordered another scone and pursued her reveries as they oscillated between the sordid and romantic. Both were absorbing.

On the way home she pondered, not for the first time, what kind of celebration the lovers were planning and why. (Yes, Charlie had been quite clear about that she remembered.) Perhaps it was something to mark the anniversary of their meeting. Or Ted's election to the Rotary Club. (He had been angling for it long enough.) *Or* maybe a chance of amorous bliss while Mrs H visited her sister in Hunstanton! A vision of mice cavorting in a cat-free pantry came to mind. But it quickly vanished, for as she passed the news-stand on King's Parade her eye was caught by the poster's headline: STARLET ELOPES WITH FILM MAGNATE: WIFE SUES.

She stopped and scanned the words again. Elopement! Was *that* what they were planning, what they were going to celebrate? The word buzzed in her mind, teasing her imagination. Would Ted Higgs really go that far? It was amazing the number of people who did, or so the papers frequently claimed... But Ted? Unlikely: too lazy. Still, she brightened, people did act out of character; and as her friend Elsa was forever saying: you can't judge a book by its jacket. Well, Ted Higgs's jacket was dull enough (a bit like Arthur's really) but who knew what intensities might lie beneath!

By the time she reached home the elopement was a virtual fait accompli; and preparing Charlie's tea she found herself humming Doris Day's *Que Sera, Sera.*

Later that evening when Arthur returned from work she confided her suspicions. 'It's not out of the question you know. Ted's always had an eye for the girls, and now that he's fifty he may want to break out.'

'What do you mean *break out?*'

'Well, you know, break away from *her* and start a new life.'

'I'm fifty too,' replied Arthur stolidly.

'Ah, but you know which side your bread's buttered on, Arthur Penrose.'

'That's as may be; but you've forgotten one thing.'

'Oh yes?'

'Two things really: *she* holds the purse strings – well most of them. In fact I strongly suspect that it's Hester Higgs who actually owns the business; not Ted at all. But either way, they make a nice little income from that bookshop. Quite a lot to give up for the Cecily Joneses of this world.' He started to light his pipe.

His wife brushed aside both smoke and objection. 'Ah, but this may just be the start. Cecily Jones may be the stepping stone to other things.'

'What other things? A higher class of debauchery do you mean?'

'No of course not,' she giggled, 'but it may be his gateway to a freer, a more fulfilling life, something more – more *adventurous.*'

'Can't see it myself,' Arthur scoffed. 'Besides, as I said, there's the other thing.'

'What thing?'

'Apart from the money angle there's Mrs H herself. Being so toffee-nosed you don't think she would let him go just like that, do you? It's always the same with that type, can't bear to lose face. I tell you, she would cling to him if it killed her – cling like a rabid limpet out of sheer cussedness! Sorry old girl, your theory doesn't hold up. The wronged wife: a definite stumbling block; in fact from what I know of Hester Higgs I'd say an insuperable barrier. No, the one solution to old Ted's needs would be to bump her off. That might fix things!' He laughed again and leant over to switch on the six o'clock news. *Disappointed hopes have cast a shadow over ...* came the announcer's voice. With a rueful sigh Mrs Penrose withdrew to the kitchen to prepare supper.

When she went upstairs to check on Charlie's nightlight she was glad to see the boy fast asleep, the grizzled teddy clasped tightly in his arms. She gazed down fondly at her slumbering son, and mused that perhaps when all was said and done some things were more valuable than the freedom for adventure...

Tip-toeing out of the room she noticed the blue exercise book lying open on the chest-of-drawers. She picked it up, and by the light from the landing idly started to scan the pencilled scrawl – of which there seemed an awful lot. He had obviously been busy. Was the story really about a murder? Perhaps he had changed its topic to something more seemly; she hoped so. However, discerning the words *blood, knife* and *slit from ear to ear* she feared that was not the case. Where on earth did the child get those ideas from? Certainly not from herself and Arthur! Perhaps it was Mickie, although he had always seemed rather a nice little boy... She must have a word with his mother. It really wouldn't do!

Curious to decipher more of the scrawl, she took the book and settled herself on the landing chair, where perseverance yielded further revelations. Mrs Penrose's eyes widened as she read: *'I wonder who that can be?' said Miss Jenner. She looked a bit surprised.*

'Anyone can see who it is,' said the big policeman, 'that is Mrs Higgs. You can tell from the hairs and braces.'

'Oh,' Miss Jenner said, 'that lady is always in the way and sometimes she is very rude. She deserves to come a blooming cropper.' The next lines faltered into indistinct runes, but then cleared again. *'Be quiet,' the policeman said, 'I have just seen a footprint by her left ear. Somebody has been here with muddy boots. That footprint is very big. I think it belongs to Mr Higgs.'*

'Well I never,' Miss Jenner said, 'I do think he should have wiped his shoes first.'

At this point the writing became impossible to follow being overlaid with scribble and criss-crosses, and then stopped completely. Presumably the muse was in suspension.

Fascinated, Mrs Penrose flicked back the pages and scrutinized earlier passages, before getting up and carefully replacing the book on the chest-of-drawers. She went downstairs to the living room, and giving Arthur a bright smile silently pursued her knitting while cogitating upon her son and his inventive imagination. She wondered where he had got it from: *not* her maligned brother; and certainly not her husband, that was for sure! Still, it was funny both of them hitting on the same idea of Mrs H's dispatch. Just went to show, there must be some sort of father-son similarity!

The following evening Cambridge had a bit of a jolt. SLAUGHTER IN BOOKSHOP! roared the headlines of the local paper. 'Police throw a cordon round Higgs's Book Emporium. Owner assassinated.'

'Owner assassinated!' mouthed Mrs Penrose to herself. 'Surely not! Oh my God, it can't be true, it really *can't.*' She started to read the item again but was interrupted by the slamming of the front door. 'Arthur!' she yelped. But it wasn't Arthur, it was Charlie home from Cubs and ready for his tea. His mother thrust the evening paper behind the cushion, and zombie-like rose to gut a kipper in the kitchen. 'Do you want chips?' she asked dully.

'You bet,' the boy replied, and started to run up the stairs.

'Where are you going?' she demanded.

'To finish my story.'

'Oh no you're not, my lad. You are going to sit down in the front room and wait quietly until your supper's ready. It won't be long.'

Naturally this was met with a barrage of protest but Mrs Penrose stood her ground. 'Writing stories isn't everything,' she said stoutly, 'there's your auntie's jig-saw puzzle for example. It was a lovely birthday present and you haven't even started it. It's high time.' She took the box from the cupboard and plonked it down in front of him.

'Oh, *mum!...*' the boy began.

'Just *do* it,' his mother said with gritted teeth, and disappeared to scrape the potatoes.

Which was worse, she pondered, Hester Higgs being murdered or Charlie's dreadful prediction? Was her son psychic? Had Ted Higgs gone berserk and, as Arthur had joked, done it because the wife had been the barrier to his illicit desires?

She stared down at the discarded potato peel and darkening water, seeing an image of two people in the cinema sharing an ice-cream. Was that what they had been laughing about and what they had been hoping to celebrate? Not elopement, but *death!...* She tried to recall Charlie's exact words when he had casually reported their conversation. 'If all goes to plan' – yes that's what Ted had said. What plan for God's sake? To do her in, grab the money and live happily ever after? Preposterous... *Exciting!*

In fact Mrs Penrose was so excited that in the act of giving an extra sharp gouge to a potato eye, the knife slipped and she nicked her finger. It bled copiously into the muddied water rendering the liquid a murky vermilion. She thought of the child's story – 'blood everywhere' he had written – and flinched. Poor little mite, how was he to have known! Yes it had obviously been that Mickie putting ideas into his head. The boy had no right! She emptied the water and staunched her finger with a tea towel, mentally preparing her reproaches to Mickie's mother. She had got as far as, 'And what's more, Mrs O'Malley,' when the front door slammed again; and wiping her hands on her pinafore she rushed into the hall to greet her husband.

Unused to such onslaughts, Mr Penrose was startled; even more so when his wife, plucking at his arm, gasped, 'Arthur, have you heard? She's dead – done in! For goodness sake don't tell Charlie!'

Unable to think of a suitable response, her husband said, 'What?'

'Hester Higgs, she's been killed!' breathed his spouse. 'It's all in the evening paper. Haven't you seen?'

'No,' Arthur said, hanging up his hat, 'no I have not. And what's Charlie got to do with it?'

Mrs Penrose propelled her husband into the living room. 'It's his *story* – he's predicted the whole thing. It's all in that exercise book!'

'Clever little bugger,' said Arthur. 'Where's the paper?'

She retrieved it from behind the cushion and thrust it under his nose. There was silence as he scanned the lines. There weren't many. He shrugged. 'Doesn't tell us anything; leastways no more than the essentials. All it says is that the owner has been murdered. No details or any mention of her or Ted, just goes on about the cordon and the police being non-committal.'

'Yes, but bound to be a lot in tomorrow. I mean I suppose it's only just been discovered. Oh my God, Arthur, how could he have done it!'

'Who?'

'Well *Ted* of course! Don't you realize? That's what they must have done, he and the girl ... and like I said, our Charlie has got it all in his book! And as for Ted, well who knows, perhaps he's on the run!' Pictures of fog-ridden fens and a floundering fugitive rose in her mind; and in the far distance, minus typewriter and heels, the luckless Cecily Jones stuck in a windswept bog.

'Hmm. How about a nice cup of tea?' said Arthur.

Over the cup of tea, supper and subsequent cocoa they discussed the matter and speculated about the victim, the perpetrator and whether their son could indeed be clairvoyant (the last being Mrs Penrose's particular concern).

The following morning the sun came out, as did the national newspapers. Mrs Penrose's assumption that more would be revealed proved correct. It transpired that Hester Higgs – despite her bossiness and Arthur's strong suspicion – was not in fact the owner of the bookshop. It was Ted Higgs. And he and his secretary had been found shot on the premises the previous afternoon, early closing day. How were they discovered? A passer-by strolling down the alleyway next to the shop had paused to adjust her hat in the side window. What she confronted was not merely her own reflection, but behind it the body of Cecily Jones sprawled incongruously across her desk. The subsequent police arrival revealed the corpse of her employer strewn on the floor under a fallen book ladder. The till was open and emptied of all contents save a few shillings. A further detail informed readers that the murdered man's wife was away at the time but had been apprised of the situation.

'The kid blundered there,' was Arthur's observation. 'Wrong corpse, wrong number, wrong method. He'll have to do better than that.'

'Is that all you can say?' his wife cried. 'It's simply horrible! Fancy the two of them gunned down like that, who'd have thought it!'

'Well evidently not Charlie.'

'Oh *shut* up about Charlie! Think of poor Ted lying there under that ladder. He had probably been trying to escape... And he was only fifty.' Her face crumpled.

'Think of the girl,' replied Arthur soberly, 'she was only nineteen.'

They stared at each other in confused dismay... And yet even as Mrs Penrose felt the tears welling she also felt something else; something she cared not to acknowledge: disappointment. Appalling though the events were they lacked a certain element: the frisson of scandal. As a motive for murder petty larceny struck her as a trifle humdrum; and Mrs Higgs's detachment from the crime – as either victim or perpetrator – did rather take the edge off things. Naturally such thoughts were far from the front of Mrs Penrose's mind ... but in the nether regions they tiptoed forlornly.

Matters took their course, i.e. the opening of the police enquiry, arrangements for two funerals, and from Hunstanton the reappearance of the grieving widow impressive in black and stoical dignity.

'You have to hand it to her,' Arthur admitted grudgingly, 'she's put a brave face on things. Can't be easy really, what with the shock and then having to cope with selling the business and everything. I mean it's not as if they had any children to give her a hand. Quite an upheaval I suppose.'

'Bound to be,' his wife agreed. 'And then of course she'll have to buy a whole new set of clothes.'

'What clothes?'

'For her cruise of course. You can't go on the *Queen Elizabeth* in any old thing. You have to dress up ... or so I've heard. And she'll need at least two bathing costumes.'

'Hester Higgs is going on a *cruise!'* Arthur wasn't quite sure whether to feel impressed or indignant, and his passing sympathy for Ted's widow waned somewhat.

'Didn't I tell you? Elsa mentioned it a couple of days ago. Said she had bumped into Mrs Higgs coming out of the travel agent's holding a sheaf of brochures. She dropped one and when Elsa picked it up she said, "Oh that's the one I've chosen, the *Queen Elizabeth* sailing round the Pacific. First Class naturally; I deserve a good break." She didn't say any more, just swirled off in that sniffy way. I suppose she imagined she was already on board hob-nobbing with the nobs! Elsa said you could have knocked her down with a feather.'

'The number of times Elsa Tomkins has been felled to the ground by a feather you'd think by now she would be crippled for life,' grunted Arthur.

Thus while Hester Higgs hob-nobbed on the high

seas, the police investigation into her husband's murder took its unproductive course. No arrests were made, no one was reported as assisting police with their enquiries and not a soul came forward. The *Cambridge Courier* declared that the thugs had undoubtedly escaped abroad, and pronounced the enquiry a dead end. Local curiosity revived briefly when, fresh from her cruise, the widow let it be known that she and her sister would be emigrating to Vancouver where she and Ted had spent their honeymoon and where, given the circumstances, she would feel more uplifted. Elsa Tomkins was of the opinion that she had a fancy-man waiting there, a fellow cruiser; but naturally nobody took any notice of that.

Two years later, when the bookshop had been transmuted into a chemist, and Charlie a pupil at the grammar school, the Penroses were gathered in their living room: Arthur doing the inevitable crossword and his wife darning an inevitable sock. Their son, an eager neophyte to football, sat in the corner engrossed in the ritual of waxing his boots and surrounded by newspaper and tins of Dubbin.

'I was in that chemist today,' said Mrs Penrose brightly, 'they've got a new range of scent and soaps, ever so smart. They seem to be doing very well.'

'What chemist?' asked Arthur, grappling with an anagram.

'Ted's place – well what used to be his before she sold it to that pharmacist.'

'I thought you always went to Boots; said you

couldn't bear being reminded of Ted and that girl.'

'Ah but Boots doesn't have Elizabeth Arden.'

'Who's she?'

'Oh of course you *know!* The perfume firm! That lovely Blue Grass soap, it's really so–'

'What's wrong with Lifebuoy?'

'Everything,' was the terse response.

Mr Penrose laid aside the crossword. 'You know,' he mused, 'they never did get to the bottom of that business. You would have thought by now they'd have dug something up. Still, I suppose...'

'Bet I know who did it,' Charlie suddenly said, looking up from the boots.

'Oh yes?' said his father. 'Then who do you think did it, clever clogs? You were only a kid when it happened, still are.'

The boy shrugged. 'I've been thinking.'

'Hmm. You think too much. Take the back door for instance – you *thought* you had locked it after the cat came in last night. But there it was this morning: still on the latch and all ready for us to be burgled.'

'Well we weren't,' Charlie muttered.

'That's not the point, it's–'

'Oh don't keep on, Arthur, the boy means well,' sighed Mrs Penrose. 'Like that Miss Jenner says, there are different sorts of thinking. According to her Charlie has a real gift for exploring ideas, a real gift! And she should know. Now that she's back from that training college in Ipswich she's his English teacher. I suppose being in the bookshop was just a temporary job, sort of filling in before going off to study–'

'Huh! Filling in his head with too many fantasies you mean, and she's obviously still at it.'

Mrs Penrose ignored this, and turning to her son said, 'Now don't mind your father, he's had a busy day and needs his supper. It's always the same: you'll see, once he's sniffed the stew he'll feel much better.'

Charlie nodded. 'Oh yes, just like Percy in his hutch. Give him his rabbit food and he gets all sort of...' he groped for the word, 'uhm, all sort of *mellow.'* He grinned triumphantly.

There was a silence as Arthur absorbed the term. 'Mellow,' he repeated thoughtfully. He couldn't recall ever being described as such and on the whole the novelty rather appealed. 'Mellow,' he murmured again. 'I see ... well that's not a bad word I suppose. Although,' he added, reaching down to cuff his son with the rolled newspaper, 'if you compare your *mellow* parent to that poncey rabbit again I'll tan your blooming hide!'

Silence once more as Charlie resumed his polishing and Arthur, smoothing out the paper, settled to the sports page. Mrs Penrose meditated upon the stew.

A couple of minutes passed. And then Arthur cleared his throat, and discarding the sports page said casually, 'So what's your theory then, Sherlock? Give us the benefit of that *exploratory gift* Miss Jenner seems to thinks so highly of. Come on, let's have it.'

He took out his pipe and Charlie put down the cleaning rag. 'Well,' the boy said earnestly, 'I think it was definitely Mrs Higgs.'

Arthur sighed. 'That's a dead duck. Everyone wondered about that, but she had a cast-iron alibi: on one of her visits to the sister in Hunstanton. The police down there had to break the news to her. Papers full of it; you wouldn't remember.'

'Anyway, Charlie,' his mother objected, 'they said the gun must have had a silencer. How would Hester Higgs know about that sort of thing? I mean it wasn't as if she was a Chicago hoodlum!' She giggled, imagining the stuck-up Hester in mobster mode.

The boy waved his hand impatiently. 'No, no. I don't mean that she did it herself; she got someone else to take them out.'

His parents exchanged doubtful glances. '*Take* them *out?*' echoed Mr Penrose. What sort of expression is that?' He turned to his wife: 'It's that Miss Jenner again. I'm not convinced she's suitable as a teacher, puts ideas and words in their heads.'

'Well,' Mrs Penrose replied mildly, 'isn't that what teachers are for – you know, to be sort of stimulating and…'

'Hmm. Sometimes you can have too much of a good thing,' retorted Arthur darkly, 'there's stimulus and stimulus.'

And having delivered himself of that profundity he was about to return to the newspaper when Charlie exclaimed, 'But there's more. Listen!'

Arthur sighed again. 'If you say so.'

'Like I said, she got someone else to do her dirty work, someone she could trust and who knew about guns.'

'Oh yes? And who would that be exactly, the

Archbishop of Canterbury?'

There was a silence as Charlie eyed each of his parents in turn. Then assured of their attention, he said: 'It was the sister, the one she was staying with. She gave Mrs Higgs a nice hot breakfast of bacon and stuff, borrowed the key to the shop, drove down here with the pistol and silencer, parked the car in a side street, went into the shop just after it had closed, shot them both, grabbed some cash from the till to make it look like robbery, got back in the car and drove home just in time to cook a nice supper.' He beamed, while his parents stared, and as an afterthought he added, 'Most probably she was in disguise – baddies, they're often in that you know.'

Although refraining from comment, what struck Mrs Penrose most about her son's narrative was its emphasis on meals. Perhaps he would become a famous chef. She pictured him resplendent in white strutting the kitchens of the Ritz.

'You've forgotten one thing,' his father said woodenly, 'why should the sister know anything about guns? Ladies don't.'

'She was a widow,' the boy said simply.

Arthur raised his eyes to the ceiling. 'And what's that got to do with it?'

It was Charlie's turn to look impatient. 'It was *you* who told me. You said that the sister's husband had been a gunsmith – just like old Tanner on the Madingly Road – and that Mr Higgs didn't like him and was forever saying that with all those weapons in the shop one day the old codger would shoot himself in the butt.'

'Not the butt, dear: *derrière* is politer,' Mrs

Penrose murmured.

'All right,' replied Charlie dutifully, 'one day he would fire a bullet up his own *derrière.*'

His mother flinched. 'No I don't think that's quite–'

'Be quiet,' snapped Arthur. 'Go on, son.'

Slightly surprised at his father's interest, Charlie faltered but rallied eagerly: 'You see if she lived with the gunsmith all those years I bet she got to know all about revolvers and such; probably got a lot of … uhm, a lot of–' he paused, searching, 'a lot of *expertise*, that's it!'

'Expertise, eh? That's a good word. Where d'you learn it?' Arthur asked.

'It was one of the words in the spelling list Miss Jenner gave us.'

'Silly me, I should have known.'

'Anyway,' the boy rushed on, 'it often happens. The wife gets bored with her dull husband, pals up with her sister or a friend, and together they plot to kill the chap, share out the spoils and make a – uhm – make a bid for freedom!' He paused, and then added helpfully, 'It happens all the time you know; leastways that's what Miss–'

'What Miss Jenner says,' Mrs Penrose completed wistfully.

Arthur fixed his son with a speculative gaze. 'Well you do know a lot don't you, young man,' he observed. Then turning to his wife, he said, 'The kid could just be right. It certainly makes more sense than anything the police have ever come up with. Apparently they still think it was a case of burglary gone wrong. No progress of course!' He gave a scornful snort.

'Well there wouldn't be, would there,' said Mrs Penrose, 'not if they were barking up the wrong tree there wouldn't.'

'Exactly,' said Arthur. 'Whereas it could be that our Charlie has shinned to the top of the right one.'

They regarded their son with respectful eyes, Mr Penrose making a mental note to raise the boy's pocket money.

'But I don't think we should say anything,' his wife said hastily. 'Just think, if the police start coming round wanting to interview him it might set people talking, and we wouldn't want that, would we.'

'Certainly not!' Arthur looked shocked. 'Besides there's no actual proof.'

'No. But it's quite a thought isn't it!'

Arthur agreed that it was indeed quite a thought.

'Mum,' Charlie interrupted, 'can we go to the pictures to-night? Ronald Reagan's on at the Regal in that film where I missed the best bit – you know, the bit where the rustler…'

But Mrs Penrose had not heard him, her mind being elsewhere. Mentally she held in her hand a smart literary magazine whose front page announced: *Prix Goncourt. Charles Penrose, the distinguished Cambridge novelist, triumphs yet again. 'It's just a knack,' the recipient said modestly…*

Arthur too was immersed in reverie: *On being asked how he had cracked the case, Chief Superintendent Charles Penrose replied that it was all a question of sound analysis and steady graft, qualities he had inherited from his father. 'It's facts,' he said, 'facts and common sense. You can keep all your fine theory and fancy notions; what matters is a calm head and shrewd judgement... Oh yes, I owe a lot to my old dad.' The distinguished detective allowed his features to break into a rare smile...*

Elsewhere Miss Jenner was also smiling. What story could she tell the children tomorrow? The headless corpse one with fresh variations? The tale of Al Capone and the one-eyed hit man? Or should she try out the idea of Hester Higgs (altered name, same nature!) slaying her paramour in Vancouver? Yes, the last surely had all manner of possibilities... Her smile widened. It was such *fun* being a teacher, better than cataloguing books any day!

The Problem of Stateroom 10
by Peter Lovesey

The conversation in the first class smoking room had taken a sinister turn.

'I once met a man who knew of a way to commit the perfect murder,' said Jacques Futrelle, the American author. 'He was offering to sell it to me – as a writer of detective stories – for the sum of fifty pounds. I declined. I explained that we story writers deal exclusively in murders that are imperfect. Our readers expect the killer to be caught.'

'Now that you point it out, a perfect murder story would be unsatisfactory,' said one of his drinking companions, W.T. Stead, the campaigning journalist and former editor of the *Pall Mall Gazette*, now white-bearded and past sixty, but still deeply interested in the power of the written word. 'Good copy in a newspaper, however. In the press, you see, we need never come to a conclusion. Our readers cheerfully pay to be held in suspense. They enjoy uncertainty. They may look forward to a solution at some time in the future, but there's no obligation on me to provide one. If it turns up, I'll report it. But I'm perfectly content if a mystery is prolonged indefinitely and they keep buying the paper.'

'The classic example of that would be the Whitechapel murders,' said the third member of the party, a younger man called Finch who had first raised this gruesome subject. His striped blazer and ducks were a little loud for good taste, even at sea.

'Dear old Jack the Ripper?' said Stead. 'I wouldn't want him unmasked. He's sold more papers than the King's funeral and the Coronation combined.'

'Hardly the perfect murderer, however,' commented Futrelle. 'He left clues all over the place. Pieces of flesh, writing on walls, letters to the press. He only escaped through the incompetence of the police. My perfect murderer would be of a different order entirely.'

'Ha! Now we come to it,' said Stead, winking at Finch. 'Professor S.F.X. Van Dusen. The Thinking Machine.'

'Van Dusen isn't a murderer,' Futrelle protested. 'He solves murders.'

'You know who we're talking about?' Stead said for the benefit of the young man. 'Our friend Futrelle has a character in his stories who solves the most intractable mysteries. Perhaps you've read *The Problem of Cell 13?* No? Then you have a treat in store. It's the finest locked room puzzle ever devised. When was it published, Jacques?'

'Seven years ago – 1905 – in one of the Boston papers.'

'And reprinted many times,' added Stead.

'But The Thinking Machine would never commit a murder,' Futrelle insisted. 'He's on the side of law and order. I was on the point of saying just now that if I wanted to devise a perfect murder in fiction, of course – I would have to invent a new character, a fiendishly clever killer who would leave no clues to his identity.'

'Why don't you? It's a stunning idea.'

'I doubt if the public are ready for it.'

'Nonsense. Where's your sense of adventure? We have *Raffles, the Amateur Cracksman,* a burglar as hero. Why not a murderer who gets away with it?'

Futrelle sipped his wine in thoughtful silence.

Then young Finch put in his two-pennyworth. 'I think you should do it. I'd want to read the story, and I'm sure thousands of others would.'

'I can make sure it gets reviewed,' offered Stead.

'You don't seem to understand the difficulty,' said Futrelle. 'I can't pluck a perfect murder story out of thin air.'

'If we all put our minds to it,' said Stead, 'we could think up a plot before we dock at New York. There's a challenge! Are you on, gentlemen?'

Finch agreed at once.

Futrelle was less enthusiastic. 'It's uncommonly generous of you both, but–'

'Something to while away the time, old sport. Let's all meet here before dinner on the last night at sea and compare notes.'

'All right,' said Futrelle, a little fired up at last. 'It's better than staring at seagulls, I suppose. And now I'd better see what my wife is up to.'

Stead confided to Finch as they watched the writer leave, 'This will be good for him. He needs to get back to crime stories. He's only thirty-seven, you know, and toils away, but his writing has gone downhill since that first success. He's churning out light romances, horribly sweet and frothy. Marshmallows, I call them. The latest has the title *My Lady's Garter,* for God's sake. This is the man who wrote so brilliantly about the power of a logical brain.'

'Is he too much under the influence of that wife?'

'The lovely May? I don't think so. She's a writer herself. There are far too many of us about. You're not another author, I hope?'

'No,' said Finch. 'I deal in objets d'art. I do a lot of business in New York.'

'Plenty of travelling, then?'

'More than I care for. I would rather be at home, but my customers are in America, so I cross the ocean several times a year.'

'Is that such a hardship?'

'I get bored.'

'Can't you employ someone to make the trips?'

'My wife – my former business partner – used to make some of the crossings instead of me, but no longer. We parted.'

'I see. An international art-dealer. How wrong I was! With your fascination for the subject of murder, I had you down for a writer of shilling shockers.'

'Sorry. I'm guilty of many things, but nothing in print.'

'Guilty of many things? Now you sound like the perfect murderer we were discussing a moment ago.'

Secretly amused, Finch frowned and said, 'That's a big assumption, sir.'

'Not really. The topic obviously interests you. You raised it first.'

'Did I?'

'I'm certain you did. Do you have a victim in mind?' Stead enquired, elaborating on his wit.

'Don't we all?'

'Then you also have a motive. All you require now are the means and the opportunity. Has it occurred to you – perhaps it has – that an ocean voyage offers exceptional conditions for the perfect murder?'

'Man overboard, you mean? An easy way to dispose of the body, which is always the biggest problem. The thought had not escaped me. But it needs more than that. There's one other element.'

'What's that?'

'The ability to tell lies.'

'How true.' Stead's faint grin betrayed some unease.

'You can't simply push someone overboard and hope for the best.'

'Good. You're rising to the challenge,' said Stead, more to reassure himself than the young man. 'If you can think of something special, dear boy, I'm sure Jacques Futrelle will be more than willing to turn your ideas into fiction. Wouldn't that be a fine reward?'

'A kind of immortality,' said Finch.

'Well, yes. I often ask myself how a man would feel if he committed a murder and got away with it and was unable to tell anyone how clever he'd been. We all want recognition for our achievements. This is the answer. Get a well-known author to translate it into fiction.'

'I'd better make a start, then.'

The young man got up to leave, and Stead gazed after him, intrigued.

Jeremy Finch was confident he'd not given too much away. Stead had been right about all of us wanting recognition. That was why certain murderers repeated their crimes. They felt impelled to go on until they were caught and the world learned what they had done. Finch had no intention of being caught. But he still had that vain streak that wanted the world to know how brilliant he was. The idea of having his crime immortalised through the medium of a short story by a famous author was entirely his own, not Stead's. He'd deliberately approached the two eminent men of letters in the smoking room and steered the conversation around to the topic of murder.

He wanted his murder to be quoted as one of the great pieces of deception. In Futrelle's fine prose it would surely rank with Chesterton's *The Invisible Man* and Doyle's *The Speckled Band* as a masterpiece of ingenuity. Except that in his case, the crime would really have happened.

It was already several weeks in the planning. He had needed to make sure of his victim's movements. This crossing was a God-send, the ideal chance to do the deed. As Stead had pointed out, an ocean voyage affords unequalled opportunities for murder.

He had made a point of studying the routine on C Deck, where the first class staterooms were. His previous transatlantic voyages had been second class, luxurious enough for most tastes on the great liners. His wife Geraldine always travelled first class, arguing that an unaccompanied lady could only travel with total confidence in the best accommodation, her virtue safeguarded. This theory had proved to be totally misfounded. Another dealer, a rival, had taken cruel pleasure in informing Finch after Geraldine's latest trip to New York that he had seen her in another man's arms. The news had devastated him. When faced with it, she admitted everything. Finch shrank from the public humiliation of a divorce, preferring to deal with the infidelity in his own way.

So for the first days of the voyage he observed his prey with all the vigilance of Futrelle's creation, The Thinking Machine, getting to know his movements, which were necessarily circumscribed by the regularity of life aboard ship. He thought of himself as a lion watching the wretched wildebeest he had singled out, infinitely patient, always hidden, biding his time. The man who was picked to die had not the faintest notion that Finch was a husband he had wronged. It wouldn't have crossed his lascivious mind. At the time of the seduction, six months before, he'd thought lightly of his conquest of Geraldine. He had since moved on to other lovers, just as young, pretty, impressionable and easily bedded.

He was due to die by strangulation on the fourth evening at sea.

The place picked for the crime, first class stateroom 10 on C Deck, was occupied by Colonel Mortimer Hatch, travelling alone. By a curious irony it was just across the corridor from the stateroom where Jacques Futrelle was pacing the floor for much of each day trying to devise a perfect murder story.

Mortimer Hatch was forty-one, twice divorced and slightly past his prime, with flecks of silver in his moustache and sideburns. His shipboard routine, meticulously noted by Finch, was well established by the second day. He would rise about eight and swim in the first-class pool before taking breakfast in his room. During the morning, he played squash or promenaded and took a Turkish bath before lunch. Then a short siesta. From about three to six, he played cards with a party of Americans. In the evening, after dinner, he took to the dance floor, and there was no shortage of winsome partners. He was a smooth dancer, light on his feet, dapper in his white tie and tails. Afterwards, he repaired to the bar, usually with a lady for company.

It was in the same first class bar, on the third evening out from Southampton, that Jeremy Finch had a second meeting with Stead and Futrelle. They were sharing a bottle of fine French wine, and Stead invited the young man to join them. 'That is, if you're not too occupied planning your perfect crime.'

'I'm past the planning stage,' Finch informed them.

'I wish I was,' said Futrelle. 'I'm stumped for inspiration. It's not for want of trying. My wife is losing patience with me.'

'Nil desperandum, old friend,' said Stead. 'We agreed to pool our ideas and give you a first-class plot to work on. I have a strong intimation that young Jeremy here is well advanced in his thinking.'

'I'm practically ready,' Finch confirmed.

'Tell us more,' Futrelle said eagerly.

Stead put up a restraining hand. 'Better not. We agreed to save the denouement for the night before we dock at New York. Let's keep to our arrangement, gentlemen.'

'I'll say this much, and it won't offend the contract,' said Finch. 'Do you see the fellow on the far side of the bar, moustache, dark hair, in earnest conversation with the pretty young woman with Titian-red hair and the ostrich feather topknot?'

'Saw him dancing earlier,' said Stead. 'Fancies his chances with the ladies.'

'That's Colonel Hatch.'

'I know him,' Futrelle said. 'He's in the stateroom just across from mine. We share the same steward. And, yes, you could be right about the ladies. There was a certain amount of giggling when I passed the door of number 10 last evening.'

'All I will say,' said Finch, 'is that I am keeping Colonel Hatch under observation. When he leaves the bar, I shall note the time.'

'Being a military man, he probably keeps to set times in most things he does,' said Stead.

'Even when working his charms on the fair sex?' said Futrelle.

'That's the pattern so far,' said Finch, without smiling. 'I predict that he'll move from here about half past eleven.'

'With the lady on his arm?'

'Assuredly.'

The conversation moved on to other matters. 'Are you married?' Futrelle asked Finch.

'Separated, more's the pity.'

'Not all marriages work out. Neither of you may be at fault.'

'Unhappily, in this case one of us was, and it wasn't me,' said Finch.

After an awkward pause, Stead said, 'Another drink, anyone?'

At eleven twenty-eight, almost precisely as Finch had predicted, Colonel Hatch and his companion rose from their table and left the bar.

'I'm glad we didn't take a bet on it,' said Stead.

'I think I'll turn in,' said Futrelle. 'My wife will be wondering where I am.'

'Good idea,' said Finch. 'I'll do the same. I need to be sharp as a razor tomorrow.'

Stead gave him a long look.

The next day, the fourth at sea, Colonel Hatch rose as usual at eight, blissfully unaware that it was to be his last day alive. He went for his swim, and the morning followed its invariable routine. Perkins, the steward for staterooms 10 to 14, brought him breakfast.

'Comfortable night, sir?'

'More than comfortable,' said the colonel, who had spent much of it in the arms of the redheaded heiress in stateroom 27. 'I almost overslept.'

'Easy to do, sir,' Perkins agreed, for he, too, had enjoyed an amorous night in one of the cabins on D deck. At the end of an evening of fine wine and fine food there are sometimes ladies ready for an adventure with a good-looking steward. 'Shall you be attending the service this morning, or will you promenade?'

'The service? By jove, is it Sunday already?'

'Yes, sir.'

'I've done more than my share of church parades. I shall promenade.'

'Very good, sir.'

The colonel felt better after his Turkish bath. For luncheon, he had the fillets of brill, followed by the grilled mutton chops and the apple meringue. He then retired for an hour. Perkins had thoughtfully folded back the counterpane.

The latter part of the afternoon was devoted to cards, afternoon tea and conversation. He returned to his staterooms at six to dress for dinner. His starched white shirt was arranged ready on the bed.

At ten to seven, the colonel went to dinner. The seven-course meal was the social highlight of the day. The first-class dining room seated five hundred and fifty, and there were numerous young women travelling alone, or with their parents. He was confident of another conquest.

Meanwhile, Jeremy Finch did not appear at dinner. His murder plan had reached a critical point. He was lurking behind a bulkhead in the area of the first class staterooms, aware that whilst the passengers were at dinner, the doors had to be unlocked for the stewards to tidy up and make everything ready for the night.

Finch waited for Perkins to open Colonel Hatch's staterooms. Methodical in everything, he knew what to expect. As each room was attended to, the steward left the door ajar, propped open with the bin used to collect all the rubbish.

Finch entered the cabin and stepped into the bathroom whilst Perkins was tidying the bed.

On Sunday evenings, there was no dancing after dinner. Colonel Hatch didn't let this cramp his style. He was as smooth at conversation as he was on the dance floor. He sparkled. But for once he experienced difficulty in persuading a lady to adjourn with him to the bar for champagne. The little blonde he'd targeted said the stuff gave her terrible headaches, and anyway Papa insisted she retired to her cabin by ten o'clock, and personally made sure she was there. The colonel offered to knock on her door at half-past and share a bottle of claret with her, but the offer was turned down. At half-past, she told him, she would be saying her prayers, and she always said extra on Sundays.

Hatch decided this was not to be his night. He returned to his own stateroom.

At eleven-forty that Sunday evening, Able Seaman Frederick Fleet, the lookout on the crow's nest, sounded three strokes on the bell, the signal that an object was dead ahead of the ship. It was too late. Nothing could prevent the *Titanic* from striking the iceberg in its path and having its underbelly torn open.

On C deck, high above the point of impact, there was a slight jarring sensation. Below, in steerage, it was obvious something dreadful had happened. At some time after midnight, the first lifeboats were uncovered and lowered. The confusion of the next two hours, the heart-rending scenes at the lifeboats, are well documented elsewhere. The women and children were given priority. It is on record that May Futrelle, the wife of the writer, had to be forced into one of the boats after refusing to be parted from her husband. Futrelle was heard to tell her, 'It's your last chance: go!' It was then one-twenty in the morning.

Futrelle would go down with the ship, one of about fifteen hundred victims of the sinking. The precise figure was never known. W.T. Stead also perished.

Between one and two in the morning there were pockets of calm. Many expected to be rescued by other vessels that must have picked up the distress signals. In the first-class lounge, the eight musicians played ragtime numbers to keep up the spirits. Some passengers got up a game of cards. Well-bred Englishman don't panic.

Stead, Futrelle and Finch sat together with a bottle of wine.

'Whether we get out of this, or not,' said Stead, 'I fear it's our last evening together. If you remember, we had an agreement.'

'Did we?' said Futrelle, still distracted.

'The murder plot.'

'That?'

'It would do no harm to put our minds to it, as we promised we would.'

'I thought of nothing worth putting on paper,' said Futrelle, as if that was the end of it.

and nobody saw. You left, unseen. I raise my glass to you. Perfect revenge. A near perfect murder.'

'Why do you say "near perfect"?'

'Because we rumbled you, old man. A perfect murder goes undetected. And isn't it ironical that you chose tonight of all nights?'

'You mean it may not have been necessary?'

'We shall see.'

'Is this true?' Futrelle demanded of Finch. 'Did you really murder the Colonel?'

Finch smiled and spread his hands like a conjurer. 'Judge for yourselves. Look who's just got up to dance.'

They stared across the room. In the open space in front of the band, a couple were doing a cakewalk: Colonel Mortimer Hatch, reunited with his flame-haired partner of the previous night. Some of the women had refused to leave the ship, preferring to take their chances with the men.

Stead, piqued, gave a sharp tug at his beard and said, 'I'll be jiggered!'

'Caught us, well and truly,' said Futrelle.

Finch chuckled and poured himself more wine.

'What an anticlimax,' said Stead.

'On the contrary,' said Finch. 'Do you want to hear my version? I might as well tell it now, and if either of you survives you must put it into writing because it was an undetected murder. I killed a man tonight in the Colonel's staterooms, just as you said. Strangled him and pushed his body out of the porthole. Nobody found out. Nobody would have found out.'

'Who the devil was he?'

'The degenerate who seduced my wife. They're

notorious, these stewards.'

'A steward?'

'Perkins?' said Futrelle.

'They're in a position of trust, and they abuse it. Well, Perkins did, at any rate, aboard the *Mauretania,* and I suffered the humiliation of being told about it by an acquaintance. So I took it as a point of honour to take my revenge. I made it my business to learn where he'd signed on. Discovered he'd been hired as a first-class steward for the maiden voyage of the *Titanic.*'

The two older men were stunned into silence.

Eventually, Stead said, 'You've certainly surprised me. But was it perfect, this murder? Would you have got away with it? Surely, his absence would have been noted, not least by the passengers he attended.'

'The method was foolproof. Of course there would be concern. The Chief Steward would be informed he was missing. It might even reach the Captain's ears. But the possibility of murder wouldn't cross their minds. Even if it did, can you imagine White Star conducting a murder inquiry in the first class accommodation on the maiden voyage of the *Titanic?* Never. They would cover it up. The passengers Perkins attended would be told he was unwell. And after we docked at New York it would be too late to investigate.'

'He's right,' said Futrelle. 'He was always going to get away with it.'

'What do you think?' asked Finch, leaning forward in anticipation. 'Worthy of The Thinking Machine?'

'More a matter of low cunning than the power of

logic, in my opinion,' said Stead, 'but it might make an interesting story. What say you, Jacques?'

But Futrelle was listening to something else. 'What are they playing? Isn't that "Nearer, My God, to Thee"?'

'If it is,' said Stead, 'I doubt if your story will ever be told, Mr Finch.'

At two-eighteen, the lights dimmed and went out. In two minutes the ship was gone.

Closure
by Michelle Spring

'Open up!' Stuart shouted, striking his palm against the thick glass doors. He knew – he'd checked his watch – that the meeting was due to begin in precisely two minutes. Where the devil were they all?

He rapped until his knuckles smarted, until he was rewarded by a flare of fluorescent light from deep inside the bookshop. Ha! He'd roused them at last, the dozy buggers.

Stuart shivered with impatience as he caught sight of Alex, the manager, lumbering towards him, like a man trying to hurry but not quite able to remember how it was done. The effect of despondency, Stuart supposed. Alex had devoted three decades to building Heald's up, making it into the best bookshop in the city, and now it was threatened with closure. Only last week, Alex had been seen poring over the plans of the building, as if trying to commit them to memory. How on earth would he cope when these doors slammed shut for the final time?

At last the glass panels parted, allowing Stuart a welcome gust of warmth. He'd found it necessary, since the temperature had tottered downwards, to wear an extra cardigan even in front of his own little gas fire at home. The infamous Cambridge draughts – straight off the Urals, as

Evelyn used to say – never failed to ferret out his sore shoulder. At Heald's, though, it was toasty warm. When the Conundrums book group was forced to disband, which would he miss the most: the vigorous discussions of crime fiction or the leather armchairs and the generous warmth?

'Welcome,' Alex said.

'Took you long enough,' Stuart muttered, as Alex locked the door behind them. 'I hope you've put together a bigger crowd than last week.'

It was a statement, not a question, and intended merely to provoke, but Alex refused to rise to the bait. 'At the moment, we're four,' he said. 'Paige and Jerome, and you and me.'

'So that builder – what's his name, Joe? – has deserted us for good? I never really thought he was serious. And that planning chappie – he's not coming? And that American woman?' She might not have been the brightest bloom in the bed – hadn't even known that Dorothy L. Sayers wrote poetry – but her blueberry muffins had been something to look forward to.

'Fraid so.'

'Humph,' Stuart grunted.

They arrived at their destination, a snug square-shaped reading room tucked neatly away at the back of the upper gallery, near as could be to Alex's office. Stuart continued doggedly in the direction of his chosen chair, the one he always occupied, and then stopped short. It wasn't there, his leather armchair. None of them were. Only a pile of stacking chairs, the kind of plastic tat that Stuart most despised. 'Where–?' he started to enquire, and then let the question die.

Why ask? It was obvious. They'd been already shifted to another branch of Heald's, most likely, or even sent to auction.

Alex wafted a hand towards the two people who were already seated. 'Here's our Stuart,' he boomed.

Stuart glared at the other Conundrums. Jerome sat as straight as a guardsman in his meagre chair, crossed one long thin leg delicately over the other and gave Stuart a cautious salute. His was the only participant whose surname Stuart knew, since *J. E. Pryce* was monogrammed in a pretentious script on his briefcase. Stuart noticed with small satisfaction that, in spite of Jerome's attempts to look the dandy, there was an incongruous splash of paint or was it blood? – on the back of his hand.

Paige was more demonstrative. She'd been bent over a copy of *Gone Girl,* the intended focus of today's discussion, as if swotting for an exam, but her face brightened when Stuart entered.

'Stuart!' she exclaimed. 'Oh, I was – we were, weren't we Jerome? – so worried that you might not come. People have been falling like flies. Our little club has been decimated.' She swept her jacket off a chair and gestured for him to sit.

'Decimated?' Stuart put on his reading glasses and peered at her over the top. 'Have you the slightest idea, my dear, of the actual meaning of the word?' He saw her smile crumple, and bit back further comment. Evelyn had always complained that he was hardest on women. Picking up on inconsequential errors, was her verdict, and failing to acknowledge good intentions. As far as Stuart could recall, it had been the only thing that had ever made her truly cross.

'Never mind,' he added, by way of apology, and lowered himself into the seat next to Paige.

Alex rubbed his hands together in a vague let's-get-going way, indicating that the quiz was about to begin. Meetings always started with a quiz – at the end of each year, the overall winner was presented with a prize. This year, a first edition Lee Child would go to the *Supersleuth* who chalked up the most wins. Though Harry had been neck-and-neck with Stuart through most of the tournament, Stuart was determined to add to his trophy chest before the Conundrums finally called it a day.

'We'll have to wait for Harry,' Stuart said.

Alex lowered the question sheets and stared at Stuart. The expression on his face gave the game away.

'What, no Harry? He's not coming either?'

Alex shook his head. 'No, I think he's – left us.' Alex and Jerome exchanged quick, furtive glances.

Stuart felt as if he'd been winded. He closed his eyes to conceal his panic, as images of people who'd recently fallen out of his life rumbled past like a funeral procession. Evelyn, above all. But also Roy, who'd abandoned their weekly U3A trek because of emphysema. And Chris Cameron, a long-time neighbour, who had sold up to some brash Londoners and faded away into an old people's home. Everyone whom Stuart had been accustomed to talk to and spar with and measure himself against seemed to be dropping away. And now it was Harry, too.

Stuart was surprised at how hard it hit him. It

wasn't as if he and Harry were *friends*. Harry was too ungracious, too reluctant to give credit when Stuart prevailed. But Harry was the only one in the Conundrums who could give Stuart a brisk run for his money, and a spirited contest was, Stuart realised, one of the few things that could take his mind off Evelyn's death. Without Harry and their mystery skirmish, life would be even more dreary.

'Harry's gone for good?' Stuart asked. A strange empty feeling replaced his appetite for competition. His chance of a decisive win, a satisfying win, was gone. He volunteered, and the others quickly agreed, that with so few competitors, there was no point in staging a contest.

Paige tried to fill the gap by initiating the discussion of *Gone Girl*. What strikes me,' she said, 'is how different it is from her debut novel. I mean, *Sharp Objects* turns on a twist, and so does this, but–'

Stuart couldn't concentrate on what the woman was saying. For the first time, he found their surroundings disagreeable. Everything was different. Less cosy. Less reassuring. The carpet tiles were mottled now with dust, and the bookcase shelves were at most half-full. Great gaps had opened up even in the Scandi section, which had until recently been threatening to burst its bounds. Stuart found the voids decidedly unsettling.

Craning his neck, Stuart could see that even Alex's office-cum-hideaway at the back of the shop (where after book launches, Alex squirrelled away leftover bottles of wine) looked different. Someone had tacked a KEEP OUT sign to the door. Did this mean that even their occasional tipples were forever at an end?

And as for the absentees ... the electrician Tom, the translator Edith, Rahid the city planner and all the others... Well, Stuart thought: they were like rats.

Rats deserting a sinking ship.

'I beg your pardon?'

He must have said that thing about rats aloud, because Paige stopped droning on about Gillian Flynn (whose first name she persistently mispronounced) and looked at him in alarm.

Alex bristled with indignation. 'Stuart, you've got entirely the wrong end of the stick. We're not a sinking ship. Not at all.' He glanced at Paige and Jerome, who nodded nervously in support. 'Yes, all right, Stu, I grant you that our protests haven't been successful. How could we possibly find the resources to fight a supermarket chain? If the final appeal is turned down – yes, all right, *when* the final appeal is turned down – Heald's of Cambridge will face closure, but–'

Stuart cut in. 'Permanent closure,' he boomed. He simply couldn't take any more of this Pollyanna nonsense. 'Why can't you face facts?' Stuart demanded. 'Things are at an end here. That's been clear since last July.'

It was July when the Conundrums heard the alarming news: the Heald family had put their Cambridge branch up for sale, and within a whisker, Toczick, the supermarket chain, had announced its intention to open a supermarket on the site. The Conundrums had been shocked into action. They'd set aside their discussion, and planned a campaign of resistance instead. They launched a protest in front of the Guildhall. They placed articles in the local papers denouncing Toczick as a predatory company. They mounted a public petition. Support was widespread. It was not just the members of the reading group who would suffer if their oldest and most cherished bookshop were to close. It was the dons who browsed books in their specialist field, the students who stocked up on textbooks at the beginning of term, the townsfolk who strolled in for a discounted newspaper and a thumb-through the newly-published fiction. There could be no dispute: a supermarket that sold a few best-selling paperbacks could not possibly substitute for a properly stocked and expertly-staffed bookshop.

The campaign had been to no avail.

'Face facts,' Stuart concluded. 'The jig's up. And we can't even console ourselves with caffeine.' Stuart thought he could detect a lingering whiff of coffee, but the machine that had dispensed quite a decent Colombian brew was nowhere to be seen. 'Sold that, too, have they?' He didn't even try to disguise the acid drop of bitterness in his voice.

Again, it was Paige who broke the uncomfortable silence. Leaning towards him, she spoke soothingly, in the kind of tone his bereavement counsellor had used before he'd sent her packing. 'Tell me, Stuart, how are you feeling now?'

Damn the woman! What business was it of hers? Though Stuart didn't doubt that the other Conundrums followed the more sensational stories in the local news, and soaked up every sordid detail, they had, after a few mumbled *sorry-to-hears,* studiously avoided the subject of Evelyn's demise. Paige displayed no such sensitivity. Only a month ago, she'd asked him, straight out, whether he'd been satisfied with the findings of the inquest.

'Satisfied!' he had spluttered. 'Are you serious? Burglars battered their way into my home while I was asleep. The next thing I knew, my wife lay dead at the bottom of the stairs with a broken neck. *An accident,* they said.'

Stu had paused. In the months since Evelyn's death, he had learned to say these words – 'broken neck' – in a dispassionate way, as if they described a neutral event. But the words still conjured up an image that pierced him to the bone.

'Oh, Stuart–' Paige had looked and sounded as if it might be she who would collapse in tears. She had reached out a hand in his direction.

He had dodged her touch and carried on. 'Evelyn and I lived in that house for over thirty years. She was not a careless woman, nor a clumsy one. So when the police and the coroner say that the burglars had nothing to do with her death, that there is no sign she was pushed ... when they refuse to seek justice for Evie, refuse to challenge those little thugs–'

Stuart had seemed then to balloon with rage. He had risen ponderously to his feet and had loomed over Paige, his face livid. 'Satisfied, Paige? Never! My wife was murdered, that's my view, and no penny-ante inquest will make me feel differently.'

After that outburst, the anger had suddenly drained out of Stuart. He had seemed to deflate. The men had formed a kind of honour guard to guide him back to his chair. They knew better than to touch him. Paige and the American woman had remained seated, but there was no mistaking the look on their faces. They'd been appalled.

This time round, Stuart didn't lose it. He merely barked at Paige: 'I'm feeling fine.' There followed a few half-hearted attempts at discussion: Jerome ventured the opinion that *Gone Girl* was *'brilliantly constructed'* – except for the final few pages when its clever-cleverness became contrived; Alex spoke with passion about the skilful way the characters developed as the narrative went on; Paige praised the distinctiveness of the principal voices.

Stuart didn't join in. He closed his eyes but he couldn't escape from a vision of rough hands that seized Evelyn's shoulders, that pushed and shoved, until she toppled headfirst over the railing on the landing. He put his hands over his ears to try and drown out the crunch of her skull on the floor. Gritted his teeth in an attempt to subdue the guilt, the unbearable guilt, of his failure to save her.

'Don't you hear it?' Stuart asked.

'Hear what?' Alex said.

'The sound of drilling. Those bloody Toczick people must have started work already.' The others shook their heads.

In the fortnight that followed, Stuart tried to put Evelyn out of his mind but she'd pop back in whenever his guard was down. Especially when he was asleep.

The nightmares multiplied. Sometimes he

heard her slip out of bed, heard a scuffle on the landing – even heard her call his name – but he never reached her before she fell. Other times, jolted out of sleep, he awoke convinced that he was clutching Evelyn's hand as she dangled over the banister; that he snatched at her as she toppled, but his dodgy shoulder gave way, his arthritic fingers snapped open, and she fell.

The worst came one cold morning when, disturbed by the sound of the dustcart, Stuart rolled towards the middle of the bed and was shocked into wakefulness. There, just inches away, was his wife. The mound of Evelyn's soft body swelled the duvet; her head was buried as always in a nest of pillows.

Evelyn! Alive!

A thrill raced like lightning through Stuart's aged body as he realised Evelyn's death had merely been a vicious dream. The burglars, the fall, the inquest: he had imagined it all.

Caribbean sunshine flooded the bedroom and Stuart felt he might explode with relief. He wanted to shout out Evelyn's name, to hold her close, to tell her how much she was loved. But he refrained from disturbing her sleep.

Instead, he edged a hand towards her and stroked the air above her body, tracing her beloved shape. He thought he heard her breathing, and his heart filled to the brim with joy.

Stuart raised himself on one elbow and edged a little closer, aiming to plant a stealthy kiss on Evelyn's cheek. But as he leaned forward, the duvet changed shape. He slid his palm along the bed where she lay, and felt the cover flatten beneath his hand. In horror, he wrenched the pillow away. Nothing underneath except another pillow.

No Evelyn.

In some ways it was a bigger shock than the death itself. The sense of a second chance had lifted Stuart; the collapse into loss that followed was all the more intense.

For a very long time, Stuart didn't get dressed. He spent days slumped in an armchair, with a blanket clutched around his shoulders. There was little food in the house, but after the first 24 hours, he found he didn't care. There were no books he wanted to read, no decent programmes on the telly, but he didn't care about that either. The next meeting of the Conundrums came and went and Stuart scarcely even noticed.

But Stuart did at last rouse himself. Some stubborn instinct told him it was do or die, and wretched as he felt, he wasn't ready yet to snuff it. What he needed, he decided, was to be with other people.

He rang an old school chum whom he hadn't seen for ages, but Mark was out, and though Stuart left a message, Mark never rang back.

Stuart contacted Evelyn's sister; their stilted conversation only served to remind him how little she and he had had in common.

He thought of the other members of the Conundrums. Once, when Stu's hip was playing up, Rahid had offered him a lift. Another time, he'd had an interesting exchange with Ozzie about Chandler. Perhaps the three of them could meet up for a drink? But Stu had no idea how to contact the two men. Any of the Conundrums, for that matter. It had never crossed his mind that he might want to be in touch.

Finally, on the following Tuesday, Stuart swigged a tot of brandy for courage and set forth. Moved by desperation more than hope, he limped along Trinity Street towards Heald's.

As he'd expected, the shop was locked, but the glow from a light in the upper gallery gave him hope. From the pocket of his corduroy jacket, Stuart pulled a torch and gave several sharp taps on the glass doors. Within seconds, a young woman appeared on the other side of the partition. Her expression was sceptical. 'Yes?' she mouthed, silver earrings swinging as she spoke. 'The shop is closed,' she shouted, loud enough this time for him to pick up a Polish accent. 'No one here.'

So, no reading group. As he'd feared, it had dwindled to nothing. But perhaps...

'May I come in? Just for a moment? I think I left something behind. Up there,' he pointed, 'in the gallery.' The girl frowned. 'Please?' he said.

She held up a finger and dredged in her pocket for a phone. Dialled a number. Had a brief exchange, put her phone away again, and opened the door. 'You will be quick,' she said. 'I have a lot of work to do.' She gestured in the direction of a hoover that was parked at the foot of the stairs.

Stuart made his way as swiftly as he could (which wasn't very swift; he felt a twinge of regret for his impatience with Alex) up the stairs and along the narrow passageway to the farthermost corner of the gallery. The reading room looked even more bereft. All the books had disappeared from the shelves, and even the ghastly plastic chairs were gone. One thing stood out: a small crate with a pile of books on top, and on top of the books, a sticky note that bore the words: *STUART. TONIGHT.*

The Polish girl stood with a duster in hand, looking at him curiously.

'Do you know who put these here?' he asked.

She shrugged. 'They've been there for days. Since last Tuesday, I think. When the book group met for the last time.' She shook the fringe off her forehead and peered at him. 'I'm Lenka,' she said, 'the cleaner. Are you Stuart?'

Stuart nodded. He had no idea what to do now. 'Do you mind if I stay here for a few minutes?' he asked. 'Have a quick look at these books?'

She scanned the alcove as if to confirm that there was nothing for an old man to steal, and then nodded. 'When you want out, follow the noise of the hoover,' she said, and left Stuart alone.

STUART. TONIGHT.

Stuart didn't know what 'tonight' meant. Did *tonight* refer to last Tuesday, when, if the cleaner was correct, the message might have been left? But why on earth would a Conundrum leave a message for Stuart *tonight* when he clearly wasn't present? It didn't make sense.

The only alternative was that the writer had been thinking ahead to this very evening: to *tonight*.

Gingerly, using one of the bookshelves as a prop, Stuart lowered himself onto the carpet. He lifted the books, one by one, and spread them out in front of him.

Ha! First to hand was a copy of the award-winning novel, *Don't Look Back*. Not *a* copy, he realised, when he flicked to the title page. This was *his* copy, the one he'd lent to Paige some weeks ago. *'For Stuart Savage'* was scrawled on the title page in the author's extravagant handwriting.

But what of the other books? There was *a vintage* James Bond *(For Your Eyes Only);* a lesser-known Ruth Rendell *(The Water's Lovely);* and *Meet Me at the Morgue,* a classic Ross Macdonald. There were oldies but goodies: Louis Trimble's *You Can't Kill a Corpse;* Jeremy Ane's *Kill Him Tonight* and even the 1919 oddity, *The Further Side of the Door,* which the jacket attributed, quaintly, to a Mrs. Marjorie Douie. Stuart hadn't come across that one in a good forty years.

More recent works – though whether or not some were crime novels could be debated – included Lionel Shriver's *We Need to Talk about Kevin,* Gerald Seymour's *The Waiting Time,* and Emma Donoghue's *Room.* There was *Hidden,* by someone called Derick Parsons, whom even Stuart had never heard of. A most eclectic mixture, to say the least. So why had they been piled up here, and why had Stuart's name been stuck to the top of the stack?

Could the books constitute some sort of message intended for him? A farewell message? One last puzzle, perhaps? Stuart smiled in spite of himself.

Well, he might be lonely, and he might be down. But he certainly wasn't out. If there was a message here, he was the man to winkle it out.

Shifting his position, Stuart arranged the books alphabetically, by author. The fact that the initial letters of Ane and Donoghue and Douie produced the word *ADD* gave him hope. But he got no joy from the others.

He arranged the books by date of publication, which was far from straightforward given that some titles – such as *For Your Eyes Only* – had been re-published dozens of times. He tried every variation he could think of, but no message jumped out.

So absorbed had Stuart become in the puzzle, that he was startled when the cleaner reappeared. She had abandoned the duster in favour of a bottle of bleach. 'So,' she said. 'You're still here? You're reading?'

Stuart managed with difficulty to raise himself from the floor.

'No, not reading. Not really,' he said, brushing dust from the knees of his trousers. 'I'm trying to work out if there's a meaning of any kind behind this stack of books.'

Lenka looked bemused.

'You know,' Stuart said. 'A secret message. A message for me.'

'Oh.' The girl came closer and looked down at the books arrayed along the floor of the alcove. 'Maybe in the titles?' She balanced on one leg, and began to shift novels around with the toe of her other sneaker. 'There's lots of instructions in these names,' she said. 'But I don't see how *You Can't Kill a Corpse* could be part of a message, no?'

'Agreed,' said Stuart, easing his back against the bookcase. 'And *We Need to Talk about Kevin* or *Meet Me at the Morgue* are equally unhelpful.'

'Kill Him Tonight?' Lenka asked.

'I hope not,' Stuart said, and they both laughed. Lenka turned as if to leave.

'Would you mind,' Stuart said, reddening just a little. 'Would you mind staying a little longer? It helps to toss ideas off somebody else.'

'OK,' she said, 'But first things first.' She padded off down the corridor in search of a glass of water.

First things first. Such a simple phrase... Stuart scanned the books again, picking out the first word in each title. *Room. Don't. We. The. The* again – three times in all. *For. Tonight. Hidden. You. Meet.*

Hmmm. This seemed more promising. *We. Don't. Meet...* Ha! Was it, as he'd thought at first, a farewell statement? No, that wouldn't work. *For* didn't fit. Or *You.* Or those blasted *Thes.*

Hang on, Stuart thought. When it comes to ordering items – entries in an index, say – wasn't the definite article at the beginning often dropped? Four Horsemen of the Apocalypse, not The Four Horsemen? Black Dahlia, not The Black Dahlia? and so forth? Removing the definite articles would mean that the first word of *The Waiting Time* would be *Waiting.* And so on.

Stuart put a hand on the bookcase to balance himself, and used his right foot to shift the books around one last time. *We. Meet. Waiting. For. You. Hidden. Room.* And if he broke the rule in one instance, and chose the third word from *Kill Him Tonight...*

'You've done it,' Lenka said, peering over his shoulder. 'There's your message, yes? *We meet tonight. Waiting for you. Hidden room.* Your friends want you to find them.'

Friends? Stuart thought. It was a new idea. 'But what about *Further?* And *Water's?*' he muttered. 'And where exactly is this hidden room?' He took the plastic bottle that Lenka held out to him, and drank deeply. He hadn't realised how thirsty he was. 'I'm most grateful,' he said.

Suddenly he got it. The answer was as clear as a newly-scrubbed window.

'The Further Side of the Door,' he exclaimed. 'The hidden room is on the further side of Alex's door. His hideaway.'

Could it be true? Stuart tore along the passageway as fast as his knee would allow. He headed straight towards the Keep Out sign. The door was boarded up, but as he got closer, he could see that the boards were a decoy. They criss-crossed the door itself, but didn't overlap the frame.

Uncertain now, anxious that he might be wrong – might be trying to pull hope out of an empty sack – he hesitated.

He turned for a final look at Lenka.

She held up the Fossum book so he could see the cover. *'Don't Look Back,'* she whispered.

Stuart put his good shoulder to the unhinged side of the door and rammed with all his might.

The Conundrums celebrated that night with three bottles of good red wine, left over from a launch the month before. Even Joe took a break from his work to raise a glass. He was busy replacing the Keep Out door with a wall of bricks; after Stuart's arrival, no one would enter this room from the former Heald's ever again. The only access would be via a small insignificant opening from the adjoining alley.

The room was smaller than their alcove had been, but every bit as inviting. The walls were dense with books – not only detective fiction, but novels of espionage and intrigue, caper novels and noir fiction, historical mysteries and thrillers. It would be many a year before the group ran short of reading material. There was their treasured coffee machine and a biscuit tin. Thanks to the American woman (whose name turned out to be Sara Jane) there was a platter of blueberry muffins. Best of all, there was a circle of leather armchairs, and enveloping warmth from an electric heater. Stuart helped himself to a muffin, settled into his favourite chair, and sighed with something suspiciously like pleasure.

In the moment when Stuart had burst through from the shop, he'd encountered total darkness. Then suddenly the lights flashed on to reveal a crowd of Conundrums: not only Joe the builder, and Rahid from the planning department, not only Jerome and Paige and Alex, but also Ozzie the architect and Rina and Tom and Howard. All the other members of the group. Stuart blinked in amazement. Paige was the first to speak. She waved a copy of a Ruth Rendell novel, and pointed to the title. 'Come on in, Stuart,' she said. *'The Water's Lovely'*. She planted a kiss on Stuart's cheek, and in his astonishment, he didn't even flinch.

They all let out a massive cheer: 'Hurrah! We thought you'd never get here.'

Stuart gazed in astonishment at the books, the

chairs, the carpets. 'All this! How–?'

'It was Ozzie's idea,' Alex explained. 'Trust an architect! When it became clear that we were going to be ousted, he suggested we commandeer a small area at the rear of the shop for ourselves.'

'But surely there are building plans,' Stuart objected. 'Drawings. Well be found out.'

'Not when we have the city planning department on our side.' According to Ozzie, lodging modified plans of the building with the appropriate authorities had proved surprisingly easy. 'This part of the building has a small entrance into the alley,' he said, 'and the supermarket is left with the much larger loading bay. Toczick's will never even notice.'

Then came the really awkward question. 'But why did you keep me in the dark?' Most of the group had the grace to look a little sheepish at that.

'You see, Stuart,' Paige began, but Harry interrupted.

'It's like this, Stuart. We all knew – couldn't help but know – how brutally unhappy you've been. We doubted that you could apply yourself to a project like this. But now that it's done...' Harry stepped forward, and with a flourish, handed Stuart a hardback book. 'Check out the title page,' he said.

For Stuart Savage, Supersleuth,
Winner of the Conundrum Award 2014.
With best wishes, Lee Child.

Stuart closed his eyes so his friends couldn't see

the tears that were welling. And for the final time, he stood at the bottom of the stairs. He saw Evelyn catch her slipper on the edge of their new rug, and tumble over the banister, and he saw himself reach out, strong and sure, and catch her in his arms.

Waiting for Mr Right
by Andrew Taylor

I live in a city of the dead surrounded by a city of the living. The great cemetery of Kensal Vale is a privately-owned metropolis of grass and stone, of trees and rusting iron. At night, the security men scour away the drug addicts and the drunks; they expel the lost, the lonely and the lovers; and at last they leave us with the dark dead in our urban Eden.

Eden? Oh yes – because the dead are truly innocent. They no longer know the meaning of sin. They can never lose their illusions.

Other forms of life remain overnight – cats, for example, a fox or two, grey squirrels, even a badger and a host of lesser mammals, as well as some of our feathered friends. At regular intervals, those splendid security men patrol the paths and shine their torches in dark places, keeping the cemetery safe for its rightful inhabitants. Finally, one should not forget to include, perhaps in a special sub-human category of their own somewhere between life and death, Dave and the woman Tracy.

In a place like this, there is little to do in the long summer evenings once one's basic animal appetites have been satisfied. Fortunately I am not without inner resources. I am never bored. In my own small way I am a seeker after truth. Perhaps it was my diet, with its high protein content, which helped give me such an appetite for learning. In my youth, I taught myself to read. Not for me the sunlit semi-detached pleasures of Janet and John. My primers were the fruity orotundities of funereal inscriptions, blurred and sooty from decades of pollution. Once I had mastered my letters, though, I did not find it hard to find more varied reading material.

We live, I am glad to say, in a throwaway society.

It is quite extraordinary what people discard in this place, either by accident or design. The young prefer to roam through the older parts of the cemetery, the elderly are drawn to the newer. Wherever they go, whatever their age, visitors leave their possessions behind. Litter bins have provided me with a range of periodicals from the *Spectator* to the *Socialist Worker*. The solar-powered tablet computer on which I am typing this modest memoir was carelessly left behind among the debris of an adulterous picnic on top of Amelia Osbaston (died 1863).

I have also been fortunate enough to stumble upon a number of works of literature, including *Jane Eyre* and *Men Are From Mars, Women Are From Venus*. Charlotte Brontë is, without doubt, my favourite author. How could she peer so penetratingly into the hidden chambers of the heart? Jane Eyre and I might be twin souls.

On one occasion, after an unexpected shower, I came across a damp but handsomely illustrated copy of *Grave Conditions*, a scholarly survey of Victorian funerary practices. This enabled me to identify the Bateson's Belfry of Kensal Vale.

Perhaps the term is as unfamiliar to you as it

was to me. Bateson's Belfry was a Victorian invention designed to profit from the widespread human fear of being interred alive. In essentials it consisted of a simple bell pull, conveniently situated in the coffin at the right hand of the corpse, which would enable one, should one find oneself alive and six foot under, to summon help by ringing a bell mounted above the grave.

Usually, and for obvious reasons, Bateson's Belfries were designed as temporary structures. But there were circumstances in which a longer-lasting variant was appropriate. Thanks to *Grave Conditions,* I learned to look with fresh eyes at what I had previously assumed was a purely decorative feature of the family mausoleum of the Makepeace family.

The mausoleum, which is illustrated in full colour on page 98 of *Grave Conditions,* was situated in a relatively remote corner of the cemetery, an area where the dead lie beneath a coarsely-woven shroud of long grass, thistles and clumps of bramble. A flight of steps led down to a stout, padlocked door leading below the monument into the chamber itself, which measured perhaps eight feet square. Two banks of four shelves faced each other across the narrow gangway.

Only three of the shelves were occupied – with the remains of the Reverend Simon Makepeace, the first incumbent of St. George's, Kensal Vale, his wife, Charlotte, and their son Albert Victor, both of whom had predeceased him. The rest of the family had apparently preferred to make other arrangements. On ground level there was a rather vulgar monument consisting of four weeping angels clustered round the base of a miniature campanile, at the top of which hung the bell.

Having studied *Grave Conditions,* I was not surprised to find that a fine brass chain passed from the top of the bell through a pipe which penetrated the roof of the chamber. It emerged at the end of the gangway, opposite the door, within easy reach of the upper ends of the coffins. I imagine Mr Makepeace stipulated that the lids should not be screwed down.

During the day, especially around lunchtime and in the early evening, the cemetery can become almost crowded. But the gates are locked half an hour before sunset, and once the security men have done their sweep (and they are commendably efficient at this) the only people left are – or rather were – Dave and Tracy in their cottage by the gates in the majestic shadow of the cemetery chimney.

Dave and Tracy did not get on – and as Dave was very deaf, owing to a passion for the music of Aerosmith, Black Sabbath and Led Zeppelin, one sometimes heard his wife's trenchantly expressed opinions about his sexual inadequacy and his low income. Tracy was tall and big breasted, with dyed blonde hair, sturdy legs and a taste for very short skirts. She and Dave rarely had visitors and never indulged in nocturnal rambles through the cemetery. Often Tracy would go off by herself for days at a time. I sometimes surprised myself by entertaining a certain sisterly regard for her.

So, given their habits and the secluded nature of a cemetery at night, you will understand my surprise when I saw Tracy arm in arm with a tall, well-built man, guiding him through the gravestones by the light of a small torch. At the time I was sitting on a table monument, and eating a light snack of Parma ham and wholemeal bread. I was interested enough to discard my sandwich and follow the couple. Tracy led the man to the Makepeace vault. Her companion was carrying a briefcase. They went down the steps together, and I heard a rattle as she unlocked the padlock.

'Christ,' I heard the man say in a hoarse whisper. 'You can't leave me here. Fucking hell – they're coffins, aren't they?'

'There's nothing here could harm a fly,' Tracy told him. 'Not now. Anyway, beggars can't be choosers, so you might as well get used to it.'

'You're a hard woman.'

For an instant she shone the torch on him as they stood at the foot of the steps. He was broad as well as tall, with a stern, dark face. I noticed in particular his big eyebrows jutting out above his eyes like a pair of shelves. I am not a sentimental creature, but I must confess a jolt went through me when I saw those eyebrows.

'Stay here, Jack,' Tracy said. 'I'll get you a sleeping bag and some fags and stuff.'

'What about Dave?'

'He wouldn't hear a thing if you dropped a bomb on him. Anyway, he's drunk a bottle of vodka since teatime.'

She left Jack with the torch. I slipped under the lowest shelf on the right-hand side and watched him. When he thought he was alone, he squatted down and opened the briefcase. I was interested to see that it contained an automatic pistol and piles and piles of banknotes. He rummaged underneath the money, took out a mobile telephone and shut the case.

He stared at the telephone but did not use it. He lit a cigarette and paced up and down the gangway of the vault. Despite his agitation, he was a fine figure of a man.

My hearing is good, and I heard Tracy's returning footsteps before he did. She dropped a backpack on to the floor of the vault. It contained a sleeping bag, several cans of Tennents Super Lager, a plastic bucket, some crisps and a packet of Marlboro cigarettes. Jack watched as she unrolled the sleeping bag on one of the lowest shelves and arranged the other items on the shelf above.

'Listen,' he said when she had finished. 'Get some passport photos done and go and see Frank.' He snapped open the case, took out a wad of notes and slapped it down on the shelf. 'That'll cover it.' He took out another wad and added it to the first. 'Buy a motor. Nothing flashy, maybe two or three years old. There's a place in Walthamstow – Frank'll give you the name.'

Tracy stared down at the open briefcase. 'And where do we go then, Jack? Shangri fucking la?'

'What about Shangri fucking Amsterdam for starters? We take the ferry from Harwich, then move on from there.'

'I got nothing to wear. I need some clothes.'

He scowled. Nevertheless he gave her another bundle of notes. 'Don't go crazy.'

'I love it when you're masterful.' Tracy dropped the money into the backpack. 'Careful with the torch. You can see a glow round the edge of the door. And I'm going to have to lock you in.'

'What the fuck are you talking about?'

'The security guys check the door at least twice a night. We had a bit of trouble with kids down here earlier in the summer. Orgies and what not. Pathetic little bastards.'

'You can't just leave me here,' Jack said.

'You got a better idea?'

'I can't even text you. There's no signal. So what do I do if I need you?'

'I can't bloody wait,' she said. 'Big boy.'

'For Christ's sake, Trace. If it's an emergency.'

She laughed. 'Ring my bell.' She leant over and touched the handle that hung between the shelves. 'You pull that, and the bell rings up top.'

'Sure?'

'We had this weirdo from the local history society the other month who tried it. Built to last, he said. But for God's sake, Jack, don't use it because if anyone hears it but me, you're totally fucked.'

'You're really sure? Really, really?'

'Yes. Trust me.' Tracy put her hand on his shoulder and kissed his cheek. 'See you tomorrow night, all right? Got to get my beauty sleep.'

She slipped out of the vault and locked the door. Jack swore, a long monotonous stream hardly above a whisper. His torch beam criss-crossed the vault and raked to and fro along the dusty shelves. Finally he reached floor level and for an instant the beam dazzled me. He let out a screech. I dived into the crack between two blocks of masonry that was my usual way in and out of the vault. A moment later, as I emerged into the cool night air, I heard the frantic clanging of the bell.

Tracy came pounding through the graves. She ran down the steps and unlocked the door.

'Jesus, Jack, what the hell are you up to?'

He clung to her, nuzzling her hair. He muttered something I couldn't hear.

'Oh, for God's sake!' she snapped, drawing away from him. 'I bet it's a damn sight more scared than you are. Give me the torch.' A moment later, she went on, 'There you are – it's buggered off.'

'Can't you do something? Can't you put poison down?'

'It won't be back,' she said as though soothing a child. 'Anyway, they seem to quite like poison. I'm sure there's more of them than there used to be. And they're bigger.'

'I can't stay here.'

'Then where the hell else are you going to go? It's not for long.'

'But how am I supposed to sleep? They'll crawl all over me.'

'Jesus,' said Tracy. 'And I thought women were the weaker sex. It won't be back.'

'How do you know?'

'You probably scared the shit out of it. Listen, I tell you what I'll do: you can have some of Dave's pills. A few of those and you'll be out like a light.'

Off she went again, and returned with a handful of capsules, which Jack washed down with a can of lager. He insisted she stay with him, holding his hand, while he went to sleep.

Despite this display of weakness, or perhaps

even because of it, there was something very appealing about Jack. I came back down to the vault and listened to them billing and cooing. Such a lovely deep voice he had, like grumbling thunder. It made something deep within me vibrate like a tuning fork. Gradually his words grew thicker, and slower. At last the voice fell silent.

There was a click and a flare of flame as Tracy lit a cigarette. Time passed. Jack began to snore. Edging out of my crack into the lesser shelter of the space beneath the lowest shelf, I had an extensive though low-level view of the vault. I saw Tracy's legs and feet, wearing jeans and trainers. The cigarette fell to the floor. She ground it out beneath her heel.

I saw the briefcase, and Tracy's left hand with its blood red nails and big flashy rings. I watched in the torch light as her fingers made a claw and hooked themselves through the handle of the case. The trainers moved across the vault. The door opened and softly closed. The padlock grated in its hasp.

After a while, I scaled the rough stone wall to the shelf where Jack lay. I jumped lightly on to his chest and settled down where I could feel the beating of his heart. I stared at his face. Through my breast surged a torrent of emotions I had never known before.

Was this, I wondered, what humans felt? Was this love?

So it began, this strange relationship, and so it continued. I do not intend to chart its every twist and turn. There are secrets locked within my bosom which I shall never share with another soul.

Late in the afternoon of the day after Jack's arrival, I happened to glance through a copy of the *Standard* which I had found in a litter bin on the other side of the cemetery. His face loomed up at me from one of the inside pages. Those prominent eyebrows were quite unmistakable. The police, it seemed, were anxious to interview him in connection with a murder at the weekend in Peckham. The dead man was said to have been a prominent member of a south London gang.

On the second day, the police arrived. They interviewed Dave in the lodge cottage. They did not search the cemetery. Halfway through the morning, Jack finished his lager, his crisps and his cigarettes, in that order. Early in the evening, the bucket overflowed. He tried to ration his use of the torch, but inevitably the battery died. Then he was alone with me in the darkness.

Is it not strange that a grown man should be so scared of the dark? If only I could see, he would mutter, Christ, if only I could see. I have no idea why he thought the faculty of sight would have improved his plight, but then I have found little evidence to suggest that humans are rational animals.

Just before dawn on the third day, it occurred to Jack – bless him, he was not a fast thinker – that Tracy might not be coming back, and that he would be able to escape from this prison and move into one of Her Majesty's if he rang the bell in Bateson's Belfry long enough and loud enough.

Alas for him, I had anticipated just such an eventuality.

The bell wire was sound for most of its length, I believe, but, at the upper end, it met a metal flange which was in turn attached to the spindle from which the bell depended. Where the wire had been inserted, bent and twisted into a hole in the flange, rust and metal fatigue had already caused many of its constituent strands to snap apart. All one needed to deal with the remaining strands was a certain physical agility, perseverance and a set of sharp teeth.

So it was that when Jack gave the bell wire a sharp tug all that happened was that he pulled the wire down on top of him. He clenched his fists and pounded them against the oak and iron of the door. That was one of the occasions when he wept.

Later, after he had sunk into an exhausted slumber, I licked the salty tears from his cheeks, my tongue rasping deliciously on the abrasive masculinity of his stubble. It was one of those small but intimate services which seem to be peculiarly satisfying to the females of so many species.

The days passed, and so did the nights, and they passed agreeably enough for me. When he was awake, Jack was increasingly distraught. He was still terrified of me, poor lamb. Are we always scared of those who love us? When he was asleep, though, and defenceless, he became mine. I spent as much time as possible with him – indeed, if possible on top of him or curled into some snug crevice of his person.

Can one ever be close enough to the man one loves? Oh, that oft-imagined bliss of perfect union! One soul, one flesh!

Sometimes he screamed, and banged on the door, and yelled, and wept; but no one except myself heard him. On one occasion, Dave was only twenty yards away from the vault when Jack began to wail, but of course Dave was too deaf to hear.

There remained a possibility that a passer-by might hear his cries, even in this remote and overgrown quarter of the cemetery. Here, however, the British climate played its part, as it has in so many courtships. Rain fell with unlovely determination for most of three days. As a result, the Kensal Vale cemetery attracted far fewer visitors than usual.

Among those who braved the weather was a brace of middle-aged ladies from Market Harborough searching without success for the last resting place of an ancestor. They left me the remains of a very acceptable chicken mayonnaise salad and – even more to the point – they discarded their newspaper. For hard news and sound principles one cannot do much better than the *Daily Telegraph.*

My eye fell on a short but intriguing item to the effect that Jack Rochester and an unnamed lady friend were believed to be in Rio de Janeiro. Knowing Tracy as I did – a special sort of knowledge unites two females with a man in common – I had little doubt that this was a false trail designed to throw the authorities off the scent.

I come now to the final act in my story, to a resolution which is both melancholy and edifying. All passion spent, blind in his own darkness, my poor Jack sank slowly into a coma. I grieved and rejoiced in equal measure. I sat on his chest and felt the beat of his heart growing slower and feebler. My night vision is good, and I gazed for long hours at his manly features. A lover is like a beloved city. I explored Jack's public squares and great thoroughfares. I strolled through his tree-lined suburbs and splendid municipal parks. I wandered through twisting side streets and lost myself in the labyrinth of his bazaar.

In his final hours, as he drifted inexorably towards another city, to the dark heart of this metropolis of the dead, Jack rested his hands on my warm fur. Then, to my inexpressible joy, he stroked me.

Soon afterwards, the life left him altogether – or very nearly so. And then?

Reader, I ate him.

Murder in Trumpington
by LC Tyler

Inspector Reeve looked out of the window at a white world. Snow in April. Of course it was April only by the narrowest of margins and it had been the second coldest March on record. Still, snow in April…

His view of the silently accumulating drifts was limited to the police station car park but, somewhere out there, snow was coating the many spires of Cambridge. Flakes would be falling onto the roof of King's College chapel; they would be clinging like moss to the walls of St John's and they would be landing and melting, one by one, in the icy waters of the Cam. The roads outside Cambridge had been barely passable last night – seven accidents reported so far. You'd have thought that one compensation for weather like this would have been that it would keep criminals indoors, but no, not even that. They'd just had a phone call to say that thieves had removed fifty yards or so of signal cable from the local railway line. Last night had been the weather for brass monkeys rather than copper cable, Reeve thought to himself – but the thieves had calculated correctly that nobody would be out watching for them. At least it was nothing worse. Expensive for Network Rail of course and, on the roads, the icy surface had provided a nice bit of repair work for the Cambridge garages, but no lives lost.

There was a knock on the door. The duty sergeant poked his head round. 'I've got a Dr Clark from Trinity College here, sir. He wants to report a murder.'

Dr Clark was one of those people that it was difficult to age exactly. He had a greyish beard, but an unlined, relatively youthful face. Forty maybe? Or younger but prematurely grey? He wore a tweed jacket and a college scarf. The story he had to tell was a strange one.

'You see,' he began, 'I tried to persuade him not to go out to Trumpington. The snow had already started and I was doubtful he'd be able to drive back, even if he managed to get hold of Mr Miller.'

'He being who?' asked Reeve.

'Dr Clarke,' said Dr Clark. 'Clarke with an E. There are two of us at Trinity – a bit confusing for people. We're always being mistaken for one another. I'm a history tutor. He's the college bursar. I'm always getting emails about building work or protests from the undergraduates about the quality of the breakfasts. He sometimes gets history essays to mark.'

'I see. How inconvenient. But you think that Dr Clarke – Clarke with an E – has been killed? The duty sergeant said something about murder?'

'That's right. Sorry – I'm not explaining myself properly. You see the reason Dr Clarke went out to Trumpington was to tackle Ted Miller over some building work he's done for us – or rather that we've paid him for but he hasn't completed. Miller's a bit of a rogue, but he gave us a very cheap quote for the job. Should have known better. No such thing as a free lunch is there? Anyway, we paid him week by week and then, as builders do, he vanished. We tried to contact him but he always seemed to be out on some other job. Once he'd gone we discovered how behind the timetable he was. He'd charged for all sorts of things he hadn't really completed. We were several thousand pounds down. He wouldn't reply to phone messages, so Dr Clarke went out there yesterday to beard him in his lair.' Clark paused and stroked his own beard for a moment. Then he continued: 'He left late morning – phoned me at about one o'clock to report on progress. Predictably, Miller had been giving him the run-around. No sooner had Clarke arrived than Miller rushed off, saying that somebody's pipes had burst. Clarke was left sitting in Miller's kitchen kicking his heels.'

'How annoying for him ... but he seems in no danger so far.'

'That's right. Had he done no more than that, he'd have been fine. Miller's wife was very attentive – kept his mug of tea topped up, gave him chocolate digestives.'

'I'm still not sure why you are fearful for his safety…'

'I'm coming to that. When I say Miller's wife was very attentive, I mean she was *very* attentive. Clarke's in his fifties but he's still regarded as pretty good looking – a sight better looking than Miller. He and Mrs Miller were left to amuse themselves as best they could. One thing led to another.'

'I bet. They don't hang around, these college bursars, do they? From chocolate biscuits straight to unbridled passion?'

Dr Clark seemed unaware of the irony in Reeve's voice.

'Via cheese scones and Victoria sponge obviously,' he said.

'Obviously. So are you saying he was poisoned?'

'No. At least, not then. Three or four hours later I got another call. Mrs Miller had let on she'd been texting Ted Miller every hour to say that Clarke was still there. Ted wasn't coming back until Clarke was out of the way and couldn't question him on building work not done.'

'So, she had a way of ensuring that her husband remained absent.'

'Precisely. She sent him a text saying that, on account of the snow, Clarke was stuck there all night and she'd be putting him in the spare room.'

'And did she? Put him in the spare room, I mean.'

'Not according to Clarke in his penultimate call. Miller's bed was a lot more comfortable. He reckoned that the college had lost its money for good, but he'd get something back from Mrs Miller.'

'Risky if Miller came back unexpectedly.'

'Very much so. Mrs Miller let slip that he'd once said if he caught her with another bloke again...'

'Again?'

'Clarke was hardly the first. Next time, he said, he'd kill both of them and bury them in the yard.'

'What yard might that be?'

'Miller's a scrap dealer as well as a builder. He's

got a yard behind the house full of rusty old cars and bits and pieces lifted from the houses he's worked on. I got a fireplace from him once. Marble. Very nice. I didn't ask where it had come from.'

'Did Miller return unexpectedly? Is that where this is leading?'

'I got the last call from Clarke around three in the morning. He was whispering and it was difficult to make out all he said, but the gist of it was that Clarke was hiding somewhere on the property without his trousers on. He reckoned Miller wouldn't find him. He said it was too bloody cold there for one thing. In the morning he reckoned Mrs M would bring him his trousers and his car keys and he could make a get-away. But he said if I heard nothing by ten this morning, to contact the police.'

Reeve looked at the clock on the wall. It was seven minutes past ten.

'He could have phoned us last night if he was in any danger. 999 is an easy number to remember.'

'I suggested that. He said he didn't think you'd be impressed if he phoned and said he was screwing somebody else's wife and needed police protection. Anyway, it really was snowing by that time. He thought even the police might not have got through.'

Reeve tapped his fingers on the table. 'Have you tried phoning him?'

'I think he's turned the phone off ... or maybe...'

The various possibilities hung in the air for the moment. Reeve looked again at Dr Clark (without an E). English dons didn't usually send the police on wild goose chases. And if the bursar of Trinity was really lying dead in a house in Trumpington... That would make the local papers all right. Especially if he'd been there a couple of weeks before the police thought to check on him.

'The duty sergeant will take your contact details,' said Reeve. 'Keep your mobile on. We'll need to talk to you again, whatever happens.'

Reeve drove the police Land Rover the few miles over to Trumpington. A young constable sat in the passenger seat. He doubted he'd need him, but it was always useful to have back-up. The roads at least were better than he had thought. The gritting lorries had been out and the traffic was moving well, if a little cautiously.

Trumpington clung tenaciously to its village status but was, if truth were told, now little more than a prosperous suburb of Cambridge. Reeve noted the evidence of building work on all sides. Billboards proclaimed the development of new executive homes. He wondered if his police salary would run to a deposit on the cheapest of them. Probably not.

Miller's place, at the southern end of the village, wasn't difficult to locate – a large sign over the entrance to the yard admitted both of Miller's occupations to the world in general. Reeve parked the car outside the half-timbered house that fronted the street and knocked on the door.

'Mrs Miller?'

'That's right. What can I do for you?'

Dr Clark had reported accurately. Even with her dishevelled hair and no make-up, Mrs Miller was a looker sure enough.

'I'm investigating a ... disappearance,' said Reeve. 'We think your husband may be able to help us. Might I come in for a moment?' He flashed his warrant card, not that most people had any idea what a warrant card was supposed to look like. And what was it meant to add? If you could fake a police uniform and a police 4x4, then frankly it was a piece of piss to come up with a dodgy warrant card. He snapped the wallet shut and tucked it into his top pocket.

'Sorry – we've only just got up,' said Mrs Miller. 'What with the snow and everything and Ted not being able to get to work. You'd better come into the kitchen. I'll get you some tea.'

A voice from the upper part of the house called: 'Who's that?'

'Police,' replied Mrs Miller. 'For you.'

There was some muffled cursing and the sound of two feet hitting the floor. Inspector Reeve was drinking strong tea with three sugars by the time Ted Miller entered the room. He was a large, red-faced man with a snub nose and no hair of any sort on his head. He showed no sign of liking the police.

'What's he want?' he asked his wife, jerking his thumb at Reeve.

'Best ask him yourself.'

'I'm looking for a Dr Clarke,' Reeve intervened, putting his mug down.

Miller blinked a couple of times but his face was untroubled. If he had just committed murder, he was covering it up well. 'Never heard of him,' said the builder, giving one armpit its morning scratch. 'If that's all, you can sling your hook. I've done nothing and that's my chair you're sitting in.'

'I'd like to search the house,' said Reeve.

Miller looked at him incredulously.

'Got a warrant have you?'

'No, but I can get one. And the constable outside in the Land Rover will stay to make sure nothing leaves here in the meantime.'

'Just the house?'

'I can't promise, but that will do for a start.'

'Go ahead then. Search it. I've got nothing to hide.'

'Thank you. And, for the record, you're saying Dr Clarke wasn't here yesterday?'

'I keep bloody telling you. I don't know any Dr Clarke.'

'I'm surprised if that's the case. He's bursar at Trinity, where you're doing some work.'

Miller frowned. 'I'm doing a job at Trinity, but I don't know Clarke.'

'Maybe you deal with somebody else?' Reeve wracked his brains for who this might be. Some assistant to the bursar? 'The steward?' Reeve suggested. 'Or the building manager?'

'Building manager, I think he calls himself. What's that to you?'

'Dr Clarke came out here yesterday to talk to you about the job you're doing. He'd tried phoning before. You didn't reply. He seems to think you owe them some money for work not done.'

'I told them – I'll finish it when the weather gets warmer. You can't get the concrete to set when it's like this.'

'Can't you?'

'No, you bloody well can't. Don't tell me how to do my job and I won't tell you how to fit somebody up for the possession of drugs.'

'That sounds like a deal, Mr Miller. So, is that what you told Clarke?'

'Jesus! I've told you – I don't know the geezer.'

'His college says that he came out to Trumpington yesterday.'

'Probably never made it. It's been snowing, unless you missed it.'

'No, I didn't miss it. I drove through it. I'll take a look round the house then.'

'You won't find him here.'

'I'll look anyway.'

Reeve toured the house. It was bigger than he'd expected – five or six bedrooms, all leading off each other, as was not uncommon with houses of this age. But ultra-modern bathrooms – if Miller had installed them himself he was not at all bad at his trade. Smart kitchen too. There was clearly plenty of money in building these days. Those units wouldn't have been cheap and the cooking range might have graced an upmarket restaurant. Acres of granite worktop. You wouldn't get a kitchen like this for under fifty grand.

The Millers followed him at a distance. They didn't seem overly worried – puzzled certainly, but not anxious. Not until Reeve looked out of a bedroom window and pointed to a long, single storey on the far side of the yard.

'What's that?'

'Just a shed. I keep stock there.'

Ted Miller had suddenly tensed up.

Though fat flakes of snow were still drifting down, this morning's fall could not quite disguise the evidence of car tracks crossing the yard or of footprints by the far doorway. Somebody had been up to something in the yard in the early morning.

'I might take a look there too,' said Reeve.

'Got a warrant?'

'The answer's still no, but that I can get one if you'd like. Something to hide, have you?'

'Not me.'

'No reason why I should go and take a quick look, then.'

'He won't be there.'

'Who?'

'Clarke. It's freezing out there. Nobody in their right mind would spend a night in that shack.'

'He might if he was dead.'

Miller appeared to be weighing up something that was pretty heavy.

'Sod it. Go and look for dead bodies if that would amuse you. I hope you find one.'

Reeve was half way across the yard when the phone rang. It was the duty sergeant.

'You won't like this, sir,' he said.

'Tell me anyway.'

'I phoned the number that Dr Clark gave us.'

'Yes?'

'It doesn't exist. So, I phoned the lodge at Trinity. No Dr Clark. Not even one. The bursar's actually called...' The desk sergeant paused as if to consult some notes.

'Not Clark anyway,' said Reeve with a sigh.

'It's not only that,' said the Sergeant. 'Just think for a moment. Trumpington. A Miller. Two Clarks – or rather clerks – one of whom screws the Miller's wife. And yourself of course.'

'The Reeve's Tale,' said Reeve. 'Chaucer.'

'And the date today…'

'April the First,' said Reeve.

'I thought Dr Clark looked a little young, except for his grey beard,' said the Sergeant sadly.

'An undergraduate?'

'I'd say so. From Trinity or elsewhere. He was very insistent that he spoke to Inspector Reeve personally. We've been had, sir.'

'Seems likely,' said Reeve. 'Still, while I'm here…' He put his shoulder to the door of the outbuilding. It creaked open. The air smelt of rust and damp soil. Half a dozen pine doors were stacked against one wall and a couple of dismantled stone fireplaces against another. In the dim light Reeve also made out a Victorian roll-top bath – dusty but containing no college bursars. 'No sign of any foul play,' he said, half to the phone and half to himself. 'I think we'll be heading back into Cambridge shortly.' Then, at the far end of the shed he noticed a strange mass concealed by a new looking tarpaulin. Damp footprints led up to it. Miller probably hadn't reckoned on how long it took a floor to dry when it was this cold.

'We could get him for wasting police time,' the Sergeant was saying. 'Not many undergraduates up at the moment, it being so close to Easter. Shouldn't be too difficult. We could probably start by tracking down who sold him that bloody fake beard.'

Reeve made no reply but walked slowly across the shed and knelt down by the tarpaulin. He carefully pulled back a corner, then whistled under his breath.

'Are you still there, sir?' the Sergeant asked.

'I thought I'd just found a body,' said Reeve, 'but it isn't.'

'Wasted trip, then,' repeated the Sergeant.

'Not exactly,' said Reeve.

He went out in the yard, where Ted Miller was standing in the snow, an old donkey jacket now pulled on over his crumpled pyjamas. Melted snow glistened on his bald head. He scowled at Reeve.

'Find a body?' Miller asked sarcastically.

Inspector Reeve shook his head.

'Edward Miller,' he said, 'I am arresting you for receiving stolen goods, that is to say about fifty yards of copper cable. Property of Network Rail. Is there anything you would like to say?'

Ted Miller did say something and expressed himself forcefully.

Inspector Reeve nodded. 'Interestingly,' he said, 'most of those words are derived from Middle English. I think Chaucer would have approved.'

The publishers hope that this book has given you enjoyable reading. Large Print Books are especially designed to be as easy to see and hold as possible. If you wish a complete list of our books please ask at your local library or write directly to:

Magna Large Print Books
Magna House, Long Preston,
Skipton, North Yorkshire.
BD23 4ND

This Large Print Book for the partially sighted, who cannot read normal print, is published under the auspices of

THE ULVERSCROFT FOUNDATION

THE ULVERSCROFT FOUNDATION

... we hope that you have enjoyed this Large Print Book. Please think for a moment about those people who have worse eyesight problems than you ... and are unable to even read or enjoy Large Print, without great difficulty.

You can help them by sending a donation, large or small to:

The Ulverscroft Foundation,
1, The Green, Bradgate Road,
Anstey, Leicestershire, LE7 7FU,
England.
or request a copy of our brochure for more details.

The Foundation will use all your help to assist those people who are handicapped by various sight problems and need special attention.

Thank you very much for your help.